What Others Are Saying about *Guardians of the Heart*...

Thanks to *Guardians of the Heart*, I'm an official Loree Lough fan! She has the magic touch when telling a story. I really enjoy the way she gives her characters life and a voice. I always find myself immersed immediately in her books. Her gifted presentation of dialogue is amazing. I read other authors daily, and I am making all of Loree Lough's novels a priority now.

—*Doran Ingram*
SAG/AFTRA Actor
Author, *Blood Brothers*, *Dark Secret*, and other reader favorites in
The Mark Ingram Adventures series

Author Loree Lough's latest novel, *Guardians of the Heart*, challenges us all with the age-old question: "Can you think of one person who has no regrets?" In it, Loree takes us on a journey of discovery as Nell and Asa try to camouflage deeply hidden secrets. You do not want to miss this book!

—*Kevin James O'Neill*
Writer and director, Olive Ranch Road Productions

Loree Lough has long been a favorite author among readers. She never fails to deliver memorable stories packed with emotion. Her latest novels in the Secrets on Sterling Street series are no exception. Truly, you will always remember a Loree story.

—*Andrea Boeshaar*
Editor, writing coach, and best-selling author of the acclaimed
Fabric of Time series

Loree Lough has done it again—penned yet another story about letting go of the past and loving in the present. With beautiful historical touches, *Guardians of the Heart* takes readers on a journey that many men and women need to take, from hiding secrets to guarding each other's hearts under God's watchful eye.

—*Robin Bayne*
Award-winning author of the Gardner's Gazebo series: *Prodigal*,
Samaritan, and *Christmas Pearl*

Weaving faith seamlessly into her stories, award-winning author Loree Lough gives images of grace and forgiveness that are compelling and heartwarming as she mixes them with a healthy dose of love. Secrets impose a heavy weight on one's heart, and she illustrates that truth beautifully as well as she does the joy of having that burden relieved. Lough brings surprises around every corner, keeping the reader intrigued, satisfied, and glad to have spent the time within the pages of her novel.

—*Susan M. Baganz*
Author, *Pesto and Potholes*

From the first sentence, I was hooked on Loree Lough's newest novel, *Guardians of the Heart*. The title alone speaks volumes, bringing to mind the biblical admonition to guard one's heart. Loree's writing is engaging, and her hero and heroine, Asa Stone and Nell Holstrom, are captivating characters. With this fresh storyline, readers will not be disappointed. Loree always comes through, offering inspiring stories that keep getting better and better.

—*Rita Gerlach*
Author of the Daughters of the Potomac series

In *Guardians of the Heart*, Loree Lough has woven a Western of heart-rending proportions, as hero, Asa Stone, seeks to keep the dark secret from his past hidden from the heroine, Nell Holstrom. Asa and Nell's journey is proof that love and faith can restore what is thought to be lost, and foster new beginnings. I found myself devouring every word to find out where the story would lead. If you enjoy Westerns with strong heroines and battle-wounded heroes, look no further!

—*Cerella Sechrist*
Author, *The Paris Connection* and *Love Finds You in Hershey, Pennsylvania*

Along a road of tragedy and triumphs, we follow Nell as she sparkles with pioneer spirit in the frontier town of Denver, Colorado. The young woman encounters quandaries and unanswered questions regarding her employer, Asa, who hides deep and disturbing secrets while appearing to be a good and moral man. But their employer/employee relationship could alter both their lives, if they can overcome the regrets of the past to bring the opportunity for a new and joyful life. *Guardians of the Heart* is sure to please fans of Western fiction.

—*Elaine Fields Smith*
Author/publisher, *Ridin' Around: Taillights in Chrome, 8-Tracks on Wheels* and the inspirational novella *The Perfect Place of Knowledge*

Engaging and suspenseful, with an unforgettable cast of characters and a plot that keeps the pages turning, Loree Lough's latest novel, *Guardians of the Heart*, is a masterful collaboration of history, romance, redemption, and forgiveness. A must-read for every historical romance fan!

—*Rachel Muller*
Best-selling author, *Letters from Grace*

I thoroughly enjoyed *Guardians of the Heart*. Loree Lough knows exactly when to throw in a twist here or a surprise there to keep readers fully engaged. I found myself hoping for the best for Nell and Asa, and fearing any mishap that might come their way; just as I felt the two were settling on a predictable path, Loree turned their entire world upside down! It was refreshing to fade back in time to an era when struggles were very real and life could be harsh, yet the triumph of spirit overcame obstacles for those with dogged natures. Loree Lough is a genre-bending, talented story teller whose multi-layered characters ring true. Call me a romantic, but I want to read more of her uplifting stories.

—*T. C. Miller*
Author, the Black Star Ops series, including *BlackJack Bomber* and *Black Star Bay*

GUARDIANS OF THE
HEART

LOREE LOUGH

WHITAKER
HOUSE

Unless otherwise indicated, all Scripture quotations are taken from the King James Version of the Holy Bible. Scripture quotations marked (NIV) are taken from the *Holy Bible, New International Version*®, NIV®, © 1973, 1978, 1984, 2011 by Biblica, Inc.® Used by permission. All rights reserved worldwide.

GUARDIANS OF THE HEART
Secrets on Sterling Street ~ Book 2

Loree Lough
www.loreelough.com

ISBN: 978-1-62911-565-8
eBook ISBN: 978-1-62911-587-0
Printed in the United States of America
© 2015 by Loree Lough

Whitaker House
1030 Hunt Valley Circle
New Kensington, PA 15068
www.whitakerhouse.com

Library of Congress Cataloging-in-Publication Data (Pending)

1 2 3 4 5 6 7 8 9 10 11 **W** 22 21 20 19 18 17 16 15

Dedication

This novel is dedicated to anyone, anywhere, who has ever worried that the secrets of the past will cast shadows on the present or the future: *"Then you will call, and the Lord will answer; you will cry for help, and he will say: 'Here am I'"* (Isaiah 58:9 NIV).

It's also dedicated to handsome young actor Taylor Kitsch, who served as the visual model for my hero, Asa Stone.

Acknowledgments

I'd like to thank my talented writer friend Rachel Muller for suggesting that I offer "Secondary Character Roles in the Novel" as prizes in a fund-raiser for her children's school. Thanks to the funds they contributed via the auction, the DiMaggio and Held families of Mt. Airy, Maryland, became an integral part of the story and helped make it more realistic, believable, and fun. Thanks, too, to Janet Marie Dowell, who, as winner of a separate random drawing in *Loree Lough & Friends* (an uber-fun, friendly Facebook group), became the town librarian and the heroine's best friend, adding yet another layer of warmth and realism to the story.

Also, a very special thanks to Robert Crutchfield, Senior Pastor of the Compassion Church in Katy, Texas, editor of *Faith That Inspires Action*, and author of The First Responders Prayer used in the First Responders series novels. He has also written many faith-moving sermons, and he graciously gave me permission to quote portions of one of them in *Guardians of the Heart*. And when he found out that a family emergency required our beloved Pastor Truett to leave the church in Denver, Robert also agreed to become a character in this novel...and the next!

A Note from the Author

Dear Reader,

Close your eyes for a moment, take a deep breath, and try to picture just one person in your life who doesn't have regrets, sad memories, or a secret that has the power to darken even her happiest mood.

Couldn't think of one, could you?

That's because every human who ever walked this planet has done something he or she is sorry for. (Well, except for *one*, and I think you know who He is!)

We all know how uncomfortable secrets can make us feel, even at the slightest threat of having them exposed. But did you know that the damage caused by keeping secrets is not limited to the metaphysical realm?

Studies have shown that when the brain's prefrontal cortex (responsible for reminding you how awful it would be if your secret was exposed) communicates with the cingulated cortex (which activates the fight-or-flight response), stress hormones are released. Blood pressure rises. The gastrointestinal tract releases acids. Memory is impacted, and sleep patterns change. Guilt provokes supersensitive or argumentative behavior. There's an oft-quoted, anonymous saying that goes, "You're only as sick as your secrets."

Thankfully, we need not be prisoners of our secrets. Carl Bard has said, "Though no one can go back and make a brand new start, anyone can start from now and make a brand new ending." Like many of us, the protagonists of this story, Nell and Asa, are working hard to guard the secrets of their hearts. Whether they decide to fess up or keep mum, one thing is sure: The Father knows every secret of His children's hearts. In the words of the apostle Paul, *"We have renounced secret and shameful ways…for God, who said, 'Let light shine out of darkness,' made his light shine in our hearts to give us the light of the knowledge of God's glory displayed in the face of Christ"* (2 Corinthians 4:2, 6 NIV).

My wish for you, dear reader, is that you will open every dark corner of your heart to the Lord so that you may experience the joy of His merciful light.

Blessings to you and yours,
Loree

Chapter One

Fourteen-year-old Asa pulled up the collar of his too-thin jacket and willed his teeth to stop chattering. Four months ago, he'd tried to talk his way out of joining the Colorado Volunteers, but he hadn't stood a chance against his big, determined pa. When he saw how much pain his father was willing to inflict on his three older brothers, he'd quietly pledged allegiance to Colonel John Chivington's Third Regiment.

Oh, what he wouldn't give to go back in time to the little house on the outskirts of Denver that always smelled of fresh-baked bread, where he'd never gone hungry and never felt cold, thanks to his ma's talent for turning scraps of cloth into warm quilts.

None of his fellow cavalrymen—nearly seven hundred in number—was complaining about the biting wind or the skin-stinging snow pellets. But then, they'd all been swigging whiskey since long before this latest march had begun. Some might have been drinking to stay warm, but Asa believed most of them were hoping a gutful of tangle-leg would dull any fears of becoming the next victim of Chivington's bloodlust.

About halfway into the seven-hour march, Asa overheard a handful of men whispering about the Treaty of Fort Laramie of '51, which had pretty much negated every promise the U.S.

government had made to the tribes in the Treaty of Fort Wise. One man opined that Black Kettle, White Antelope, and other Cheyenne chiefs didn't trust the whites, but that, desperate to secure hunting lands for their starving people, they'd reluctantly agreed to winter near the south bend of Big Sandy Creek.

"I hear-tell them Ind'ans are all sick as dogs," one soldier said, "so they sent their healthiest bucks in search of food."

"Yep, I heard the same," a third man agreed. "Also heard Chivington say that'll make easy pickin's of them that's left."

"And he won't tolerate no excuses," added the first, "iffen any Ind'ans are still breathin' when it's over."

The words sent chills up Asa's spine, and he sought out his brothers to get their take on things. It surprised him when even Chester, the oldest and the toughest, looked just as scared and disgusted as Asa felt.

"They're all drunker than skunks," Asa whispered. "We could belly-crawl south awhile, then make a run for it. Why, I'll bet we could be halfway home before they even notice we're—"

His pa stepped out of the shadows, filled both his meaty fists with bunches of Asa's threadbare jacket, and lifted him off his feet. Nose to nose with his youngest son, Daniel hissed, "Desertion?"

Asa turned away to avoid his father's baleful glare, as well as his rank, boozy breath.

"Can't even look me in the eye, can you, coward?" he growled, turning Asa loose with a blow that sent him sprawling into the snow.

"You'll stand and fight, same as the rest of us, you hear me?" Daniel aimed a forefinger at Asa, then at three two brothers. "Same goes for you, and you, and you." He glanced over his shoulder, where a half dozen officers were orchestrating a line of artillery aimed at the all-quiet Indian camp. "You're lucky no one else heard you, or I'd-a had no choice but to shoot the lot of you, right where you stand."

Asa scrambled to his feet and deliberately stood apart from his brothers.

"They had nothing to do with it, Pa. I was just telling them what I heard the other men saying. Don't hardly seem right, sneaking up on the camp. The Indians are just doin' what the government told 'em to. Besides, they're sick, and it's just old folks, women, and young'uns, since most of the men are off huntin'—"

"Don't matter how old they are or whether they wear skirts or trousers. They're *Injuns*, you stupid boy. That's all the reason we need to kill 'em." Daniel took one step forward, and all four of his sons flinched. "I'll say this just once: Try to run, I'll put a bullet in you, myself."

Asa's mouth went dry, and he glanced at his brothers.

"Do you believe I'd do it?"

Chester took off his cap and ran a shaky hand through his dark waves of hair. "Yes, Pa. I do believe you would."

Duncan hung his head, and Edgar nodded.

Now Daniel aimed that fierce gaze at Asa. "And what about you, coward? Do you believe I'd shoot a deserter, even if he was my own son?"

"Yessir," he said, rubbing his still-throbbing jaw. "Ain't a doubt in my mind that you would."

For an instant, Asa got a glimpse of the man who'd patiently explained how to drive a nail with one strike of the hammer, the man who'd cried while burying the family dog. Where was that man now?

"Next time I see you boys, you'd better be belly-down in a rifle pit, aimin' your Springfields at them Injuns and shootin' like you mean it!"

The hours that followed seemed to Asa like a hazy nightmare; and when he came out of hiding the following afternoon, the air was heavy with the scent of gunpowder and blood. The war whoops and screams of women and children had fallen silent, but Asa knew nothing would quiet his memories of the guttural moans of the dying, some of them pleading with the murder-hungry soldiers to spare their lives.

He fought the urge to retch as, in search of his pa and brothers, he was forced to step over and around the scalps and entrails of slaughtered warriors. Then he saw Chester, down on his knees in the blood-soaked snow. He'd taken a round to the shoulder, but Asa knew instantly that it wasn't the injury that had painted the ferocious expression on his eldest brother's face.

"Look what you've done," Chester growled.

Edgar cradled their father's head in his lap. "You've killed Pa."

Anguish and fear roiled in his gut as he stared in slack-jawed shock at his father's lifeless body. But how could he have killed his pa, even by accident, when he hadn't joined them in the rifle pit? He hadn't aimed or fired a single shot.

"One more gun might have made the difference," Chester snarled, answering his unspoken question, "but you ran like a scared schoolgirl. Ran and hid behind a rock." He jerked a thumb over his shoulder. "And now, Pa and Duncan are both dead."

Duncan, too? Asa followed Chester's gaze and recognized the black and brown scarf—one of the last gifts their mother had made for Duncan before she died—fluttering in the cold breeze.

A quaking started in his boots and quickly climbed all the way to his scalp, and Asa knew the temperature hadn't caused it.

In the next moment, his brothers pounced on him like wildcats, scratching and growling, kicking and hissing. But Asa didn't lift a finger to defend himself, because Chester and Edgar were right. He'd earned the beating. When they tired of pummeling him, the brothers stood, oblivious to the confused stares of cavalrymen milling nearby.

"Better get to crawlin' on outta here like the spineless snake you are," Edgar said. "If the colonel gets word that you deserted, he'll hang you, sure as you're standin' there."

"But not before he skins you, like he done them outlaws awhile back," Chester added.

The scene flashed in Asa's mind of those men—accused of robbing settlements, wagon trains, and banks—being rounded up and manacled, then butchered and left for the coyotes and vultures. In Chivington's twisted mind, they weren't worth the time or effort that would be required to bring them back to stand trial.

Asa had never known a fear that was more raw or real. Nor had he known such self-revulsion. Was Chester right? If he'd stayed and fought, could his participation have made the difference between life and death for his pa and Duncan?

Aching from head to toe, humiliated, cold, and more alone than he'd felt since his ma's passing, Asa started walking. He didn't stop until three days later, when he passed out from hunger, exposure, and exhaustion.

∼

April 15, 1883 • Denver, Colorado

Shortly after sunup, Nell Holstrom passed through the heavy wrought-iron gate of the cemetery, cradling five bouquets of Granny's Bonnet in the crook of her arm. The winter had been hard on the zigzagging brick path, and she took care to avoid tripping on the sharp edges that protruded from the dirt.

On her way to the far corner, she passed a child-sized stone angel sitting atop a rounded headstone, then a ten-foot obelisk, three intricately carved crosses, and a giant clamshell. If she'd had the money to afford elaborate memorials, would she have immortalized her loved ones that way? Not likely, because they'd been simple people who'd lived simple lives. Anything more than an unembellished stone would have made their strict frugality a lie.

The path ended where the low-hanging branches of an Engelmann spruce shaded a small group of plain markers. She brushed away the crisp leaves and pine needles that covered their names, birthdates, and deaths, and replaced them with flowers—blue for her grandpa, pa, and brother; pink for her mother and grandma.

Many of those who'd suffered the hardships of mining were rewarded with great wealth. The Holstrom Mine, on the other hand, gave nothing and took everything and everyone. Her pa, the last to go, had held fast to his belief—even as a sobbing Nell had scrambled to free him from the dirt and rocks and rotting wood trapping him—that, one day, the family claim would prove the naysayers wrong. He hadn't used his last breath to say goodbye or to tell her he loved her. Instead, he'd told her where to find charges, maps, and a small cache of gold to help her get by until she uncovered the vein.

If he truly had left money and other treasures in the tumbledown shack, she would not be the one to find them, because on the day Nell had laid him to rest, she'd vowed never return to the detestable place that had turned first her grandpa and then her pa into men so obsessed with striking it rich that no sacrifice was too great. As much as she loved them, Nell also hated them for allowing their greed to make her an orphan.

Her mission fulfilled, Nell got to her feet and brushed the dirt from her skirt. While it was true that she had no living relatives, God had blessed her with a loving church family, as well as friends who'd become almost as important as the people buried here.

But self-pity never got anyone anywhere. And life had taught her that the only way to smother it was through hard work and good deeds. She had mastered the "hard work" part, thanks to her job at the DiMaggios' store, as well as the eighteen months it had taken her to transform Joe's unused tool shed into the warm and cozy cottage she called home.

Any day now, she would put the "good deeds" part into action as never before, because when the grocer's mother-in-law arrived, Nell would have to give up her job and the cottage, too. She understood that the grieving widow needed some occupation to fill her lonely hours. And, having shared many Sunday dinners with the DiMaggio family, Nell knew they couldn't fit even one more person into the cramped apartment above their store. What choice did they have but to move the poor woman into the cottage?

Joe had given her a small sum as reimbursement for the work she'd done to the interior and exterior, for the cast-off furniture she'd refinished, and for the curtains she'd sewn, all on her own time and at her own expense. But good jobs were scarce. Would the money tide her over until she found new employment and another place to live?

Nell glanced at her father's headstone and fought tears, remembering how he'd used the last of his strength to tell her that if she were to pry up a certain floorboard under his rickety cot, she'd find a small sack of nuggets and a stack of folding money. Had that been the truth, or merely the ramblings of a dying man? Hopefully, she'd never feel so desperate that she'd need to go back there and find out, one way or the other.

She said a prayer for his soul—and for the soul of every Holstrom buried near him—before leaving the graveyard with her chin held high. There wasn't time for regrets. She needed a job and a room to rent.

Shop by shop, Nell made her way through town, inquiring in every store, regardless of whether there was a "Help Wanted" poster in the window. She refused to give up because, surely, in a city the size of Denver, an able-bodied, honest person who was willing to work hard could find work and a place to live!

Regrettably, it seemed no one was hiring. Few things scared Nell more than the prospect of being homeless and destitute. She sat on the steps of the bank, held her head in her hands, and tried to pray. She'd said countless prayers for others but couldn't remember the last time she'd prayed for herself. Did she even remember how?

Lord, You have always provided for my most basic needs, every day of my life. All I ask now is that You would lead me to a job that will put a roof over my head and food in my stomach. Anything more than that, I'll consider a blessed gift from—

The sound of fluttering of paper drew her attention to the bulletin board behind her. Nell stood, thinking to secure the flyer before the spring winds sent it sailing down the street. Smoothing it flat, she read the words printed upon it.

IMMEDIATE OPENING
Experienced Housekeeper and Cook
See Asa Stone, Proprietor, Stone Hill Inn on Sterling Street

Her heart pounding, Nell grabbed the advertisement and stuffed it inside the front pocket of her jacket. All her life, she'd heard people say that God worked in mysterious ways. Could this be His answer to her prayer for a job *and* a home?

Chapter Two

Even in its current state, with faded white clapboard siding and sagging black shutters, Stone Hill Inn was a sight to behold. Situated high on a hill two streets behind Denver's main thoroughfare, it stood three stories tall and boasted a towering turret. Intricate dentil mouldings followed the roofline, and the deep porch supported a double-wide balcony that was accessible from two second-story rooms.

In recent months, Nell had seen a man working there, all on his own. Day by day, he labored from dawn till dusk, whether balanced on a ladder or bent over his sawhorse.

On her way there, Nell had to pass the DiMaggios', so she stopped in for a quick visit.

"There he is again," she said, pointing across the street. "Hard at work, as usual."

Joe nodded. "Yeah, that's Asa Stone for you."

"How odd that in all the months I've worked for you, Mr. Stone and I haven't been formally introduced." God willing, that fact would change within the hour.

"Guess keeping to yourselves must be a Holstrom family trait," Joe muttered. "Your people never were big on socializing when you came into town."

She couldn't argue with that. The mine had occupied her family day and night during their years in Colorado. On the few occasions they'd come to town, there hadn't been time for polite chitchat.

"If you were nosier, you would've heard the stories." Joe chuckled good-naturedly. "I declare, I've never met a woman like you, Nell Holstrom. You're not the least bit interested in his past, are you?"

"It isn't that I'm not interested, exactly." In truth, Nell was very curious, especially now that he stood to become her next employer. "But, based on what little I've heard, Mr. Stone hasn't had an easy life. I'd hate to compound his pain by asking questions that might unearth ugly memories."

Joe eyed the advertisement poking out of her pocket. "Are you thinking of going to work for him?"

"Yes," Nell admitted. "As a matter of fact, that's where I'm headed next."

"Then, curious or not, there are a few things you need to know. If he seems taciturn, don't be offended. It's just his way. The man's quieter than the proverbial church mouse."

"I suppose there's something to be said for a person who doesn't waste words."

"He wasn't always that way. Fifteen or twenty years ago, before his pa dragged him and his brothers out of town, he was quite the prankster. It was all in good fun, mind you, but he got into his share of mischief. So did the other boys." Joe shook his head. "Don't think I'll ever understand how Asa's pa could up and leave his own parents with no one to look out for them, as old and sick as they were."

He went on to explain how Silas and Abigail Stone had held their own for a while, but then, before long, as their health had deteriorated, so had the hotel. Nell got the picture: With so many other options for lodging in town, why would anybody choose to rent a room in a falling-down place?

"There at the end, the Stones were down to eating whatever the good ladies of the church brought by." Joe heaved a great sigh. "And then, from out of the blue, Asa rode into town on a sway-backed nag. Most folks didn't even recognize him, all grown-up and bearded, lookin' like he was carrying the weight of the world on his shoulders. Nobody ever found out why, 'cause he guarded every word he spoke…and nobody expected he'd stay once he got an eyeful of that mess." He nodded toward the inn. "Good thing I'm not a gambler, 'cause I'd-a lost my shirt on that bet."

But, to Asa's credit, Asa had stayed; and, according to Joe, he'd cared tirelessly for his grandparents, right up until the day Jesus had called them home.

"How did they die?" Nell asked. "Old age, or…?"

"Silas went first," Joe said "The consumption, if I remember right. Abigail…guess you'd say she died of a broken heart. Never got over losin' Silas, and so, 'round three months after we buried him, we buried her, too."

"How long ago?"

"Oh, nine or ten months now, I guess."

And yet, Asa had stayed and continued working on the old place. On a handful of occasions, she'd seen him in the store. Joe hadn't exaggerated when he'd said Asa didn't say much and preferred keeping to himself. But what had turned a once-gregarious boy into a near hermit?

"Whatever became of his pa and brothers?" Nell asked next.

Joe held out his hands. "Don't rightly know. Some say they signed on with the cavalry, got themselves killed during the Indian wars. Others say they joined up with an outlaw gang, got shot robbin' a bank." He leaned forward, propping his elbows on the counter. "Wish I could keep you on, Nell. I hate to think of you over there, day after day, trying to please that sour-faced fella."

Nell shrugged. "If he hires me, I'll consider myself blessed, and get my fill of conversation at church or when I come here to shop for groceries." She started for the door. "Wish me luck," she added over her shoulder.

Nell hurried down the steps, lifting her skirts, and crossed the street, pausing to kick a ball back to a group of boys playing in the street.

"Thanks, Miz Holstrom," said one.

"Could-a kicked it my way," the other yelled, grinning. "He's already ahead by three!"

"Sorry!" she hollered, starting up the hill that led to the inn. "Next time!"

Nell rarely had reason to venture to Sterling Street, so it was odd to see the entire facade of the inn rather than simply the roof peaks and turret, visible from below. She tried ringing the bell, but it produced no sound, so she rapped on the door, instead. When that, too, proved futile, she tried the door and, finding it unlocked, went inside and followed the scent of fresh-cut wood and the sound of a wood saw.

There he was, at the opposite end of the foyer, his shirtsleeves rolled up and his handsome brow furrowed as he concentrated on cutting through a thick board.

"Hello, Mr. Stone?" she called.

He turned, looking slightly annoyed by the interruption. "Yes?"

She took a few steps closer. "I'm here about the job?" Nell slid the ad from her pocket and held it up. "The one you posted on the bank's bulletin board?"

"I see." Straightening from his work, he wiped his hands on a bandanna. "You're the girl who works at the DiMaggios' store. Name's Holstrom, right?"

"Yes. Nell Holstrom." And in the event he considered age a factor in his hiring decision, she quickly added, "But I'm hardly a girl."

"Is that so?" He tucked the bandanna into a back pocket of his trousers and gave her a quick scan. "And just how old are you, Nell Holstrom?"

"Twenty-five."

He arched one of his dark eyebrows, as if to signal that he didn't believe her. Arms crossed over his chest, he began walking a slow circle around her, nodding all the way. She'd seen men do the same thing at the stockyards. If she didn't need this job so badly, Nell would have told him she didn't appreciate being inspected like a cow on the auction block!

"You're barely bigger than a minute," he said. "I'd say you weren't cut out to work here, if I hadn't seen you hefting sacks of meal and wearing down the bristles of Joe DiMaggio's push broom." He came to a stop directly in front of her. "But I presume your duties there included more than sweeping floors and stocking shelves."

Nell cleared her throat. "You presume correctly. I was in charge of the children when they weren't in school. I also tended the garden, cleaned the house, scrubbed the laundry, prepared most of the family's meals, and often helped Joe balance his ledger books."

"Is that so?" His eyebrows disappeared behind the dark waves of hair overhanging his forehead. "Makes me wonder what the missus does all day."

"I'm sure you're well aware that Michelle helps run the store," Nell replied, trying to keep the indignation out of her tone. "It keeps her very busy. Too busy to—." She clammed up, realizing it was unlikely for a man of few words to hire a chatterbox.

Strangely, one corner of his mouth turned up in a faint grin. As pleasant as the sight was—especially compared to the stern expression that had been there before—Nell had no idea what she'd said to inspire it.

Asa nodded. "I admire your loyalty. Your work ethic. Seems you made yourself indispensable to the DiMaggios."

"If I were indispensable," she said, "I wouldn't be looking for work, now, would I?"

He shrugged one shoulder.

"In addition to employment," she continued, choosing her words carefully, "I am also in need of a place to live." She proceeded to tell him how, in addition to her small salary, the DiMaggios had given her a place to live, rent free. "I turned their unused tool shed into a one-room cottage." Lest he think she expected the same from him, Nell quickly added, "I found and refinished every piece of furniture, at my own expense and on my own time. But it takes very little to satisfy me."

A frown creased his brow. "And you're leaving it all because…?"

"Because Michelle's mother is due in town any time now." *You would have known*, she thought, *if you took the time for friendly conversation while shopping for groceries!* "When she arrives, she'll assume my duties and also move into the cottage behind the store, as there is no room to spare in the upstairs apartment. I understand," she continued, "that it doesn't make fiscal sense to keep me on once she arrives. Family comes first, after all. However, I've been on my own long enough to know that *understanding* won't keep a roof over my head or food in my stomach."

With his arms still folded over his chest, Asa watched her from where he stood, leaning against the registration desk—and looking bored as ever. If she got this job, Nell intended to make a point of culling her words.

After a few moments of apparent contemplation, Asa straightened, returned to his sawhorse, and put two tenpenny nails between his teeth. "You'll find food in the root cellar," he said, his eyes on his project, "but I'm afraid the kitchen will need a good cleaning before you can put supper on the table." He punctuated the statement by pounding one of the nails into the newly sawed board.

Cooking? And cleaning? *Now?* "Does that mean…? Am I…?" *I wouldn't be the least bit surprised if he called you "Nell the numb-skull"!* she thought. Then she straightened her posture and raised her chin a notch. "Do I have the job, Mr. Stone?"

He raised his big green eyes to meet her gaze. "We'll see. Call me Asa." With that, he went back to work.

He hadn't told her where to find the root cellar, the kitchen, or anything else she'd need to give the place a thorough cleaning and get a meal on the table. If he wanted proof that she was the type who could work without supervision, that was exactly what he would get. And if he saw scrubbing and preparing a rib-sticking meal as some sort of test, she aimed to pass it!

She turned on her heel and followed her instincts down the hall to find the kitchen just where she'd suspected it would be. And, as expected, Asa had understated how much work the room needed. Nell turned in a slow circle, wondering where to begin, and how in the world she'd have time to put the room in order *and* prepare supper.

One of the walls was lined with wooden crates stacked four and five high. Beside them, an ungainly pile of rolled-up rugs and an odd assortment of chairs and side tables. Clearly, Asa's efforts since the passing of his grandparents had been dedicated almost exclusively to the inn's exterior. How had he prepared any meals with the kitchen is such disarray?

The first order of business, Nell decided, was to get something on the stove. That way, while it simmered, she could roll up her sleeves and plow through the mess.

That meant she'd need to find the root cellar. Exiting through the creaking kitchen door, she descended the steps of the covered porch and followed a messy path through the backyard to a set of double doors set into the side of the house.

"The root cellar, no doubt," she said, lifting one door and then the other. As she descended into the darkness, she wondered what manner of bedlam awaited her at the bottom of the crumbling stone steps.

Holding her hands up to protect her face from the curtains of cobwebs hanging from the low ceiling, Nell surveyed the space. There wasn't enough time to organize it now, but if she hoped to make use of the jars of food that lined sagging shelves, it wasn't a job that could be put off for very long.

Using her apron as a makeshift sack, she quickly filled it with potatoes, carrots, onions, and turnips—the makings of a good stock for tonight's supper. She also took a jar of green beans and two jars of fruit—whether apples or peaches, she couldn't tell due to the dim lighting. After delivering her cache to the kitchen, Nell made a second trip into the dungeon-like space for enough flour and sugar to make bread and cobbler.

Whenever she found time to put the place in order, she'd need a lantern, a long-handled broom, and a bucket of sudsy water, because only the good Lord knew how many mice had set up housekeeping down there.

She ran a finger across the surface of the rusty, fat-spattered cookstove. "You can't very well prepare a decent meal on this filthy old thing," she muttered with a grimace. She'd need boiling-hot water to give it a proper cleaning, but firing up the stove would only fuse the dirt and grease onto the iron surface.

Then she remembered the fireplace she'd spied out back, towering between the terrace and an overgrown vegetable patch. Like the kitchen, it had become a place to stow things. She went back outside and, after digging through chunks of wood and fallen tree limbs, found a rake. After clearing the area as best she could, she piled the fireplace with dry grass and weeds from the garden to use as kindling, then filled a battered old pot with water. As she waited for it to boil, she dragged the crates and furniture from the kitchen to the storeroom behind it, removed the threadbare curtains, gave the grimy windows a good scrubbing, and cleared a space on the counter to peel and pare vegetables for the stew.

An hour later, after scouring the kitchen stove inside and out, Nell fired it up. And an hour after that, with soup bubbling gently on the stovetop and bread dough rising on the counter, she started going through the cupboards.

In the pie safe, she found tins of salt and lard to flavor the soup; in the sideboard was a stash of kitchen linens. For now, the embroidered tea towels would serve nicely as curtains for the now-shining windows.

Next, she dragged one of the rugs out back, gave it a thorough beating, hauled it back inside, and arranged it in the middle of the sparkling floor. Then, one by one, she polished four chairs and a medium-sized round table, which she placed in the center of the rug.

Before long, having washed, dried, and stored every plate, cup, pot, pan, fork, and spoon, she had nothing left to do but set the table.

The aromas of fresh-baked bread and peach cobbler filled the air as Nell went to summon Asa for supper. She paused in front of the hallway mirror, and even through the film of grime, she could see evidence of her hard day's work. She spent a few seconds slapping the dust from her skirt and rearranging her hair in a bun, then used the hem of her apron to wipe the soot and sweat from her cheeks.

The moment she stepped into the foyer, Nell could see that Asa, too, had accomplished a lot in the hours that had passed since they'd last spoken. The reception counter shone with a fresh coat of varnish.

"Mr. Stone? Supper is ready."

"About time," he said, facing her. "The smell's been driving me mad for hours now. And please, it's Asa, remember?" He wrapped a rag around the tip of his index finger and dipped it into a jar of kerosene. "Give me a minute to clean up, and I'll be right in."

She'd just finished tying the strings of the starched white apron she'd found in the dining-room china cabinet when he entered the room. His gaze traveled from the gleaming windows to the shining floorboards to the table, where a white bowl, a silver spoon, and a tumbler of milk sat atop a red and white checkered tablecloth. In the center, she'd put the stewpot on a wooden trivet, and beside it sat a towel-lined basket of thick-sliced bread. Behind her on the counter, crusty apple cobbler cooled in a black iron skillet.

Nell plucked a towel from the shelf beside the sink, thankful that the cedar-lined buffet drawers had protected the linens from dirt and dust. She held it out to him. "There's warm water in the basin, there," she said, pointing, "so you can wash off the kerosene before you eat. I have plenty to do in the dining room, so just call me when you've finished eating, and I'll serve up your dessert."

He rolled up his sleeves as he approached the sink. "You really expect me to eat alone?" He plunged his hands into the soapy water and began to scrub. "You've made enough food for a family of six. Guess old habits die hard."

He was referring, she presumed, to her work for the DiMaggios. If he decided to hire her, it would take time to learn to cook for just one—or two.

"Please, set a place for yourself," he said as he dried his hands. "Few things irk me more than wastefulness."

Nell gratefully did as instructed—she had worked up quite an appetite—then began ladling the steaming stew into two bowls. "I hope you don't mind plain bread," she said, sliding the bread basket toward him. "There wasn't time to go purchase butter."

He looked around, then gave a small grin. "Can't imagine why."

When Asa folded his hands and bowed his head, Nell was surprised. She had never seen him in church.

Even more surprising was the way her heart suddenly started beating too hard and too fast for her to hear a word of his blessing.

Chapter Three

Asa spent most of the night pacing the downstairs rooms of the inn, stopping now and then to peek inside a drawer or cupboard to marvel at their cleanliness. Years of neglect had left the kitchen in chaos; and yet, in just a few short hours, Nell had restored it to the spotless, welcoming room it had been when his grandmother managed the inn.

Evidence of Nell's contributions didn't stop there. She'd raked away the leaves from the flagstone path leading to the root cellar, cleaned the outdoor fireplace and burned the debris that had collected inside it, and swept the back porch, rearranging the rocking chairs and side tables so that, if he had a mind to, a man could sit and watch the early-morning sun climb toward the snowcapped peaks of the Rockies.

And this morning, Asa had a mind to. He leaned back, propped his boots on the railing, and smiled.

Last night after supper, he'd issued Nell a perfunctory thank you for the meal and for all the work she had done before promptly excusing himself to resume replacing the missing shelves in the mail unit behind the reception counter. By the time he'd returned to the kitchen, she'd been long gone, but she'd left a note.

"Dear Asa," it began. "I've already measured out the water and coffee for you. Once the water comes to a boil, move the pot to this trivet." She'd drawn an arrow, so he couldn't miss it, and signed the note with a feminine flourish. Beside the coffeepot was a big old mug that brought back good memories from his childhood, for his grandmother used to fill it with warm cider in the wintertime and cool lemonade during the summer months.

He was still smiling when he crossed the street and entered the DiMaggios'. And who wouldn't grin with a belly full of leftover apple cobbler and the taste of the most flavorful coffee still in his mouth?

"Asa! Good to see you," Joe greeted him. "What can I do for you today?"

"Time to restock the pantry," Asa answered, "and I need some cleaning supplies. Related to laundry, mostly."

In a few minutes' time, Joe had collected several cartons of soap crystals, a box of starch, and a bottle of bluing, all of which he arranged on the counter.

"Did Abigail have a flatiron?" he asked. "A washtub? Mangle?"

"All of the above," Asa said, "but they've stood unused so long, they're rusted and useless."

While Joe moved about the store, filling his arms with replacement supplies, Asa wondered how the grocer would feel about Nell's coming to work for him at Stone Hill. And how long would it be until she was released her from her job here?

"Well, Asa, it's the end of life as I know it. My mother-in-law is coming to live with us." Joe rolled his eyes. "If you're smart, you'll never marry." He held up a hand. "Don't get me wrong—having a *wife* is a good thing. It's when she invites her mama to move in that things get…." He finished with a sigh.

"Could just as easily have been your ma who needed a place to stay."

"True enough. But *my* ma was a saint." Laughing at his own joke, Joe added a washboard to the assemblage of supplies. "And what about a sewing machine? Did your grandmother have one of those?"

Asa followed the man's pointer finger to the shiny Singer in the corner. Nell had hung simple tea towels at the kitchen windows, a suitable substitute for curtains. But what could she do in the guest rooms with a proper machine?

It dawned on him then that he hadn't offered her the job. Not officially, anyway. He needed to set that straight the first chance he got, before some other business owner in town snapped her up.

"How soon before you can let Nell go?" he asked Joe.

"Maria should be here day after tomorrow. I'll ask Nell to put a final shine on the cottage. Once she's done, you can have her—as early as tomorrow, if you have a place to put her."

A pang of guilt shot through Asa when he realized they'd been talking about Nell as if she were a piece of furniture. Even if she hadn't proven her worth—and she most certainly had—she deserved far better than that.

"Of course, there's a place for her," he said. "And I'm happy to have her as soon as she's available. In fact, I should have a word with her now. Is she upstairs?"

"She's in the back room, balancing the books," Joe said. He released a wistful sigh. "She's a hard worker. The apartment's never been so clean. And she presses clothes with all the right creases, even my work shirtsleeves." He held out his arm to prove it. "Takes such good care of the children, strangers have mistaken her for their mother. Word to the wise, though"—he patted his stomach—"you'd better set aside some money for new trousers."

Asa raised his eyebrows.

"She's a wonderful cook. Couple of months from now, you'll wonder what happened to that flat belly of yours." Joe looked around, then lowered his voice to add, "Between you and me, I'll miss her bookkeeping most of all. That gal can add up a row of numbers faster than you can say 'How-do.'"

"I'll just have a quick word with her, then, while you add up what I owe you for everything."

Joe picked up a tablet and a pencil. "Sewing machine, too?"

Asa nodded, then headed for the storeroom. He paused just outside the door and knocked softly, not wanting to startle Nell. He wondered how she managed such a tedious task with so little light. When she looked up, the room brightened with her smile.

"Mr. Stone—I mean, Asa. How are you this morning?"

"Fine, fine. Stopped by to offer you the job—if you still want it—and to pick up some supplies. If you can think of anything you'll need...." He noticed a large bandage on the back of her hand. "What happened there?" he asked, nodding at it.

She hid her hand in her lap. "Oh, it's nothing. Just a little splinter."

A little splinter, under a wrap that thick? Asa didn't think so. He hadn't noticed it last night at supper. Had she injured herself while cleaning up afterward?

"Yes," she said next.

"Yes," what? Asa wondered.

His confusion must have been obvious, for she added, "Yes, I'd like very much to come work for you."

It sure didn't seem like it, though, given her serious expression and monotone reply.

"But you have reservations...? Perhaps because we never discussed a salary?"

"Oh, no, it isn't that. Well, it sort of is...salary, I mean. It's just...well, I imagine you'll want to make all the rooms available for guests, so I'll need to earn enough to afford a room in town...."

He immediately thought of the storage area behind the kitchen. The woodstove in there would warm her, even on the coldest days. She'd have windows—two of them—and a set of doors opening onto the terrace. Properly furnished, it could become a suite, of sorts, that she could have all to herself.

"Something close by," she continued, "since I'll have to walk to and from work, and mostly in the dark—"

"I see no reason for you to trek back and forth twice a day," he put in. "A waste of time and shoe leather, and unsafe, too. But I have something in mind for your lodging." He paused, wondering how to ask her when she could report for duty without sounding like a greedy clod. "Has Joe said how much longer he'll need you?"

She exhaled softly. "I'm guessing he'll want me out of the cottage by morning, so his mother-in-law can move right in when she gets here."

"Well, just let me know what time you'll arrive so I can help you move in."

Nell chuckled softly. "I appreciate the offer, but I won't need any help. Everything I own fits nicely into one satchel—with room to spare, I might add—and I think I can manage that on my own." She grinned. "Perhaps I could arrive mid-afternoon, in time to fix your supper?"

"What about the furniture you bought and refinished for the cottage out back? You're more than welcome to bring it. We can load it up in my wagon—"

"Again, I appreciate the offer, but I won't be taking any of it with me." Nell averted her gaze. "Michelle's mother will need those pieces, and Joe put a little extra into my final pay envelope as reimbursement."

A woman who could fit all of her personal belongings into one bag? Asa would believe it when he saw it. And she still hadn't asked how much he would pay her. Between now and when she moved in, he'd make a point of finding out the going rate, to which he would add a small amount.

"I really ought to get back to work," she said, tapping the ledger with her pencil. "I still need to give the cottage a thorough cleaning before moving out. But I'll be happy to report for duty in time to fix your supper tonight, if you like."

Nell punctuated the offer with a smile and a smart salute, and when she did, Asa noticed that a penny-sized drop of blood had seeped through the gauze on her hand. If she was still bleeding when she showed up for work, he'd make sure she'd removed the whole splinter, and then he'd mix up a poultice of lanolin and iodine and wrap it up good and tight. That would be the easy part. The hard part would be making sure she kept it dry until it healed.

"Sounds good," he said, glancing at the clock on the wall. At best, he had six hours to make the storeroom comfortable for Nell.

"All right, then. I'll see you soon." Following a short nod, she bent over the DiMaggio Grocery books once again.

Asa paused in the doorway, wondering the reasons for her dismissive reaction—and why it had disappointed him. What had he expected—a joyful dance? From a woman who was about to trade one demanding job for another?

She looked up at him and raised her eyebrows. "Was there something else?"

"No." He felt the heat of a blush creep up his neck. "No, of course not. Guess I'd better get back out there and pay before Joe sells those supplies out from under me."

He made his way to the counter, where Michelle DiMaggio stood chatting with local reverend Meb Truett.

"Well, as I live and breathe," the pastor thundered, "if it isn't the elusive Asa Stone!" He extended a hand. "Tell me, how are the renovations coming over at Stone Hill?"

Asa took his hand in a brief shake. "Slow going, but I'm making progress."

"Your grandparents would be awful proud of you, son." Meb dropped a fatherly hand on Asa's shoulder. "I'm sure you know that you made their last days brighter, coming home when you did."

Asa knew no such thing. He'd spent years wandering aimlessly, trying to outrun the shame of his past deeds. He had no idea how their health had waned in the time he'd been away. If he'd had the heart—and the backbone—to put the past behind him sooner, they might still have been with him.

"From the looks of this order," the grocer's wife said, filling the uncomfortable silence, "you're about ready to welcome guests."

"Not quite, but it shouldn't be long." Asa pointed at the bolts of material lining a nearby shelf. "Need some fabric for curtains, too."

Meb nodded at the stack of goods. "Now I understand. All these things are for your new…what's the proper term? Assistant?"

Until that moment, Asa hadn't given a thought to Nell's title. He'd advertised for a cook and housekeeper, but he also planned on having her mind the front desk and help him balance the books from time to time. Not to mention the help he would need, redecorating the guest rooms….

"Are you looking for heavy cloth to block the light?" Michelle asked, interrupting his musings. "Or will the draperies be strictly decorative?"

"I…uh, I'm not sure."

She laughed, looking briefly at Meb. "Do *all* men avoid such decisions, or just those I'm acquainted with?" Then she returned her attention to Asa. "Let me put it to you a different way: If the purpose is to block sunlight and provide privacy, you'll need a certain type of fabric. On the other hand, if the point of the draperies is to coordinate with the rugs and furniture in a room, you'll need another type. And if you want both…." Grinning, she lifted her shoulders. "*Capisce?*"

"I guess dual-purpose makes the most sense," he finally said.

"Your new assistant's a bright, resourceful young woman," Meb said. "I'm sure she'll make some helpful suggestions."

Michelle laughed. "Nell will do more than that. She'll measure the windows and add up how much cloth and hanging hardware you'll need."

In the meantime, though, Nell would need something to cover the windows of her new quarters. Asa explained as much, then picked out two readymade curtains: a pale blue calico, because it reminded him of Nell's eyes, and white lace, like the collar of the dress she was wearing today.

"Well done, Asa Stone. Nell will love these."

"Hope so."

"I think it's just wonderful that you're doing all of this for her," Michelle said as she opened a cupboard. Lowering her voice, she added, "I feel so guilty, sending her away from here with nothing but that pitiful satchel of frayed dresses." She grabbed a colorful quilt from the middle of the stack and set it on the counter. "No charge for this," she whispered. "My way of thanking her for all she's giving up so that my mother will feel right at home the minute she arrives."

"I'll be sure to let her know where it's from," Asa told her.

"It *is* a beautiful thing you're doing," Meb said. "Nell is built of sturdy stuff, but she's been on her own for much of her life. She'd never admit it, of course, but I'm sure she's terrified of having to start all over, all over *again*." He donned his black bowler hat and gave it a tap. "Now, if you'll both excuse me, I have a sermon to write."

"Say hello to Tillie for me," Michelle told him, then turned to Asa. "Let me call little Joey to help transport your purchases. No need for you to make half a dozen trips back and forth across the street."

"Oh, don't bother the boy," Asa said. "I can transfer everything in two trips. How much?" he asked, opening his wallet.

Joe stepped up beside his wife and handed Asa a sales slip. "That's everything, with the exception of that pretty blue quilt." He winked at his wife. "And I wholeheartedly agree—Nell has been more than generous with us. It's the least we can—"

"Hold up, there," Asa interrupted him. "If the quilt's meant to replace payment for the work she did in turning that old shack into a cottage, I'll pay you twice what it's worth."

"Relax, Stone," Joe told him. "The girl has been good to us, and we'll be good to her. The quilt is a gift, just as Michelle said. And we'll pay her fairly for all her work on the cottage."

Asa studied his face and nodded slowly. "Glad to hear it." He dropped several bills on the counter—more than enough to cover the supplies *and* the quilt—then gathered as many of his purchases as he could carry. "I'll be back for the rest," he said over the stack in his arms.

Outside, Asa walked a few extra steps to the left to dodge a large puddle, putting him eye to eye with a fresh batch of wanted posters hanging on the facade of the sheriff's office. How many years had it been since his own likeness had appeared on a board much like this one?

"Not nearly enough," he muttered, his heart hammering as he dodged wagons and buggies on his way across the street. "Not nearly enough."

Chapter Four

Seeing those wanted posters worried Asa more than he cared to admit. After all this time, it was highly unlikely that anyone would recognize him from the one posted all those years ago. "Lucky for you," Jesse James had said, "nobody got a good look at you." The proof? His wanted poster hadn't looked a thing like him. "Why, they even spelt your name wrong!" Jesse had added.

Sweeping dirt and debris from the storeroom made him think back to the day when Jesse found him, dirty and hungry, mucking stalls in a Reno stable. When Jesse extended the invitation to join his makeshift family, Asa had jumped at the opportunity. Regular meals and a roof over his head? He would have been a fool to turn the man down.

If only he'd known what Jesse and his cohorts had planned for that hot July day in '81.

An engineer had died during the robbery of the Rock Island Lines train, and within hours, a posse was formed to hunt down the James-Younger Gang. No one knew for sure which outlaw killed the conductor, William Westfall, and John McCullough, the passenger who'd stepped into the line of fire. Asa knew he wasn't the guilty party—although he'd unholstered his pistol, he hadn't pulled back the hammer. And yet his likeness had appeared on wanted posters tacked to every post, pole, and bulletin board between here and Timbuktu.

Asa propped the broom in the corner and, using a shake shingle as a dustpan, scooped up the gritty dirt. Then he crouched to pry open a can of paint, using a screwdriver that was much like the one he'd used that stormy Tuesday night. Though no one had said it in so many words, the outlaws had known he wanted out and, afraid of his blowing their cover, had kept a close eye on him.

Not close enough.

One night, as they slept off the aftereffects of a rowdy poker game, Asa crawled out through a back window and started walking, stopping in towns and cities along the way just long enough to earn a few dollars for food and lodging. He walked for ten long, lonely years. North, south, and all the way to the Pacific Ocean.

And then, one day, Asa realized he'd wandered right into Denver.

Home.

He shook off the memory and looked around the room. With a fresh coat of bright white paint on the walls, it looked bigger and cleaner, a much more fitting place for Nell. Asa dipped a rag in kerosene and wiped paint spatters from his hands, awakening another bleak remembrance.

At his last job, working one month for a rancher near Golden, he'd received extra compensation for his efforts. He'd spent the money wisely and arrived at Stone Hill on the swaybacked nag the rancher had been planning on putting down, freshly bathed and wearing new clothes and polished boots, in hopes of making a good impression on the man and woman who had raised him and his brothers after his mother's death.

After what he'd seen on the battlefield at Sand Creek, few things shocked him. But that first glimpse of his grandparents, of the inn, had hit Asa hard. Then, as now, he knew the image would stick in his memory until he drew his last breath.

"Asa! Asa Stone! You in there?"

He leaned into the hallway and spied his neighbor in the foyer.

"'Mornin', Craig," he said as the man made his way to the storeroom. "What can I do for you?"

"Not a thing." Craig looked around and nodded approvingly. "The place is really starting to take shape. I can almost picture Abigail smiling down from heaven. Silas, too."

Asa took very little pleasure in the compliment. If he'd come home sooner, they might have seen the progress in person.

Craig rolled up his sleeves. "Talked with Joe earlier and he said Nell will start work here tomorrow. Is this to be her room?"

"It is."

"When does she move in?"

"Today, if all goes as planned. But you can unroll your sleeves, because I can't ask you to—"

"Craig? Craig Held, are you in here?"

"Back here, Aleta, in Nell's new room!"

Craig's wife joined them and, hands on her hips, inspected Asa's work. "Last time I was in here, it was so dark and dirty, it made my skin crawl." She met Asa's eyes. "She's going to love it. I know I would! When do you expect her?"

"Shortly before suppertime."

"My goodness! Then there isn't a minute to spare, is there?"

"Look, I appreciate the offer, but—"

"I'm guessing I'll find a bucket and some vinegar in the kitchen," Aleta said, rolling up her own sleeves.

She disappeared around the corner before he could answer.

"Is that the rug you'll put down in here?" Craig asked with a nod to the rolled-up carpet in the corner.

"Yes...."

"I'll just carry it out back and give it a couple of good whacks." He hefted the roll over one shoulder. "Where will I find the rug beater?"

"It was hanging on the clothesline last time I saw it, but really, you don't—"

He was gone before Asa could finish his sentence.

Aleta returned moments later and set down her bucket of water. Then she dragged a wooden crate closer to the windows, climbed up, and, without a word, began wiping years' worth of grease and grime from the glass.

"As soon as I've finished here," she said over one shoulder, "I'll fetch any other items or furnishings you have in mind for this room."

"Such as…?" Asa had thought he'd covered everything, but perhaps there were some items Nell would need that he hadn't anticipated

"Those curtains I washed and pressed the other day will look lovely with that rug." She hesitated, and without turning around, added, "And you can just wipe that worried look from your face, Asa Stone," she said without turning around, "because I've already hung brand new ones where the old ones used to be. Nothing will please me more than knowing Nell will have something bright and cheery hanging at *her* windows."

What could he say but thank you? "I happen to know that Nell loves to read, so you might consider bringing in a few books. And lanterns, too, so she can read after dark. And what about a bookcase? Is there one that isn't in use, perhaps in one of the guest rooms?"

"I'm sure there is." She was a whirlwind, that Aleta Held! He left the happily humming woman, now hard at work polishing every surface in sight, to search the guest rooms for the items she'd suggested.

With Craig's help, Asa brought down a headboard, a foot-board, a bureau, and two cozy chairs with coordinating ottomans. Aleta cleaned them up, then told the men where to put them.

"There's a pot of soup on the stove in our kitchen," she told Craig, shooing the men from the room. "Please help yourselves. You can sit and eat on the porch while I make up the bed. And if you notice Nell heading this way, do something to distract her. I'd hate for her to see this before it's finished!"

Half an hour later, as he left the Helds', Asa said a silent prayer of thanks for good neighbors. He'd done nothing to earn their friendship, yet they'd treated him like a long-lost relative from the moment he'd moved back into the inn. Thanks to Craig, Aleta, and their three children, the past several months had been some of the happiest in his memory. And now, with the inn taking shape, and a dependable, capable assistant stepping up to help keep it running, he had hope for the first time in years that his life might turn out to be more than regrets and bad memories.

He was standing in the storeroom, taking in the fruits of his labors, when he heard the front door click shut. A glance at his pocket watch told him it was three fifteen. *Should have changed your shirt while you had time*, he thought, running a hand through his tangled hair as he made his way to the front hall.

What he saw next stopped him in his tracks. Nell stood, cheeks flushed from the brisk wind, one hand clutching the collar of her shawl, the other gripping the ropelike handles of a shabby suitcase.

"I, uh, I've built a fire in the parlor," he said, relieving her of the bag. "There's one in the cookstove, too."

"Who'd believe a body could catch a chill just from crossing the road?" She headed straight for the kitchen. "As soon as my hands have thawed, I'll start supper."

He watched her hang her shawl on the coat rack beside the back door, thinking that it looked good there—like it belonged.

Asa was looking forward to seeing her shawl on that hook for a long time to come.

Then he noticed her surveying all the supplies he'd hauled in earlier.

"Sorry," he said. "Meant to put those away. Guess I got a bit sidetracked."

Nell started organizing them immediately, finding a place for every jar, can, and sack. "You have absolutely no reason to apologize," she said. "This is my job, after all!"

She'd spoken matter-of-factly, but there was no mistaking the note of cheer in her voice.

"It's as though you read my mind," she continued, pumping water into the teakettle. "Every item on my shopping list is right here at my fingertips. It'll make meal preparation as easy as pie."

She put the kettle down with a clang, then opened the stove and stoked the fire.

"What a peculiar saying, 'as easy as pie,'" she muttered to herself. "Anyone who's made one knows there's nothing easy about it." She rubbed her hands together. "Oh, that does feel marvelous!" Then she looked up at Asa, still holding her valise. "Goodness me! What a ninny I am, letting you stand there all this time, holding my scruffy bag! If you'll tell me which room is mine, I'll get that ugly old thing hidden away."

It had seen better days, but he hoped she wouldn't need it again for a very long time.

"If you'll follow me...." When they reached the storeroom, he stood back and watched as she stepped inside, fingertips pressed to her lips.

"This can't be the same room," she declared after a moment. "Just yesterday, this space was a hodgepodge of clutter and cast-off junk!" She turned to him with a smile. "How did you accomplish such a transformation in such a short time?"

"I can't take all the credit," Asa admitted. "Never would have finished in time if Craig and Aleta hadn't helped."

A mischievous grin lit her face. "Promise me something."

How could he refuse when she stood there, prettier than a field of wildflowers, and blushing like a schoolgirl?

"Please don't tell the DiMaggios, but this is so much nicer than the cottage. I don't know what I did to deserve this blessing from God, but if I ever find out, I'm going to do it over and over again!"

Her obvious pleasure made him remember something Aleta had said while they worked together on the room: "Nell has no family, and very little in the way of material possessions. I have a feeling she's going to settle in here quickly, and very happily, and feel right at home."

At the time, he'd acknowledged how much he and Nell seemed to have in common. But now, looking into her sweet, guileless face, Asa was struck by how very different they were. Nell was good and pure, with no shameful secrets shadowing her every step.

"Oh, my!" Nell exclaimed, striding across the room to the sewing machine. "Just when I thought things couldn't possibly get any better!" She stooped to peer inside the notions box on the table beside it, oohing and ahhing as she inspected the contents. "With all these supplies, sewing will seem more like play than pesky work!"

Asa was dumbfounded. His mother had been an optimistic woman, as had his grandmother; but Nell? He'd never met a more agreeable, merrier person.

"Enough of this dillydallying," Nell said. "I'll get supper on, and while it's cooking, I'll see how much work I can do in the dining room."

She'd already put in a long day at the DiMaggios', yet here she stood, still raring to go. Something told him Nell would be worth twice her salary, as long as she didn't keel over from exhaustion, as any normal person tasked with her responsibilities would be wont to do.

"The dining room can wait till tomorrow," Asa told her. "Wouldn't you rather discuss your salary?"

Nell shrugged and headed for the kitchen, and he followed.

"I trust you to be fair, Asa."

He couldn't remember the last time anyone had used the words "trust" and "Asa" in the same sentence.

On second thought, he could. Just days before slipping into a coma, his grandfather had summoned Asa to his bedside, pressed a crinkled sheet of paper into his hand, and insisted that he read it aloud. The mere memory of that first, shaky line was still enough to put a lump in his throat: "I, Silas Nehemiah Stone, being of sound mind and failing body, hereby entrust all that I own to my grandson Asa Jedidiah Stone."

Nell poured hot water into the dishpan and added soap powders. "I think I'll make cottage pie for supper, since we have all the ingredients," Nell was saying. "And how about egg custard for dessert? Does that sound all right to you?"

Asa shook his head, roused from his reverie by the tantalizing menu. "I'll tell you how it sounds. Sounds like I'm bound to become fat and lazy if you continue cooking this way."

Nell grinned. "Seems to me you could use a little fattening up with all the hard work you're putting in around here."

Asa left the room, grinning from ear to ear. He'd definitely made the right choice in hiring Nell Holstrom.

Chapter Five

The next afternoon, as she removed her soiled apron, Nell remembered how she'd earned every spot and stain. It had been a busy day, but rewarding, too, as the inn was starting to shape up beautifully. After rearranging the kitchen cupboards and cleaning up the root cellar, the pantry seemed twice its size. One side of the space held tins of flour, tubs of lard, jars of meat and vegetables, and baskets of produce that would spare her running out in the weather to fetch things for the cook pot. On the other side, newly scrubbed and rearranged shelves held cakes of soap, bottles of bluing, the iron, and the washboard. Where Asa's grandmother had stored sacks of sugar and corn meal, Nell stacked towels, sheets, and pillowslips, leaving plenty of room for blankets, quilts, and bed pillows in the linen closet upstairs.

Next, she rolled in the treadle sewing machine, hung an unused brass lantern on the wall above it so that if need be, she could sew after dark. On the opposite wall, she set up the ironing board and a long narrow table that, when not covered with patterns and material she'd turn into curtains, slipcovers, and tablecloths would be the perfect place to treat stains on Asa's work shirts and trousers. Best of all, being steps from the kitchen would make it easy to haul buckets of hot water from the cookstove to the washtub.

Tomorrow, she'd make curtains from the bolt of blue fabric Asa had brought home, days ago. That way, she told herself, all the windows on the backside of the inn will match!

She reached inside her skirt pocket and popped open the lid of her father's watch—the only material possession left to remind her of him. It was only three o'clock, giving her plenty of time to get herself cleaned up and head over to the DiMaggios' to retrieve the Holstrom family Bible. If she didn't dillydally, she'd be back in plenty of time to start supper.

She carried a basin of warm water into her room. "You can be such a ninny," she scolded herself. "How could you have forgotten something as important as the family Bible?" Smoothing the lace doily on her nightstand, Nell gave a nod of approval. Here, within easy reach, is where she'd put the Good Book once she'd fetched it from the cottage.

After washing up, it didn't take long to decide what to wear— one advantage of having only three outfits. She removed her gray skirt and white blouse from the hooks in the back of the wardrobe and slipped them on. "And one advantage of working hard," she whispered, leaning closer to the full-length mirror fastened to the door, "is that there's never a need for rouge!"

After draping a cream-colored crocheted shawl around her shoulders, she hurried down to the DiMaggios'. Seconds after stepping inside, Nell found herself surrounded by the grocer's children. The boys—Joey and Dom—granted her shy grins, while Sophia eagerly grabbed Nell by the hand.

"Are you back to stay?" the girl asked. "*Please* say you're back to stay!"

Nell chuckled. "No, I'm sorry to say. Would it surprise you to hear that I forgot to pack my Bible?"

"Nell *forgot* something?" Joey exclaimed. "Just this morn- ing, I forgot to dust the tops of the cans, and Pa said, 'If you'd concentrate *half* as much on your chores as Nell does, you'd never forget anything!'"

Nell tousled his thick, dark hair. "Sorry, Joey. If I'd thought he might use that against you, I'd have purposefully overlooked a task now and then."

"Are you going to marry Mr. Stone?" Sophia asked.

"Heavens, no!" Nell said with a laugh. "Wherever did you get that idea?"

Sophia frowned. "I thought it was a sin for a man and a woman to live together unless they were married."

"It isn't the least bit sinful under these circumstances," Nell explained. "Mr. Stone is my employer, you see. I'll do the same work for him that I did for your folks."

If the look on the girl's face was any indicator, she still had questions.

"Speaking of your folks," Nell said, glancing around the store, "where are they?"

"Down at the depot," Dom said, "waiting for Nonna Maria's train."

"So soon? Oh, my!" She ruffled his hair, too. "You three must be thrilled to see her."

Dom stared at the floor. "I guess."

"Well, *I'm* not thrilled." Sophia crossed both arms over her chest. "I don't want her here."

Nell tidied the ruffles on the girl's pinafore. "But why?"

"Because I've never even met her. Pa says she doesn't speak English very well. I saw a photograph of her, standing with Grandfather. She has white hair and wears little round spectacles, like Mr. Wolfe." Sophia huffed. "I'll bet she's mean and scary and smells like him, too."

Denver's resident curmudgeon spent his days in a rocker on the sheriff's porch, waiting for unsuspecting children to walk by so he could yell "Boo!" or grab a wrist, a shirt, or a handful of hair.

He'd been doing it for so long, most adults in town remembered falling victim to his ornery sense of humor.

"I'm sure your grandmother is nothing like Abner," Nell said, drawing the girl close. "She probably looks like an older version of your mother." Then she held her at arm's length. "You don't mean to say that you think your mother looks like a scary old man!"

The boys laughed, and though she tried hard not to, even Sophia giggled quietly.

"My ma is the prettiest woman in all of Denver," she said. "In all of Colorado, even! But even if Nonna Maria looks *exactly* like Mama, I won't like her."

Just the other day, Michelle had told Nell how, when she and Joe had moved from New York to Denver, Maria stayed behind with her husband, whose heart had been too weak for the long, arduous trip. Michelle insisted that the children respond to their nonna's every letter, but words on a page—especially when accompanied by stern-faced tintypes—were a poor substitute for grandmotherly hugs and loving tweaks of the cheek.

Nell smiled at Sophia. "Once you've met her, I'm sure you'll feel differently."

She was well aware that the minute the DiMaggios returned from the train station, the children would face one of the biggest changes of their young lives. But life had already changed, drastically, for their grandmother.

"Just try for a minute to imagine being in her shoes," Nell told them. "She just lost her husband, and then she got on a train and traveled for days, all by herself. Why, I'll bet she's terrified, wondering if Denver is anything like the way it's described in the New York newspapers. And let's not forget that she barely knows your pa, and she's never even met any of you!"

Sophia thought about that for a moment. "But…but she's a grown-up," the girl said. "Grown-ups don't get scared."

"Oh, but you're wrong, sweet girl," Nell said, one hand cupping the girl's chin. "We're afraid far, far more often than you know. We've simply learned to hide our fears so that we won't terrify any curious children who might be watching us."

"Do Ma and Pa get scared, too?" Dom asked.

Nell nodded. "Yes, even your ma and pa, once in a while."

The children were quiet for a moment, and then Sophia said, "I just don't understand why you had to leave."

Nell pressed a kiss to her forehead. "Of course you do, sweet girl. There's not a square inch to spare in your apartment. Where would the poor woman sleep?"

The children exchanged guilty glances—a sign, Nell thought, that the three of them had discussed this very thing. She could only imagine where they'd decided their grandmother should spend her nights!

"You know that my ma and pa died, don't you?" Nell asked them.

All three nodded.

"And that I cried myself to sleep night after night, even after I moved into the cottage?"

With eyebrows raised and mouths turned down, they shook their heads.

"You didn't hear me because I was out back in the cottage, and you were all fast asleep in your little beds. It wasn't too hard pretending not to miss my family during the day, because I had my work to keep me from feeling too sorry for myself. And I had the three of you, of course, being...being *you*, and making me laugh. I suppose it doesn't make much sense, but crying, without having to worry about being overheard, helped me miss them less." She looked at each child in turn. "Do you understand what I'm saying?"

Nell watched as understanding dawned—hopefully followed by compassion for their grandmother.

"Besides," Nell continued, "it isn't as if I'm moving to Antarctica. I'll be right across the street. You can come visit me anytime you please. And since I'm the official cook and house-keeper at Stone Hill Inn, I'll be visiting *you* whenever I need to restock the pantry and the cleaning supplies. Why, you'll probably so sick of me by the end of the first week, you'll ask your pa to bar the door!"

They were smiling when she turned toward the cottage. "Will you do me a favor, children?"

Three voices blended in a harmonious "Yes!"

"Promise me you'll welcome your grandmother with open arms. Tell her how good it is to see her. That you're happy she made it here safely."

Three heads gave reluctant nods.

"Now, if you'll excuse me, I need to fetch my Bible from the cottage before the new resident moves in."

She didn't wait for them to agree—or disagree. Instead, Nell said, "Are you in charge of the store?" she asked Joey.

"Yeah. But only until Pa gets back."

"Then I don't suppose you'll mind if I get these two," she said, winking at Dom and Sophia, "out of your hair for a few minutes."

"Mind? It'll be a treat!" he said, smirking.

Perfect!" she said, taking the younger children's hands. "Let's get out back and find that Bible, and make sure everything is ship-shape for your grandmother."

Once inside, Nell picked up her Bible as Sophia said, "Are you really going to leave all your pretty things for a stranger? Especially after all the work you did, fixing up all this furniture?"

"First of all, Nonna Maria won't be a stranger for long," Nell replied. "I'll give her a day or two to settle in, and then I'll pay her a visit to welcome her to town. Second—and more important— I'm hoping these things will make her feel comfortable and happy. There isn't a thing out here—aside from my family Bible—that can't be replaced. People, especially family, will always be more important than possessions."

"It's like what the Sunday school teacher told us last week," Dom put in. "If anybody loves the world, the love of the Father is not in him…or something like that."

"That's exactly right," Nell said with a smile. "You keep listening to your teacher."

The threesome followed the path connecting the cottage to the back of the store. Tears stung her eyes, and she did her best to hide them. Yes, it was true that she would still see the DiMaggio children fairly often, it wouldn't be the same.

And Nell missed them already.

⌣

Stone Hill Inn would be ready to open to the public in just a few weeks, thanks in no small part to Nell. While Asa had busied himself repairing nicked baseboards and doorframes, she had whipped the guest rooms into shape. As he'd painted the parlor, she'd turned the dining room into a place where guests would also feel free to read or write letters. When he'd concentrated his efforts outside, replacing rickety porch railings, it hadn't been easy to stifle his laughter as he'd overheard her talking to herself while organizing the root cellar. And while he'd been on the roof, replacing loose slate shingles, her sweet humming had drifted up to him through the chimney, making a delight of the arduous task.

Just yesterday, she'd climbed the ladder, grinning from ear to ear, to show him her latest discovery: a hand-carved briar pipe. It had belonged to his grandfather. Now, Asa studied the smooth burl wood and ran the pad of his thumb along the curved stem and the curlicue initials decorating it. How many life lessons had he absorbed, listening as his grandfather leaned back in his creaking rocker and puffed wispy columns of smoke into the air? Eyes closed, Asa held the pipe near his nostrils and inhaled the sweet scent still clinging to the bowl.

He had Nell to thank for realizing the worth of the pipe, rather than tossing it away with the trash she'd cleared out of the attic. Of course, she seemed like the type of woman who saw value in more things than most people would. And her sudden appearance in his life underscored how alone he'd felt since Sand Creek. Since long before that, truth be told. Nell brightened every room, whether with the thoughtful positioning of knickknacks and doilies she'd found in the attic, her soul-stirring songs, or her sunny smiles. Just as she'd turned the DiMaggios' falling-down shed into a cozy cottage, she'd helped him ready Stone Hill for paying guests, and, in the process, made the place feel like *home* once again. No amount of money in a pay envelope could ever compensate her for that.

Smiling, he fingered the pipe. If he had a tin of tobacco, he could sit on the covered porch and catch the evening breeze, puffing away, just as his grandfather had always done. And, God willing, someday he would share what he'd learned along life's way with an attentive grandson or two, just as his grandfather had done with him and his brothers.

The first part, he could certainly take care of. Pocketing the pipe, he left the inn and strolled down to the grocer's, cringing slightly when the door squealed.

"Hello?" he ventured. "Anyone here?"

The DiMaggios' oldest boy, Joey, stepped up to the counter. "Pa and Ma are down at the station, but they'll be back soon. Anything I can help you with, Mr. Stone?"

"I hope so. Need some tobacco."

"We sell a lot of the Five Brothers brand." The boy stretched to reach a high shelf behind him. "There's cheaper stuff," he said, grabbing a tin, "but I've smelled it." He wrinkled his nose. "If I was old enough to puff, this is what I'd buy."

Asa inspected the container, then winked as he set a Morgan silver dollar on the counter. "Keep the change," he said. "Maybe buy some penny candy for yourself and your brother and sister."

Joey stuck out his chest and tucked both thumbs under his suspenders, mimicking his father's usual stance.

Asa was halfway out the door when he saw Nell striding purposefully toward the inn, a large book that appeared to be a Bible tucked under one arm. She looked more serious than he'd ever seen her.

"There goes Nell," Joey said on a sigh. "We'll miss having her around. She stopped by to get her family Bible, and she showed it to us—it's got a family tree with lots of folks she's related to. Only most of them are dead."

Perhaps that explained her serious demeanor. Viewing that particular page surely reminded her that she'd lost every family member listed there. Asa understood that kind of loneliness better than most.

"Will that be all, Mr. Stone?"

He shook his head to snap out of his musings. "Yes, that will do it. Thanks, Joey." As he made for the door, he paused to add, "I hope your pa knows what a good son he's raising." *And I hope that you know how blessed you are to be part of a big, loving family,* he thought.

Chapter Six

Nell slipped the strap of her apron over her head, taking care not to catch it on any hairpins. Having only a few dozen in the satin-lined, white porcelain box on her bureau, she couldn't afford to lose even one.

She'd found the box in the attic while looking for figurines and lamps to decorate the tables and bureaus in the guest rooms. Chipped and cracked in several places, and with a creaking hinge and a missing foot, the box was useless to visitors but perfect for storing her sole pair of earrings and her tiny cameo pin. It, too, had seen better days, but that never stopped her from threading a narrow ribbon through the small gold link and tying it to her petticoat bodice—as close to her heart as she could wear her only memento of her mother.

She patted the cameo, smoothed the skirt of her yellow calico dress, and inspected her reflection in a silver serving spoon. It wouldn't do to come to the table with soot-streaked cheeks!

Satisfied that she looked reasonably presentable, Nell removed the roasting pan from the oven and placed it on the stovetop. Steam wafted toward the ceiling when she lifted the lid to poke at the carrots, potatoes, and onions surrounding the plump hen. "Roasted to golden perfection," she said as she ladled some of the juices into a cast-iron skillet. "And you'll make some delicious gravy, too."

Nell added flour and milk to the chicken juice and whisked vigorously, hoping that Asa would be pleased with the meal. He wasn't exactly lavish with compliments, but she figured she was doing an adequate job, at least, or else he'd complain. He seemed like a nice enough man, albeit a quiet, somewhat sullen, one. Mostly, he kept to himself; even on the rare occasion when he showed up at the hardware store or the grocery store, he rarely spoke unless spoken to. Once in a great while, a smile lit his handsome face, but it almost always vanished in an instant. It was as if he felt undeserving of even a fleeting moment of enjoyment.

What would make a man feel that way? Nell wondered as she added salt and pepper to the pan gravy.

He'd been back in Denver for quite some time now, yet Nell had never heard anyone speculate about where he'd been, what he'd done while away, or why he'd come home when he had. Either folks didn't know, or they chose not to risk receiving that hard, steady stare by asking him.

"I wonder if Janet knows—"

"Knows what?" Asa asked, taking his usual seat at the head of the table.

"I see you found the shirt I washed and pressed!" Hopefully, her comment would provide a suitable distraction from his question, because Nell had no idea how she'd explain why she wanted to talk with Janet.

"I did, thanks. No idea when you found time to do that."

She could have told him that a person who rises before the sun and works long past dark—without taking breaks—has plenty of time for such things. But because Asa kept the same hours as she, and worked even harder, Nell kept her response to herself.

"This gravy is just about ready," she said, whisking in a pat of butter. "I roasted a whole hen, so I hope you're hungry."

Even though he made no reply, Nell knew he had to be famished. His breakfast, taken at five in the morning, had consisted of a meager egg and a mug of coffee; at noontime, she'd delivered him a plate with a slab of ham and a hunk of cheese, along with a tumbler of milk. "Looks good," he'd said from the roof. "I'll come down soon as I've finished mortaring the chimney." But when she'd returned two hours later to fetch the plate, she'd been forced to scrape the food into the compost heap. The only bites had been taken by several flies and a bird or two. And now, it was after four.

She transferred the hen to a platter, arranged the vegetables around it, and poured the gravy into a deep bowl. Then, one at a time, she carried both to the table. As she sliced up the loaf of fresh-baked bread, Nell reflected that her pa had also been a man of few words. So had Grandpa Holstrom. But even those gold-greedy miners managed to comment on the aroma of the food they were about to eat.

Nell sat across from Asa and waited. The one time she could count on him to speak was before a meal, when he would offer a word of prayer.

"Father, bless this food, the cook who prepared it, and the house that shelters us from the elements. Amen."

Oh, ye of many words, Nell mused, grinning to herself. He picked up his fork and speared a slice of bread.

"Butter?" she asked, sliding the dish closer to him.

For the next few minutes, neither of them spoke. It seemed to Nell that Asa's mind was anywhere but in that room.

"Were you able to repair the chimney?" she asked, trying to make conversation.

He cut into a potato. "I was."

"That's good."

When he looked up, she noticed several flakes of sawdust clinging to his dark hair.

"Before we know it, winter will be upon us, and won't it be nice to warm ourselves in front of a cozy fire?"

She might as well have been dining alone. Good thing she enjoyed her own company and conversation.

It could be worse. If life hadn't taught her just one lesson, it was that things could always be worse. Instead of being unbearably quiet and reserved, Asa could have been cruel and abusive. And he was anything but that!

Living with a man who barely spoke was hardly the worst conceivable scenario. Those harrowing years after her mother's death came to mind, when her father had sunken deeper into despair while pursuing the sole, desperate purpose of finding gold. She remembered all too well how it felt to go days without food, shivering beneath that scratchy brown blanket in the leaky, bug-infested shack adjacent to the mine.

A minuscule wood chip fell from Asa's hair, floated down to the table, and came to rest near his elbow. Afraid that the next piece would fall into his food, Nell leaned across the table and, as quietly and unobtrusively as possible, shoved his plate aside, then brushed the remaining sawdust from his hair. The dark waves were surprisingly soft to the touch.

"There," she said, moving his plate back to where it had been. "That's much better." Then she hastily buttered a slice of bread, doing her best to ignore his wide-eyed look of confusion.

"There was sawdust in your hair," she finally said, when it was clear he didn't know why she'd done what she had.

"Ah."

"I was afraid it might fall into your food."

"Mmm."

"Wouldn't want you getting a splinter in your tongue, because I know how much you love to *talk*."

A second, perhaps two, passed. And then Asa sat back and laughed.

The only thing that surprised her more than the rich, robust sound was the series of shivers that traveled up and down her spine in response to it.

⌣

The day was raw and rainy, and Asa stopped working to massage his left hand. Thanks to the beating his surviving two brothers had administered after the battle at Sand Creek, his fingers and joints reacted to certain types of weather.

That wallop had been unlike any Asa had experienced before or since. And that was saying something, because, during his days with the James-Younger Gang, he'd been involved in plenty of fistfights. Not even those outlaws would have sent him packing with a dislocated shoulder, several cracked ribs, and two broken fingers.

No point in whining about the past, he thought, flexing his hand. He picked up his chamois and went back to polishing his grandmother's old spinet. Maybe Ambrose Brigham, the piano player at the Tivoli, could tune it up for any guests who might have a mind to pound out a tune or two.

He turned the chamois in his hand, wondering whatever had happened to the dazed, disheveled old man who'd wandered into his camp and offered up the yard of wash-leather in exchange for hot coffee and a bite of the rabbit he'd had roasting on the spit. It had seemed a foolish trade, but Asa had spent enough time in the old man's shoes to take pity on him. Between then and now, he'd probably used the chamois a hundred times, to polish his boots or filter drinking water from creeks and streams. Oh, how far he'd come since those torturous days of aimless drifting, hoping and praying for work in the next town, so that he could afford a place to sleep, a cup of coffee, a bite to eat.

But what about Chester and Edgar? Were his brothers out there somewhere, taking comfort from wives, children, and homes of their own? Had they forgiven him for the egregious mistake he'd made that night?

Asa gave the piano's now-glossy finish a final pass with the chamois. Would the instrument look better near the double doors or between the two tall narrow windows, where his grandmother had kept it? Did it matter? Asa didn't think so. He tossed the cloth aside and made his way to the front porch. If the paint had dried on the porch swing he'd found in the shed, maybe he would hang it now.

On his way, he spotted a pile of sawdust he'd neglected to clean up after sanding the banister of the main staircase. Stooping, he swept it into the trash bin, remembering how Nell had fidgeted, sighed, and stammered before plucking a flake of the stuff from his hair at supper the night before. She'd leaned close enough for him to catch a whiff of scented bath powder. Close enough to kiss.

Instead, he'd sat as still as a statue, held his breath, and looked into eyes the color of Texas bluebells, wishing he'd lived the kind of life that would made him worthy of a woman like her.

"Ah, there you are!"

She'd startled him, but his back was toward her, so he hoped she hadn't noticed.

Hope hammered in his heart as he turned around. "You were looking for me?"

"I need your advice about something."

Asa followed her up the stairs and into the smallest guest room. It was empty, save for the braided rug on the floor.

"What would you think of turning this into a nursery for guests with small children? It isn't big enough for a normal-sized bed and bureau, but a crib would fit here, and a cradle there," she said, pointing. "And there's space enough for a daybed for a mother to sleep on." She faced him, her hands clasped at her waist, face glowing with anticipation. "Down here at the far end of the hall, the cries of fussy babies would be less likely to bother the other guests. I found everything we'd need in the attic, including some old toys. I could clean it all up and have it ready well before we open for business."

From day one, Nell had thought of things he never would have, from tacking old blankets over open doorways to protect the furniture from construction dust, to sewing matching curtains and bedcovers for each guest room, to arranging the chairs, tables, and lamps with an eye for comfort and artistic balance. The entire inn smelled like the wood polish she'd made from beeswax and lemon oil. She'd even painted a sign to hang beside the front door. "Stone Hill Inn," it said. "Rest like a Nobleman at Workingman's Prices."

Every one of her ideas had been good—including the nursery—and he told her so.

"I have something to show you, too," he said.

He led her to his study, where, during the wee hours of the night, he'd refinished his grandfather's desk and chair. As he'd worked, Asa had pictured her, forever scribbling lists—chores, groceries, what to plant and when.

"I thought you might appreciate an easier writing surface than those books you're always using when you make your lists."

"Oh, my," she whispered when he uncovered it.

"Belonged to my grandfather," he said. "Did all his ciphering on it." He slid open one of the drawers. "Stored his money in it, too."

She took a few steps forward and ran her hand gently over the smooth surface.

"I thought it could go in your room," Asa said.

"Oh, it's much too lovely to hide away where I'm the only one who will ever see it." Nell met his eyes. "Unless I'm mistaken, it should fit perfectly in the parlor, right under the front windows. Plenty of natural light, and that way, we could both make use of it." With her fingertip, she drew an imaginary line down the middle of the desk.

How like her to realize how much the pieces meant to him.

Nell glanced out the window. "Have you checked on the vegetable garden lately?"

"Not since last week." It had been longer, but Asa didn't have the heart to admit it.

"You won't believe how well things are growing," she said as they left the study. "At this rate, we'll have fresh produce by the Fourth of July!"

Asa followed her outside to the garden, where she opened the tiny access gate and stepped inside the protective screen she'd built around it. Then she stooped and plucked the only weed brave enough to sprout there.

Asa walked all the way around the enclosure, admiring her handiwork. "When did you build this?"

"Oh, I worked on it here and there and now and then, usually while I was waiting for dough to rise or clothes to dry."

"Appears to be working," he said, nodding at the lush green leaves. "No evidence of deer or rabbits getting in."

His ma and grandma had often put him and his brothers to work adding sand, chopped straw, dried leaves, and manure into the heavy clay soil. Somewhere along the way, Nell must have learned a similar recipe, evidenced by the dark, rich topsoil that nourished the plants. She'd gone a step farther than the women in his family, though, making small signs on posts of twig to mark the varieties of vegetables growing there in perfectly straight rows: green beans, potatoes, beets, and peas.

"Are you looking forward to eating fresh-picked greens as much as I am?" Nell asked as she climbed back out of the pen.

Asa nodded.

"As long as I have your attention, I have another idea to pass by you," she said, fastening the gate. "It's about chickens."

"Chickens?"

"On my last visit to the library, Janet showed me a few books on building a proper coop. I could put one right over there," she said, pointing toward a shady spot under a horse chestnut. "The tree will keep the hens cool in the summer and let in enough light during the winter to provide a little warmth."

"Chickens," he said again.

She looked at him as though he'd grown a third eye. "They're relatively easy to care for, if you're willing to put some time into them—and I'm willing, if it means fresh eggs and a nice fat hen for the stewpot now and then."

Asa nodded repeatedly as she described the process of constructing a coop with a ramp and with screens that would keep the hens from wandering into the road.

"I've spoken with Joe, and he said he'd buy some eggs from me," she said as she walked toward the house. "I'll use the money I earn to buy flowers and shrubs to pretty up the yard, along with some seed packets to cultivate plants for the future."

Asa was about to say that he'd gladly give her the money right now, but before he could, she reached into her apron pocket and produced a seed packet featuring an English garden in full bloom.

"It's hard to imagine from just looking at a picture, but I believe this place could be just as beautiful."

For the first time, Asa noticed that she'd constructed a low stone wall around the flower beds. When in tarnation had Nell managed that?

"Lilacs, roses, mock orange, peonies...all different colors, and varying in scent, to greet our guests," she was saying. "We can also cut fresh blossoms to fill vases in the guest rooms."

"I...I imagine that would appeal."

"It'll take time, of course, before things look as pretty as the picture on the seed packet; a proper garden takes years to develop, after all. But I have a few tricks up my sleeve to speed things up so we can enjoy it a little sooner than that." This she said with a wink.

"Sounds good, very good. But I'll handle purchasing everything you need."

"I certainly don't mind the expense," she assured him. "After all, this is my home, too."

"Never meant to imply otherwise." Taking her hand in his, Asa pressed two silver dollars into her palm, then gently closed her fingers around them. "Don't know the first thing about flower gardens. Since you're in charge of getting them in the ground, then nurturing and maintaining them, I couldn't, in good conscience, ask you to buy them, too."

Before Nell could object, Asa decided to change the subject. "I like the idea of a chicken coop." He lowered himself onto the top porch step. "Built one years ago, near a trading post between the Columbia and Kootenai rivers."

Nell sat beside him. "Kootenai? I've never heard of that one."

"Named for the Ksunka Indians, 'People of the Standing Arrow.' Met an old chief who told me the French changed it to Kootenai. Said they were too lazy to learn the proper way to say it. Word means 'deer robes'—or 'water people' depending on who you ask." He shrugged. "Anyway, I know how to build a coop."

Nell looked a little disappointed. Clearly, she had been counting on doing all the work for that project, too. He had to look away to keep her from seeing his grin of amusement.

When he'd sobered, he turned back to her. "Hope you'll consider letting me help out at least a little," he said.

"Do you have the time?"

"Won't take long. Not with two of us working together." *Together.* He liked the sound of that. Asa swallowed and cleared his throat. "Need help getting the crib and cradle from the attic?"

"I suppose it would be easier on the furniture and the walls if we moved them together, wouldn't it?"

"Sure." He got to his feet and held open the door for Nell.

Thunder rumbled in the distance, and Asa glanced at the gathering clouds.

"Better batten down the hatches," Nell remarked. "Looks like we're in for a good one."

Chapter Seven

The following week, Asa arranged for Ambrose Brigham to come tune his grandmother's old spinet. Dinner was to be included, and Nell had invited Janet Sinclaire, the local librarian, to join them for the meal. Gently, he grasped the man's elbow and led him into the kitchen.

"Sure am lookin' forward to some home cookin'," Ambrose said. "Somethin' smells fine in here. Real fine. What you an' Miss Nell fixin' to serve up for this humble ol' black man, Miz Sinclaire?"

Smiling, Janet shook her head. "How in the world did you know I was here, Ambrose?"

He chuckled. "I might be blind, but my nose works just fine, and you the only woman I know who smell like bergamot, roses, an' spice."

"That's the Hoyt's Cologne," she explained. "Brad wore it all the time, and somehow putting it on makes me miss him less."

Ambrose nodded and lowered himself into the chair Asa had pulled out for him. "Oh, I hear that, Miz Sinclaire. Been ten years since I lost my Clara, an' sometime, it seem like jus' yesterday."

Nell carried a steaming pot of soup to the table. "How soon do you need to get back to the Tivoli, Ambrose?"

"'Long as I play for the midnight crowd, Mr. Smith don't complain."

"*Mr.* Smith, indeed," Nell sniffed.

"Now, now, Miss Nell," Ambrose said. "The man ain't *all* bad. He gave this ol' blind man a job, didn't he?"

"I suppose," she said, setting a basket of biscuits beside the kettle.

"I remember well what Mr. Smith done to your pa and gran'pa, but they wasn't the only ones what fell for his 'dollars hid in the cake o' soap' trick."

"But how many innocent people has he fooled—people who can't afford to lose so much as one thin dime!" Nell exclaimed. "What sort of person thinks up such horrible things? A criminal, that's who!"

Asa had never seen Nell angry before, and he didn't quite know how to react. Jefferson Smith had never been his favorite person, either; but, unlike Nell, Asa's reasons for disliking him were not personal.

Evidently, Janet had never seen Nell riled up, either. She met Asa's gaze with a bewildered smile and a shake of her head.

Nell filled a bowl and placed it in front of Ambrose. "Take care, now. It's hot."

"Smells like liquid heaven," Ambrose said, eyes closed as he inhaled the steam.

Nell ladled soup into the remaining three bowls and arranged them at the table. "Biscuits are in a basket at your right elbow, Ambrose, and there's a jar of apple jelly to your left."

Thankfully, the smile that Asa had come to know and love had returned to Nell's face.

"Ambrose, would you do us the honor of saying the blessing?"

"Be my pleasure, Nell." As heads bowed and hands were folded, he began.

"Lord, we thank You for good friends, good food, an' the good cooks what brung it to the table. We ask that You'd bless us with good health...and enough appetite at the end of the meal to eat them apple dumplin's I been smellin' since settin' foot in this kitchen. Amen."

When he opened his eyes, Ambrose said, "You made them dumplin's, didn't you, Ms. Sinclaire?"

"I did," Janet affirmed, patting his hand, "but you'll get one only if you promise to stop calling me Ms. Sinclaire instead of Janet."

"You drive a hard bargain," he said, buttering a biscuit, "but a man's gotta do what a man's gotta do."

~

All during supper, the room pulsed with warmth and laughter, and Nell was sorry when the meal concluded. "I'd best get to tunin'," Ambrose said, "so's I won't be late to work."

Once the men had left the kitchen, Janet helped Nell with the cleanup.

"He's such a sweet man," Janet said, drying the dish Nell had handed her. "I didn't know he and Asa were such good friends."

"Neither did I," Nell said, rinsing the suds from a soup bowl. "But then, I hardly know anything about Asa."

"Really? That surprises me. You two have worked side by side for weeks now, restoring this place to its former glory."

Nell felt the heat of a blush creep up her neck. It was good to hear that others had begun to notice the transformation, but she couldn't have anyone—not even her dearest friend—thinking that her relationship with Asa went anywhere beyond employee-employer.

"It's a big house," she said with a shrug. "We're almost always in separate places, doing different things. The only time we're together is at suppertime."

"Still, that's an hour a day, at least. Surely you talk while you eat."

Nell sighed. "He isn't exactly what you'd call a chatterbox, but you probably knew that. Mostly, I talk, and he listens. But I must admit, I wish he'd open up a little. I still don't know what happened to his family. Why did he stay away from Denver for so many years? And how did he spend that time away?"

Janet laughed. "I can't believe you haven't asked him, if you're as curious as you seem to be!"

Nell put away the last of the pots and pans, then poured them each a cup of coffee. "You've lived here all your life," she said as she sat across from Janet. "Do you know how his mother died?"

Janet shook her head. "Only that she left four boys—Asa was the youngest. After she passed, Daniel stayed drunk most of the time. He'd get into brawls and beat those boys mercilessly. One day, about a year after Hanna died, Daniel just up and left town without a word to anyone. They'd lived in a little house at the edge of town, and his folks brought the boys to live with them, right here at Stone Hill Inn." Janet exhaled a sad sigh. "Chester sat beside me in school. Such a sweet boy. And Edgar and Duncan... well, they were always getting into mischief of some sort, but they were good boys, too."

"Whatever became of them?"

"A few years after Daniel disappeared, he rode back into town wearing a cavalry uniform two sizes too big. He'd brought two horses with him, and at first, we thought he'd come home to stay.

"How wrong we were! Instead, he rounded up his boys and put them two to a saddle on those horses, and away they went." She took a sip of coffee, then released another sigh. "I'll never forget the way Abigail ran after him, crying and pleading to let her and Silas keep the boys. She was never the same after that. And neither was Silas."

Living miles from town as she had, it was no wonder Nell and her family had been oblivious to all these goings-on, and Denver residents knew next to nothing about the Holstroms—or the infernal mine that had taken loved ones from her, one by one. The first victim of the Holstrom Mine had been her grandfather, buried in a cave-in. Soon after that, her grandmother died of consumption—a disease whose effects were compounded by a broken heart. Next, Nell's sweet ma had been struck by lightning while gathering firewood during a storm…a job one of the men would have done if they hadn't been gold-obsessed. And when a hoist broke in the mine, killing her younger brother, Nell had sat her pa down and confessed that she couldn't stay, not even one more day in the place that destroyed all who entered it. She'd begged him to come with her to Denver. Or to Golden or Boulder, if he preferred—anyplace that wasn't the Holstrom Mine. "Can't leave now, girl," he'd said, "not when I'm just ten feet from striking gold!" She hadn't believed him. And why would she, when he'd always been ten feet, or fifteen, or twenty from the elusive vein? As he'd spoken those oh-so-familiar words, she'd realized that he would never leave. So Nell made the long trip to town, alone, on foot, and went to work at Sterling Manufactory, returning to the cabin on Sundays to make sure he had enough to eat. Until that awful Saturday when her worst fears were realized, and she found him halfway buried under—

⌒

"Goodness, Nell!" Janet exclaimed. "You're as white as a bedsheet. What on earth are you thinking about?"

"Oh, nothing. Just…just feeling a little sad about everything Asa and his family went through, I guess."

Janet clucked her tongue. "You can't fool me. Why, you still look as though you've seen a ghost!"

In a matter of speaking, she had. After burying her pa, Nell vowed never to lament aloud all that the mine had taken from her. For one thing, she had no desire to be the object of others' pity. For another, she was ashamed—and angry—that her family's lust for gold had been as much to blame for their demise as the mine, itself.

"I don't believe in ghosts," Janet was saying, "but if I did, I'd say Daniel met up with at least one during his years away from home. Even after all this time, when I picture the look on his face when he first came back—as though he'd looked death itself in the eye—I get chills." She shivered to prove it.

"Where is Daniel now?"

Janet shrugged. "No one knows for certain. Rumor has it that after he dragged those poor boys off to fight for Colonel Chivington, Asa's brothers died on the battlefield."

"And what does Asa say about it?"

"Asa," Janet said slowly, "refuses to speak of his pa and brothers at all."

"I can't say I blame him."

Perhaps memories of them explained why he sometimes slipped into stony silences. She and Asa had much more in common than this old house. Nell realized that now. They shared loss and loneliness, and dreams of someday belonging to a place they could call home.

Could Stone Hill Inn be that place?

Chapter Eight

Do you know 'Aura Lee'?" Nell asked during Ambrose's next visit.

"Why, 'course I sure do. You know the words?"

"Why, 'course I do," Nell echoed with a grin.

Janet leaned closer to Asa. "I've never heard it."

"I haven't, either."

Ambrose's weathered hands had been racing up and down the keys, plinking out spirited hymns and work songs. Now, his playing turned soft and slow as Nell stepped up beside him, closed her eyes, and sang the story of a man whose heart belonged to a sweet blonde beauty.

Asa found himself fighting tears as she sang the last mellow notes:

Aura Lee, Aura Lee,
take my golden ring;
love and light return with thee,
and swallows with the spring.

Janet applauded heartily. "Oh, Nell, that was simply lovely!"

Nell blushed—a most becoming sight, Asa thought.

"It was my mother's favorite song," she said. "Our wagon master sang it every night as we traveled cross-country from Boston."

"Well, li'l gal, you ever tire of workin' for Asa, here, come see ol' Ambrose. I predict that men would flock to the Tivoli from all over Colorado to hear singin' that purty."

Asa's heart knocked against his chest at the mere thought of her being ogled by drunken gamblers.

"An' speakin' of the Tivoli," Ambrose said, getting to his feet, "I best be gettin' on over there. You mind walkin' me back down, Asa?"

"Happy to." He took the man by the arm.

"I should get going, too," Janet said. "I'll walk with you partway."

"Janet and I packed up some food for you to take home," Nell told Ambrose. "Let me fetch it from the kitchen, and I'll meet you in the foyer."

The old piano player didn't move as fast as he once had, and Nell reached the door before they did. Asa smiled as she told Ambrose that she'd tucked an apple dumpling, several biscuits, a jar of soup, and a slab of chicken into the basket.

"Oh, I'll be prayin' for you ladies," he said. "I'm blessed, indeed, to have such caring friends."

Janet hugged Nell goodbye. "See you soon?"

"Likely tomorrow or the next day. I have books to return to the library, so if you have any recommendations, please have them ready!"

Janet laughed. "*If* I have any recommendations? Why, I have hundreds!"

As Asa led Ambrose onto the porch, he turned to Nell. "Shouldn't be long, but I'd like you to lock up. I'll ring the bell when I get back."

"Lock up? But we've never had to—"

"Humor me," he said, closing the door behind him.

As they walked, Janet kept up a steady stream of conversation. Under different circumstances, it might have annoyed him;

but right now, it made it easier for Asa to push Nell's frightened expression to the back of his mind. For days, he'd had an eerie, unsettled feeling, but having no tangible cause to explain it, he'd kept it to himself. Out there in the wilderness, he'd learned to trust his instincts. He'd traveled alone, for the most part, more often than not on foot, which meant treading with caution and keeping his eyes and ears open.

The first close call happened after a long, cold night in Texas. He'd prepared the coffeepot and picked up a stick to stoke his camp fire, but something stopped him from poking it into the coals. If he hadn't heeded the odd feeling that had set his neck hairs to bristling, he wouldn't have noticed the sidewinder coiled beside the fire, poised to strike. Never one to waste a bullet, he'd circled around and, wielding his hatchet, whacked off its head. Skinned and peeled, the snake made a right tasty supper that night, but that hadn't stopped him from sobering at the knowledge of how close he'd come to suffering a deadly bite.

His instincts had saved him again a year or so later, while picking his way along the Sevier River. Legends, passed down by Paiutes who described the hoodoos as "rocks that stand tall like men," made him jumpy and irritable. Without warning or reason, something told him to look up—and he'd done so just in time to dodge the cougar that leaped from one of the thousand clay spires. His guttural bellow spooked the cat, sending it out of sight into the canyon.

Then, just a few months before his return to Denver, Asa had bedded down under the stars. With one hand resting on the grip of his revolver, the other tucked under his neck, something—to this day, he didn't know what—woke him. He'd known better than to move, except to raise one eyelid, just enough to see a man towering over him. He wore a black ankle-length duster and a flat-topped, wide-brimmed hat—and the firelight glinted from the barrel of the Remington Rolling Block that rested on his shoulder. His pa had used a rifle exactly like it at Sand Creek. In one smooth motion, Asa had eased back the hammer of his pistol and thrown off the blanket, but by the time he got to his feet, the stranger was gone. Boot prints in the dirt were proof that he hadn't dreamed up the midnight visitor.

Lately, the same gut feelings told him that something was "off" in Denver.

"You're awfully quiet, Asa," Janet observed. "Is everything all right?"

He quickly collected himself. "Shouldn't've eaten that second apple dumpling of yours," he said, patting his belly. "Just feeling stuffed, is all."

Janet giggled. "Well, I'm glad you liked them." They had reached the white gate at end of her walk, and she stopped to open the latch. "Thank you for seeing me safely home."

"My pleasure."

"Denver could use a few more like this fella, couldn't it, Miz Janet?" Ambrose put in.

"It could, indeed." With that, she started up the path. "Good night, gents," she added over her shoulder.

When the door clicked shut behind her, Ambrose said, "Seem a shame she never took another husband, don't it?"

"Mmm...."

"She tol' me once it was 'cause the good Lord only made one Bradley Sinclaire."

"Mmm-hmm."

"You ever wonder why Nell never took a husband?"

Yes, he had. In fact, he'd considered that question more than a few times.

"Is she as purty as she sounds?"

Asa didn't know how to answer that.

"I'll take that as a yes. Shame 'bout her kinfolk, ain't it?"

A statement, Asa noticed, not a question. "I don't know much about her background," Asa admitted.

Ambrose slowed his pace, then proceeded to fill Asa in on the details he knew as they completed their trek to the Tivoli. The sounds of bawdy laughter grew louder as they neared the club, and by the time Asa guided the older man up the porch steps, he felt a whole new connection to Nell.

"That li'l gal is sweet on you," Ambrose advised, "so you take care to treat her right, you hear?"

"Sweet on me?" Asa grunted. "Nonsense." But Ambrose Brigham was hardly ever wrong. Anything he missed seeing due to his blindness, he perceived in some other way.

"And you's sweet on her, too! Your words say one thing, but your *voice* says another."

Asa chuckled nervously. "Too late in the day for riddles, old friend."

"Joke all you please." Ambrose squinted one rheumy eye. "Can't put my finger on it, but you don't talk to her the way you talk to ever'body else."

If that was true, it wasn't likely Nell had picked up on it. Just in case, Asa decided to pay more attention to how he spoke to her from now on.

"Thank you kindly for supper, Asa," Ambrose said at the door. "Now, you take care headin' back to Sterling Street."

The word of caution, compounded by the eerie sense he'd been feeling lately, sent a chill up his spine. He did his best to laugh it off. "No need to worry on my account," he said. "Walked that stretch a hundred times. Could probably do it in my sleep."

Ambrose shook his head. "Still got this powerful bad feelin' there's danger lurkin' in the night. And I never doubt my senses. When a man loses one, he learns to lean heavier on the rest. It's how the good Lord protects people like me."

Asa cleared his throat. "Better get on inside, before Soapy trades you for a player piano."

"Awright, funny man. But you keep your wits about you. I done lost too many good friends already."

All the way home, Asa thought he heard footsteps, matching his pace. He thought he saw movement behind every lamppost, and would have sworn he smelled the unmistakable odor of tobacco.

Fool, he thought. *You've let that superstitious old man spook you.*

The hike seemed to take ten times longer than usual, and with every step, Asa wished he'd thought to strap on his six-shooter before leaving the house.

If he'd seen the bright orange tip of a cigarette, glowing in the shadowy alleyway across from Stone Hill, he would have wished for his Springfield rifle, instead.

⌣

"There. No more loose buttons." Nell folded Asa's favorite work shirt. "I'll get this washed and pressed first thing in the morning."

"Thanks," Asa said without looking up. He spread the latest edition of *The Rocky Mountain News* on the tabletop, then raised the wick of the hanging lantern.

"I saved an apple dumpling for you."

No response.

If he showed the slightest interest, she'd plate it up and serve it with hot coffee. "Or, if you're still too full from supper to eat the whole thing, we could split it."

Asa finally met her gaze. "Sounds good."

She stood at the sideboard, dividing the dessert between two small bowls. Then she set them on the table, along with two mugs of steaming coffee, and sat.

Asa kept his eyes on the paper. Nell figured he must be reading something truly fascinating, for it to delay his diving into dessert.

"Did you hear what happened to Mr. Arkins?"

"No, can't say I did."

After pouring him a mug of steaming coffee, she slid the plate onto the table. "That awful Soapy Smith beat the poor fellow with a cane. His face is all swollen and bruised. It's only by the grace of God he wasn't killed!"

"Not that I approve of Smith's actions, mind you, but Arkins does tend to stir the pot."

"Far as I can tell," she said, sitting across from him, "he just prints the truth about crime and corruption in town. Hardly cause for Smith's actions!"

"True enough. But even you have to admit, Arkins crossed the line when he cast aspersions on Smith's wife and children."

Nell sipped her coffee. "True enough," she echoed. "But…why couldn't he have demanded that Mr. Arkins print a retraction, instead?"

"Unfortunately, some men prefer intimidation to civility."

She shook her head, and just as suddenly as it had appeared, her frown faded. She leaned forward and pointed at an advertisement for the Denver-Pacific Railroad's new Pullman cars.

"This reminds me of an idea I had just this morning while sweeping the front porch…."

"Oh?" Asa smiled around a bite of the apple dumpling and waited for the explanation he knew would follow.

"I saw the conductor, buying up stacks of the newspaper, then deposit one on each table in the dining car. Think of all the passengers who will read each edition. Hundreds, I'd guess, between here and the next depots! The inn has been closed for years, and an ad gives us an opportunity to let potential guests know that we're open and ready for business again. Even if only a few of them decide to stay with us, it'll be well worth the cost of an ad."

DiMaggio had been right about her talent for numbers. But Nell also had a gift for coming up with money-making ideas. Asa met her eyes. "You know, that's about the best porch-sweeping idea I've ever heard."

Smiling, Nell sipped her coffee.

"How soon can you get the ad written and submitted?"

She reached into her pocket and withdrew a folded sheet of paper. Smoothing it on the table, she said, "I was just jotting down ideas, so if you can think of any way to improve it...."

Asa refolded the page and handed it back to her. "I'm sure it's perfect, just like every other idea you've come up with. Let's just hope the editor doesn't bury it in the back, with the obituaries and crime reports."

Something told him he'd see that happy, enthused expression long after he turned in tonight.

⌒

Three days later, Nell showed him the ad, smack in the middle of page three.

"How much did that cost me?" he asked.

"Not a penny more than it would have if the editor had mixed it in with the obituaries."

Pride—not only that she'd written a winning add, but that its placement guaranteed a wider audience—beamed from her face. It was good to see her so happy. So good that he reached across the table to pat her hand.

"Great job," he said. "But then, I'm not surprised. I've yet to find anything you *don't* do well."

She blushed like a schoolgirl as delicate eyebrows disappeared behind thick blonde curls. The reaction told him Nell wasn't accustomed to compliments. After turning the falling-down house into a showplace, she'd earned some praise, and he was happy to deliver it. In his opinion, not even the upscale Remington Hotel could hold a candle to Stone Hill, thanks in large part to her willingness to dig in and work hard. Nell picked at a tiny nub in the tablecloth, drawing his attention to the faint scar on the back of her hand.

"Healed up pretty well," he said, nodding at it.

She smiled. "Yes, thanks to your poultice. If I'd heeded your advice and kept it dry and covered, it probably wouldn't have left a scar."

She was right, but Asa didn't want to spoil the moment by saying so.

"I've been meaning to tell you how welcoming the front porch looks," Nell said next. "I know it was backbreaking work—all that scraping, sanding, and painting—but the hours and effort really paid off. And the back porch looks just as lovely." She met his eyes to add, "You've provided our future guests with places where they can enjoy the sunrise *and* the sunset, if the weather cooperates."

"Thanks."

"First thing tomorrow," she continued, "after I've hung the wash on the line, I'll go back to the newspaper office and see how much Molly Vernon will charge to place the ad in next Friday's edition of the paper." Winking, Nell added, "Maybe if I bake some cookies, she'll talk her father into printing up a few copies of the ad, all by itself, so we can tack them up around town."

Almost from the start, Nell had used words like "we" and "our" when talking of work to be done at the inn. It pleased him that she felt at home here, but he wondered how much time would pass before she figured out what a mistake it would be to link her happiness to a good-for-nothing like himself.

He felt like a presumptuous pig, even entertaining the notion that a woman like Nell might fancy a future with him. But if Ambrose had been right about her being sweet on him, Asa owed it to her to put a stop to such thoughts, *now*.

He'd been in love once, and believed with all his heart that Suzannah loved him, too. Believed it so strongly that, for the first time in years, he'd given serious consideration to putting down roots in Texas. But his opinion that a solid Christian marriage should be built on a foundation of faith and trust compelled him to confess everything to her. And nothing could have shocked or hurt him more than when Suzannah ran home and repeated it all to her pa, who dragged her to the sheriff's office to tell the story again. If not for the goodwill Asa had built up with an underpaid, underappreciated deputy, he wouldn't have gotten a two-hour head start on the posse that had formed to bring him in.

Having been in love, even just that once, Asa recognized the feelings that stirred in him every time he looked at Nell, or heard her voice, or noticed some little thing she'd done for him, like sewing on a button or taking a hot iron to his work clothes. He recognized, too, the importance of extinguishing those feelings, right down to the smallest ember. For if he let them flare and grow, he'd slide into that same rabbit hole, and this time, he might never emerge.

Far more important than his freedom was believing that Nell was a fine woman with a steadfast heart. Someday, a good man—not a fraud hiding behind a facade of decency—would recognize and appreciate her positive attributes and give her the life she deserved. A woman with a heart like hers, if she pledged her loyalty to Asa, wouldn't even notice that good man.

Knowing what he needed to do restored the gloomy mood he'd tried so hard to shed. Asa didn't like the feeling, so he decided to focus on the prickly dread provoked by Ambrose's premonition the previous evening, instead.

"Well, it's getting late," he said, standing so quickly that he nearly upended his chair. "Better get some shuteye, 'cause the sun will be up before we know it."

Whether it had been his sudden action or his gruff tone of voice that inspired Nell's tiny gasp, Asa couldn't say. But if her being afraid of him—just a bit—helped to keep her distanced from him, then so be it.

Better to hurt her feelings now, he thought, *than to let her get close enough to have them destroyed when she learns what you really are.*

Chapter Nine

Teo, you know very well that I hate, hate, hate guessing games!"

No matter how many times Nell had said this to her little brother, he'd always persisted in tormenting her with "How many beans am I holding?" or "I know why the early bird gets the worm...do you?" Since she was six years older, Nell's parents had expected her to exercise patience and self-restraint—which sometimes annoyed her as much as Teo's incessant questions.

Lately, Asa's behavior left her feeling just as frustrated. She didn't see how her work performance could be to blame, but just in case, she pushed herself harder to accomplish more and more with each passing day. As a result, every room at the inn was now ready to receive guests. The gardens were bursting with flowers of a dozen colors and varieties. The root cellar shelves were stacked with dry goods, vegetables, and produce Nell had put up in jars—more than enough to see them through even the harshest of winters.

The first thing this morning, even before Asa finished his breakfast, Nell gathered the supplies she'd need for today's mission: a hammer, a box of nails, some binding wire, a paintbrush. She tied it all up in an old bedsheet, then, slinging it over her shoulder, grabbed a bucket of paint and marched up the knoll to the Stone family burial plot. Like everything else at Stone Hill, the little cemetery had fallen into disrepair. She'd figured, why not kill two birds with one stone and put things right by taking out her frustrations on the thick weeds choking out every headstone?

The sheet was piled high with bindweed, common mallow, dodder, and yellow alyssum when she got back down on her knees to take the bristle brush to the stone markers. Before long, Nell could easily read the names: Silas and Abigail, Asa's grandparents; Hanna, his mother; and one that said "Baby Girl, died on the day she was born." In the row behind these, markers that presumably belonged to aunts, uncles, and cousins.

She dragged the weed-covered sheet into the woods and shook it free of its load. Next, she rolled it into the shape of a log and used it to protect the tilting stones as she hammered them straight. Once they stood upright, she applied the same technique to the leaning picket fence that surrounded the graveyard.

Then she stepped back and, hands on hips, admired her handiwork. *With a fresh coat of paint on that fence, perhaps Asa will be inspired to pay his respects,* she thought, nodding.

Using the hammer's claws, she pried the lid from the paint can, only to realize she'd forgotten to bring along something to stir it with. Muttering to herself, Nell found a sturdy stick at the edge of the woods, wiped it clean with the edge of her apron, and plunged it into the pail.

She was nearly finished when an ugly red blister popped up on the web of skin between her thumb and forefinger. "Oh, of all the irksome things," she grumbled, blowing air across it. "You can't quit now. Not with just two more pickets to go!"

Squatting to reach the lowest part of the last board, Nell whispered through clenched teeth, "It doesn't sting. You can do this. Don't be a whiny baby. Think how surprised Asa will be when he sees what—"

"Well now, what's all this?"

His deep-timbered, stern-toned voice startled her so badly that she toppled backward, upsetting the paint bucket. "Asa Stone, don't you know better than to sneak up on a body that way!" she exclaimed. Nell got up slowly, so as not to splatter any paint on the newly scrubbed tombstones.

He wore a sheepish expression and said, "Sorry."

Despite the fact that he sounded sincere, Nell wasn't satisfied. She owned just one other dress—the one she wore to Sunday services—and only this pair of shoes. Hopefully, the paint hadn't soaked through her apron and onto her ma's cameo or her pa's watch.

"You're like a magician when it comes to getting stains out," Asa muttered. "I'm sure you can make easy work of—"

"This is *paint*, not dirt or sweat!" Nell fumed. "I could scrub until I rub my fingers raw and never—" *Oh, why bother trying to explain? It's not as if you'll improve his disposition. Why, he hasn't said a word about the work you did on the burial plot!*

"Well?" she couldn't help asking.

His expression transformed from remorseful to confused. "Well, what?"

"This," she all but shouted, pointing a paint-covered finger at the plot. "What do you think of *this*?"

His astonished expression told her that he hadn't commented because he honestly hadn't noticed. Nell didn't know whether she felt more annoyed or disappointed.

"Heard hammering," Asa said, stepping among the headstones. "Thought I should see what was happening."

"That was me, hammering the markers and the fence posts upright."

Asa frowned slightly and ran a hand along the top of one tombstone.

Exercise a little patience, Nell, she told herself. It was impossible to know what state the cemetery had been in the last time he'd visited—or how long ago that might have been.

"It took a little doing," she said, forcing composure into her voice, "and I'm sure that if we laid your carpenter's level on top of them, they could use a few more whacks; but at least now the place doesn't look...." She wanted to say, "*...like a hideous, disrespectful mess.*" Instead, Nell finished with "forgotten."

His frown intensified, and a tiny pang of guilt shot through her for having roused a bitter memory.

"I just, well, I thought...." Nell exhaled an exasperated sigh. "I thought they deserved a better final resting place."

"You're right, of course."

And there it was again...that bad-tempered demeanor that had her tiptoeing for days now. "What is *wrong* with you?" *Easy, Nell.* But it was no use. She'd reached the end of her patience.

"What? Wrong? I don't understa—"

"You've been in a short-tempered mood for nearly a week. If it's because of something I did—or didn't do—I wish you'd just say so, straight out, so I can make the appropriate adjustments."

He sighed. "Everything you do is exemplary. I'm sorry if anything I've done or said has led you to believe otherwise." He slapped a hand to the back of his neck. "I would have gotten around to this, eventually."

Would he have? Nell wasn't so sure. She crossed both arms over her chest. "Well, now you won't have to."

She followed his gaze from her apron to her skirt and boots. Covered in white paint as she was, it looked as though she was wearing that bedsheet. And her hair, having fallen loose, now whipped around her face, blown by the wind. She started to tuck a wayward curl behind her ear.

"Don't!" Asa exclaimed, grabbing her wrist. In a softer, gentler tone, he quickly added, "You'll get paint in your hair."

In all the weeks she'd been at Stone Hill Inn, she'd been this close to him only once, on the night she'd brushed the sawdust from his hair. In that instance, Nell had been in full control. But right here, right now, Asa had the upper hand, literally and figuratively. And she didn't quite know how to feel about that.

He blinked once, twice, then swallowed hard and turned her loose. The chill on her skin where his warm hand had touched her made Nell instantly regret taking a step back. She needed something—anything—to focus on other than the handsome face so near her own.

"Was this your baby sister?" she asked, turning to the nearest headstone.

Asa followed her gaze, sadness dulling his dark-lashed green eyes. He nodded somberly.

"Did you lose your mother at the same time?"

Tucking his hands into the pockets of his trousers, he nodded again. "Doctor said the cord was wrapped around her neck."

"That must have been so hard for you. For your pa and your brothers, too."

"Loss is always hard," he murmured. "From what I hear, you know that about as well as I do."

"Oh? And what have you heard, exactly?"

Asa took his hands from his pockets. "Let's leave that discussion for another day." He hammered the lid back on the paint bucket, then picked it up and started down the hill. He'd gone just a few feet when he stopped and turned back to her. "After all you've done here, 'thank you' seems real inadequate. I just hope you know how much I appreciate...everything."

With that, he left her standing alone at the freshly painted cemetery gate. Nell took note of his strong, sure stride. Of the sturdy shoulders that had easily hefted fifty-pound sacks of flour, sugar, cornmeal...and carried the memories of loved ones lost. The wind ruffled his dark collar-length waves of hair. It tousled her own curls, too; and as she moved to tuck them behind her ears, she remembered how he'd spared her the ordeal of trying to get paint from her hair. She groaned, because it would probably take half an hour and half a quart of kerosene to clean herself up.

Nell picked up the bedsheet and flung it over her forearm—the exact spot Asa's callous yet gentle fingers had held just moments ago.

"See you at supper?" she called out.

He raised one hand, and if she'd blinked, Nell would have missed it. Was the gesture his way of acknowledging her question? Or had she been unceremoniously dismissed?

"What a puzzle you are, Asa Stone," she said, following the path his boots had left in the tall grass. "And you, Nell Holstrom, are a ninny and a fool."

For, in spite of the many reasons he'd given her not to, she was falling in love with that strange, sometimes difficult man.

Chapter Ten

One evening the following week, Nell found Asa in his tiny office, hunched over a thick ledger book.

She knocked quietly. "Asa?"

Turning slightly, he ran a hand through his hair. "How can I help you, Nell?"

In the bright light of the lantern hanging above his desk, he looked even more haggard than he sounded. Not that she was surprised. His study was directly above her room, and the past few nights, she'd heard him up there, pacing long into the early-morning hours. No wonder he'd put too much money in her latest pay envelope—it was a mistake any sleep-deprived person would have made.

"There must be some error," she said, holding up the envelope. "There's nearly twice the usual amount in here."

Asa made no move to accept it. "No error, Nell. I ruined your boots and dress, sneaking up on you the other day. Least I can do is pay for replacements. If that isn't enough—"

"Oh, it's more than enough. In fact, it's beyond generous! But I can make do with what I have."

Nell pictured her six-drawer bureau, empty, for save the bloomers and two pairs of long black stockings. On the floor of the tall wardrobe was one pair of black slippers. On the shelf, a plain black bonnet. There were ten brass hooks attached to the back of the big cabinet, but she needed only three: one for the boiled wool jacket with frayed sleeves and a missing button, one for her gray skirt, and one for the white blouse she always wore with it.

"It isn't as though I'm attending operas or fancy tea parties," she teased.

Either Asa didn't get the joke, or he simply wasn't amused.

"You ever been?" He swiveled in his chair to face her directly. "To the opera, I mean."

"Me?" A giggle bubbled forth from her lips. "My pa was a miner, and not a successful one. We considered ourselves blessed to have watered-down soup to share in that barely-standing one-room shack."

He nodded slowly, his gaze directed just beyond her left shoulder. His expression told her what words needn't: Asa had survived many lean years, too.

"I never bought a ticket to go inside," she continued, "but I once stood outside, listening in on a performance." She could still hear the beautiful music that had filtered through the walls of the elaborate Tabor Opera House that night.

Asa sat up a bit straighter. "Alone?"

What a peculiar question, Nell thought.

"Can't imagine any right-minded father allowing his lovely young daughter to meander around that part of town on her own, especially at night."

"He didn't...exactly. Nor did I take a leisurely stroll." She grinned. "I'd found a cast-off newspaper earlier that day, you see, and in it was printed a wonderful review of the Denver Opera Company. They were performing *Rigoletto*, and the story sounded so fascinating that I made up my mind, right there in the middle of the muddy street, to find a way to hear as much of the opera as possible."

"And did you?"

"But of course!" Another out-of-character snicker escaped her mouth, and Nell hoped he wouldn't think she'd completely lost her mind. She took a step closer, tucking the pay envelope—and her hands—into the front pouch of her apron.

"It was my turn to accompany my father into town, to trade a small sack of gold for cash to purchase a few rudimentary supplies. It made me so angry when he ducked into the saloon. He'd done it before, and, despite his promises to save enough to fill the pantry, I knew better. So," she said, shrugging, "I decided that if I had to be outside, cold and alone, I might as well make the most of it. And while he was squandering the family's food money on whiskey, I made my way to Curtis Street. The music was faint out there in the alley, but I heard enough to fall in love with it."

The hint of a smile replaced his frown. "Why do I get the feeling there's more to your story?"

"I suppose that's because there is." She grinned. "After that night, I sang all the time, trying to duplicate the notes, the vibrato, the mood. I sang while sweeping the cabin, gathering firewood, doing laundry down by the creek…. But my favorite place was deep inside the mine. The echo was the only thing I didn't hate about that miserable place."

"How old were you?"

Nell gave it a moment's thought. "I'll never forget that day, exactly one week before I turned fifteen." The answer woke a happy memory. "On my birthday, I was in an especially good mood, because my mother gave me her cameo…the one that had belonged to my grandmother. Teo clapped his hands over his ears and said 'If you don't stop this confounded singing, night and day and day and night, I'll tie you down and cut out your tongue!'"

She laughed yet again. "He was a silly goose, that little brother of mine."

"Well," Asa said slowly, "I'm very glad he didn't carry out his threat." Suddenly, everything about Asa seemed to mellow, from his smile to his posture to his eyes, now beaming with kindness. But she'd learned better than to bask in it, for Asa sometimes reminded her of Aesop's satyr—warm one minute, cold the next.

"Have you ever attended the opera?" she asked him.

Just that quickly, the joy vanished, as if he didn't think he deserved so much as a moment of pleasure.

"Yes. Once. In San Francisco. Heard Inez Fabbri sing in *Don Giovanni*. But I'd rather listen to you any day."

Nell didn't know which surprised her more—that he'd attended an opera, or that he'd heard her singing at all.

What she did know was that Asa could use a good night's sleep. She thought of her grandmother's remedy: warm milk with butter. "I was about to wash down a slice of pie with some warm milk before turning in," she told Asa. "Care to join me in the kitchen? Or, if you'd prefer, I could bring it in here, so you can finish your bookkeeping?"

He blinked a few times, then faced his ledger again. "I'll wrap up here and join you in a few minutes."

So much for the friendly conversation they'd been carrying on. She'd been abruptly dismissed, and for no apparent reason, just like that day on the cemetery hill.

Nell knew that if she didn't control her every step, she would stomp from the room. *Of all the nerve!* She thought, hurrying toward the kitchen. She wasn't the least bit hungry. Didn't even want a piece of pie. Yet she'd extended the invitation anyway, exclusively out of concern for his well-being.

That isn't true, and you know it, Nell thought as she uncovered the pie. She'd been enjoying their pleasant exchange and was hoping to prolong it as much as possible. It made perfect sense that if she got to know him on a more personal level, she might better understand his mercurial mood changes. Armed with a rationale, perhaps it wouldn't be as difficult to exercise patience and compassion.

But, since patience and compassion were two virtues she possessed in abundance, she spread a tablecloth embroidered with blue flowers over the table, folded matching napkins into fancy triangles, and lay a gleaming silver fork atop each one. She made sure that the slice of mixed-berry pie on his porcelain plate was a fair bit bigger than hers, then arranged teacups and saucers at the two o'clock position above the dishes. In the center of the table was an amber-colored glass vase of lyre leaf greeneyes, pale yellow stork's bill, and common daisies she'd picked from the side garden. *Did he notice any of these things?* she wondered.

When the milk began to sizzle in the saucepan, Nell added a spoonful of sugar and whisked it until it looked thick and frothy. Once the cups were filled, she added a dollop of butter and a sprinkling of cinnamon to each. Then came the pièce de résistance: singing "Come and get it" in her loudest, most operatic voice.

Soon, Nell heard boot heels thundering down the hall.

"What happened?" Asa demanded as he burst into the kitchen. "Heard this awful caterwauling. Thought maybe you'd scalded yourself!"

Caterwauling indeed! Nell felt a wave of indignation rise up within her, but a look at his handsome, smiling face told her he'd been teasing.

"Looks great," he said, eyeing the table. "Smells great, too."

She sat across from him and took a sip of warm milk. "So, Monday's the big day—Stone Hill Inn, open for business!"

"Indeed," he said around a bite of pie.

"I hope we haven't overlooked anything important."

Asa raised one eyebrow and put down his fork. "You're joking, right? This place looks better than it did, even when my grandparents ran it. Can't think of a single thing that needs doing—on your end, at least." Now he looked slightly apprehensive. "Is there anything you can think of that *I've* overlooked?"

"Now *you're* joking," Nell retorted. "Why, you haven't had a decent night's sleep since I got here. Probably since long before that." Then she ran down a summarized list of his accomplishments—everything from transforming the storeroom into her living quarters to repairing the roof to patching the leak in the root-cellar wall. "You've worked hard to make Stone Hill Inn the most desirable hotel in Denver. In fact, I'm so confident that we'll run out of rooms that I've compiled a list of all the other local lodging options, with instructions on how to reach them from the inn. You'll find it in the drawer under the reception counter."

Asa shook his head as he finished his pie. "Never could have done it without you, Nell. Can't tell you how grateful I am that nobody else answered the ad I posted. You've gone above and beyond the job description, that's for sure."

After the most articulate of compliments he'd ever issued her, Asa pushed back from the table, cleared his dishes, and retired with customary silence.

Nell still couldn't figure him out, but she figured she would take what she could get.

⌐

Asa wondered if he looked like a giant oaf, because that's exactly how he felt, lumbering along beside this pretty, petite, personable woman. Only a minute or so into their Sunday-morning walk, he realized that Nell was almost having to run to keep up with him. He tried taking smaller steps to alter his pace, but it only made him feel more awkward and unnatural.

It wasn't just the length of his stride that caused him feel self-conscious. He'd been to church exactly twice since returning to Denver, to attend the funeral services of his grandparents, who'd died just three months apart—and everyone who attended Meb Truett's church knew it as well as he did.

If he'd worn a hat with a wide brim to block his view, Asa would have been able to ignore the sideways glances and long, curious stares. But here he was, clean-shaven and wearing a tie for the first time in years, doing his best not to bark like a mad dog when Nell's happy greetings obliged them to smile.

"You're awfully quiet," Nell said, looking up at him from beneath her bonnet. "Aren't you feeling well this morning?"

"Fine," he grunted. "Just not accustomed to being gawked at like a sideshow freak."

She laughed, and the light, melodious sound helped to brighten his dark mood a little.

"Yes, I've noticed." She gave him a playful bump in the shoulder. "If you think *you* feel conspicuous, try tripping over your own skirt sometime. Believe me, folks'll do more than stare—they'll accuse you of sipping the cooking sherry!"

He couldn't help but chuckle at the mental image of her, arms flailing as she struggled to stay upright.

"I imagine the sight of me tripping over my skirt would raise a few eyebrows."

"My, my, my." Nell clicked her tongue. "I don't know what to make of witnessing *two* marvels in one morning."

His decision to attend church must be the first marvel, but he didn't have a clue about the second.

"No, wait—make that *three* marvels."

"Three?" he echoed.

"The always serious Asa Stone, on his way to church, laughing and making a joke—at my expense, no less. But never mind that. It's Sunday, and forgiveness should come naturally."

"Much obliged."

Forgiveness. The word unnerved him, because it was the very thing he'd been seeking his whole adult life.

"We'd better hurry inside," Nell said as they approached the church, "or we'll have to sit in the back row."

"That'd be just fine with me," Asa murmured as they stepped over the threshold.

Nell giggled, and out of the corner of his eye, Asa caught the disapproving glance of Beryl Clements. Just then, it occurred to him that folks weren't staring because he'd shaved or worn a tie. Nor were they gaping at him for having decided to show up at church. They stared because he'd showed up *with Nell*. He was hardly the only employer who provided his employee with room and board, but by accompanying her to the Sunday service, he'd unwittingly sent the message that a relationship beyond that of employer-employee existed between himself and Nell—something inappropriate. If only the townsfolk knew that he couldn't afford to entertain any relationship with Nell, even a chaste, proper one—and why.

Many nights, when sleep eluded him, Asa walked the main streets of Denver, where he witnessed questionable things—so-called respectable citizens stumbling home from the saloon or scurrying away in the shadows from Jennie Rogers's establishment to avoid notice. Even in the bright light of day, he'd watched the city's most reputable ladies sneak more eggs than they'd paid for into their shopping baskets, then gamble those saved pennies on games of chance. How dare those hypocrites judge this woman whose heart was even more beautiful than her face!

Asa had seen how quickly rumor and innuendo could destroy a reputation, and he refused to allow that fate to befall Nell.

"Go on in without me," he told her. "Woke up with a headache. I thought the walk would help, but it's still pounding away."

She searched his face, as if looking for a sign that he was merely making up an excuse to get out of sitting through the service. "There's a tin of headache powders in the top drawer of my bureau," she told him. "If you haven't used them before, the dosage instructions are on the label."

"Wouldn't feel right, going through your things, but thanks all the same." Asa tipped an imaginary hat and turned to leave. "You staying after for the social?"

She shook her head. "No, I'll see you at home."

When Nell lifted her skirts and hurried up the steps into the sanctuary, Asa breathed a sigh of relief. If tongues got to wagging, they could report only that he'd escorted her to church. *Let them speculate about that!* he thought.

With his head down and his hands stuffed into his pockets, he took his time walking back to Stone Hill.

"See you at home," she'd said.

Home.

It had been decades since Asa had felt as if he belonged somewhere. Coming back to Denver had not fulfilled the desire. Neither had restoring his grandparents' hotel. But Nell, with her eye for detail and her never-quit attitude, had turned Stone Hill into a home.

As he climbed the porch steps, he smiled. *Really* smiled for the first time in decades.

Chapter Eleven

So, tell me, Miss Holstrom, are you enjoying this bright June day as much as we are?"

Nell placed the tray of tea and cookies on the porch table between the governor hopeful, James Grant, and his wife, Mary.

"Oh, yes. And I'm happy to see someone else taking advantage of the balmy weather."

"You really must introduce me to your gardener," Mrs. Grant said. "I'd love to ask him to share his secret." She pointed at the brilliant red blossoms growing along the waist-high retaining wall that surrounded the terrace. "I've never had a talent for roses."

"They're a lot like children, I think," Nell said, "for they require daily tender loving care. I spend almost as much time clipping spent blooms as I do cooking in the kitchen!"

Mrs. Grant perked up. "Oh, you simply *must* share some of your secrets. Perhaps after James' speech?"

"Now, now, Mary." Mr. Grant patted his wife's hand. "We aren't the only guests. I'm sure Miss Holstrom has better things to do than give horticultural lessons." He looked up at Nell. "Isn't that right, Miss Holstrom?"

Nell thought of all the chores still left on her list, but how many people could say they'd taught the future governor's wife about cultivating roses? She certainly hoped Grant would become the state's next governor. If she could vote, that's who she'd choose!

She faced Mrs. Grant. "My system is very basic, so it'll take only a few minutes to explain. I'm happy to share what little I know."

"Aren't you sweet?" The woman beamed. "We have some hands to shake and some personal thank yous to deliver before James addresses the town council, but I seriously doubt my mind will be on the speech." She turned to her husband. "Sorry, dear—just being honest!"

Another guest, Cooper Preston, called to Nell from the top step of the back porch.

"I'll be with you in one minute," she told him. Facing the Grants once more, she added, "I'll be in the kitchen if you need anything—anything at all."

She soon discovered that Mr. Preston had used his bath towel to sop up a coffee spill in his room and needed another for his bath.

"And can you recommend a good restaurant?" Preston asked. "I'd like a rib-stickin' breakfast in my belly before I meet with your banker." He winked. "If all goes well, I might need to make arrangements to rent a room by the week."

"Oh?"

"I'm trying to buy the empty building beside Joslin's Department Store." He tucked in his double chin and thrust out his chest. "I'm a tailor, you see, and my wife's a seamstress. We're hoping to open a men's haberdashery and sell all manner of gentlemen's clothing. Shoes and hats, too!"

Nell wished him well and suggested the Windsor for breakfast. As he headed back up to his room, an idea began to take shape in her mind. Would Asa agree that it had merit?

Only one way to find out! But first, she had some research to do.

After finishing her morning chores, Nell took a walk up and down Denver's bustling main streets, stopping only to inspect Stone Hill's primary competitors. Then, armed with the information she'd gone looking for, she loaded a tray with coffee and a slice of jellied bread, and carried it to Asa's office.

"What's this?" he asked as she set the tray on his desk.

"I thought you could use a little sustenance."

"You thought right." He bit off one corner of the bread. "Thanks. Been sitting here trying to ignore my rumbling stomach."

"That's what happens when you skip breakfast," she said, shaking a forefinger at him.

Asa smiled as he studied her face. "Now, why do I get the impression you didn't come in here just to deliver a mid-morning snack?"

"Am I that transparent?" She chuckled quietly. "I was out in the garden just now, and Mr. Preston asked for directions to the nearest restaurant. It got me to thinking…why send our guests to competing hotel restaurants and cafés when we could serve them breakfast right here? Most of them check out by lunchtime, so we wouldn't be obliged to offer supper, as well. I'm thinking a light snack, tea and cookies—not just for special guests like the Grants—but for anyone who registers after noon."

Asa pushed back from his desk and nodded toward the empty chair beside it, so Nell sat down.

"You're already doing so much, practically single-handedly. Where you find the time to get everything done—and so well— I'll never know, but you can't possibly add yet another duty to your list. It's too long as it is."

"Oh, but I could! I'm already preparing a morning meal for you and me. Frying up a little extra bacon or poaching a few more eggs won't be any bother at all. When Tillie Truett sold us the chickens, she told me not to expect more than an egg or two from each of them per week, at first; but they're producing so fast, I can barely keep up with them. Our expenses for providing the meal will be next to nothing."

"It isn't the cost of the food that concerns me," he said. "You'd have to set the dining room table. And serve the meal at whatever time the guests decide to roll out of bed. Then clean up after them. You're an amazing bundle of energy, Nell, but not even you can be in two—or five—places at once."

"You're right, of course; but I've given that some thought, and I think I might have a solution for that, too."

"Now, why doesn't that surprise me?"

Leaning closer, Nell explained, "We'll set a fixed time—say, eight o'clock—and require that they register in advance: 'Please notify hotel staff if you'd like us to wake you for breakfast.' That way," she said, leaning closer still, "we'll kill two birds with one stone. First, it's a lovely service...offering to rouse them for important meetings or whatever, and second, I'll know ahead of time how much food to prepare. We could test it out for a few weeks. If it isn't working, we'll stop offering the meal. But if it *is*, we could charge twenty-five or fifty cents more per room, per night. I've done a little research." Nell paused, clasping her hands in her lap. "No other hotel in town is offering this service. As for getting it all done, well, I wouldn't need to do it by myself if, say, we were to hire Sophia DiMaggio to help out."

She sat back to study his reaction.

Asa nodded slowly. "I see only one problem with your idea."

Nell held her breath and said a quick silent prayer that whatever the problem was, she could counter it with more facts—or a simple solution.

"Working to help out the family is one thing, but do you think Joe and Michelle will allow their daughter to take an actual job?"

"A very good point," she admitted, "and it raises another issue. We'll need to settle on an hourly wage before we offer her the job. I realize that summer is right around the corner, but we'll still need to firm up a schedule that won't interfere with school—or her chores at home, for that matter." She bit her lower lip. "Can we afford the added expense?"

"If the DiMaggios are willing to let her work, I'll find room in the budget for her salary." He took a sip of his coffee. "What do you think would be a reasonable salary for a girl her age, doing that sort of job?"

Nell thought for a moment. "When I first left the mine and went to work at Sterling Manufactory, Sloan paid me six dollars a week, plus a free room at his hotel." She started counting on her fingers. "But I worked forty hours, and we'd need her for only an hour or so a day. I'll ask around, see about hiring another girl to help out on weekends. Maybe the girls could collect eggs for me, too. But there I go, off on a side issue." Nell groaned good-naturedly and got back on track. "If Joe and Michelle say yes— and Sophia wants the job—we could offer ten cents an hour to start. Explain that she'll be on probation for a week or two, and if things work out, we'll raise it to fifteen."

"Makes perfect sense to me."

"I don't think Joe will have a problem with the arrangement. And if I were in Sophia's shoes, I'd jump at the chance. She and her brothers are well taken care of, but I know for a fact that it's rare for them to get any spending money of their own."

"Hmm. That raises the possibility of another problem...."

Oh, no, Nell thought. *What now?*

"When Joey and Dom see Sophia running around with money she's earned jingling in her pocket, they'll want the same."

"Hmm," she echoed. "And wouldn't it be nice if you had some help with things like stacking wood? Carrying it inside for the fireplaces and cookstove? Running errands? I realize it isn't winter yet, but when the snow falls, think of how nice it'll be to have help shoveling the walks!"

"Same offer, then," he said, mostly to himself. "Ten cents an hour...at first." Asa jotted the numbers on a piece of paper, multiplied them by three, and looked over at Nell. "And when all the other children in town hear about this, how will you handle *that?*"

"Why, I'll simply tell them, as sweetly as possible, that there are no openings at this time. That there are dozens of businesses in Denver where they might find work." She slapped her knee. "And then I'll give them a cookie."

They shared a moment of companionable laughter, and Asa was still smiling when he said, "This place wouldn't stand a ghost of a chance of surviving if not for you. I don't say it near often enough, but I really appreciate everything you do."

Nell sensed a blush coming on, so she jumped to her feet, not wanting him to see it. "I have a few minutes before I start supper," she said, walking toward the door. "Might as well make good use of the time to see what Joe and Michelle think of our little plan."

"Our?" He chuckled. "Oh, no you don't. This scheme has your name written all over it. If it succeeds, you can be sure I'll give you all the credit."

And if it fails, she finished, hurrying down the hall, *who do you suppose he'll blame?*

Two days later, Nell was in the kitchen working on a shopping list when Mary Grant came in to ask for a cup of coffee.

"I believe this is the first time I've seen you sitting down," the woman exclaimed as Nell stood to serve her beverage. "And I can plainly see that's only because you couldn't make a list while standing up!"

Nell smiled. "Did Mr. Grant's speech go well?"

"Oh, I suppose," the woman said with a dismissive wave. "He does so many of those things that I hardly even listen anymore. At least today, I had a valid excuse—daydreaming about a beautiful garden for the governor's mansion."

Nell recapped the ink bottle, thinking she might as well get the rose-growing lesson over with. "Would you like to carry your coffee outside and walk among the roses?" she asked.

"Why, that would be lovely."

Nell started by describing the anatomy of a rose, pointing out the stamens and pistils, filaments and anthers, and the part each plays in producing the flower.

"Colorado soil is mostly heavy clay, and not the best for growing roses. Their roots need air, and if you'll pardon the pun, they don't like wet feet." Nell explained how she'd gone into the woods to retrieve wheelbarrow after wheelbarrow of rich loam to mix in with the soil. "I come out here every other day or so and poke my finger into the dirt to see whether the plants need water." Cupping a bloom in the V between two fingers, Nell added, "This one is just about spent, so I'll snip it off, using very sharp shears, right here." She pointed to a five-cluster of leaves that sprouted beneath the rose. "That way, the plant won't have to work at keeping the spent blossom alive. Instead, it can send energy to buds that haven't yet opened."

"Amazing. Simply amazing." Mrs. Grant beamed. "You're a virtual fount of knowledge. You should come to work for me. I'll need someone smart and capable at my side if James wins the election."

Nell pictured the governor's mansion, clear on the other side of town, and tried to imagine taking care of a place that large, plus hosting state dinners and galas.

"I'm serious as serious can be, Nell."

"I'm sure you are, Mrs. Grant."

The woman shook her head. "I can see you have reservations. Will you at least take some time to think about it?"

"I'm very flattered by your offer, but it wouldn't be fair to let you think I might eventually say yes. I'm very happy here, but I wish you all the best in finding someone else."

The woman's penciled-on eyebrows rose slightly as she considered Nell's answer. Then she laughed and gave Nell's forearm a gentle squeeze. "What a diplomatic reply," she said with a wink. "Have you given any thought to writing speeches for men like my husband?"

"Write speeches! Why, I can barely manage a grocery list."

"No offense intended, Nell, dear, but I don't believe a word of that. One need only look around here to see what you're capable of. I've hired enough housekeepers, cooks, and assistants to know proficiency when I see it."

Nell hoped she'd stop pressing the issue, because her answer would be the same. Instead—thankfully—she began talking about her husband, a former Confederate soldier. After the war, he'd enrolled at Iowa's agricultural college, transferred to Cornell, then traveled to Germany to attend the Freiberg School of Mines. "It was all excellent training," she boasted, "for when he moved to Leadville. And just last year, James and his uncle became partners in a very successful venture. Perhaps you've heard of their company...Omaha and Grant Smelting?"

Nell nodded. Who in town hadn't heard of it?

"And *then*, that industrious man I married was appointed vice president of the Denver National Bank. I still haven't quite figured out how he decided running for governor was a natural next step, but there you have it," she said. "So you can trust me when I say money is no object. You can pretty much name your salary, and I'll happily pay it."

There didn't seem a polite way to say that money didn't matter to her. So, Nell merely said, "Do you have any more questions about the roses?"

Mrs. Grant's laughter frightened the birds perched in the branches of the limber pine. As they fluttered to the next tree, she said, "Oh, no. You were very thorough." She grasped Nell's hand and gave it a gentle squeeze. "Thank you for taking time out from your busy day for that lesson. And if you ever change your mind, the offer stands, no questions asked."

Nell knew she wouldn't change her mind, not even to work for the woman who could very well become the next first lady of Colorado.

"Listen to me, going on and on like an old hen, while you have things to do." Mary Grant started down the flagstone path. "James is inside, paying our bill. When he comes looking for me, you let him know that I'll be out back, enjoying all the other lovely flowers growing in your gardens."

"I will," Nell assured her.

Half an hour later, she went to the foyer and found Asa studying the framed sign she'd put on display earlier that day. It read, "Please advise the staff if you wish to join us for breakfast, served promptly at 8:00 AM."

"What do you think?" she asked. "Does it say everything it should?"

Asa met her eyes. "It's perfect. Succinct and easy to read." Squinting one eye, he began counting on his fingers. "She sews and embroiders, she cooks and bakes, she gardens and builds chicken coops that no fox or coyote can break into, she entertains gubernatorial candidates, and now I can add 'calligraphy' to the list of her many talents." One corner of his mouth lifted in a playful smile. "Tell me, Nell Holstrom, is there anything you *can't* do?"

Her face flamed with the heat of a blush, so she turned away, not wanting him to see. "Do you think it'll be conspicuous enough on the post behind the counter?"

Asa made a slow turn, stopping when he faced the wall of mail slots. "Yes, that's ideal. This is the first thing they see, so I could drive a nail right here," he said, knocking on the center support post, "and you could hang your sign right here."

Nell bit her lower lip. "Unless...."

"Unless...?"

"Unless the glass reflects light from the door and windows, and makes it difficult for guests to read." Nell stepped toward the door. "If you'll just hold it in place, I'll check to see if there's a glare."

While Asa held up the sign, Nell walked back and forth in the entryway, checking it from every angle. Then she groaned.

"What's wrong? Is it too high? Too low?"

"No. At least, I don't think so. It's just that most people who come in here will be taller than me. Let's trade places."

She pressed herself flat against the cubby wall as he squeezed past her. They didn't touch, save the flutter of her apron hem, brushing his trousers as he went by. She had gone behind the counter dozens of times, to dust and mop, to straighten the registration book and pen, and to polish the brass service bell. Had it always been this narrow, or did it just seem that way with the presence of Asa's muscular frame?

"You'll probably need a stool," he said.

"No, I won't." To prove it, Nell boosted herself onto the counter beneath the mailboxes. In no time, she was on her knees facing the wall. "Oh, good grief," she muttered, turning around. "I forgot to pick up the—"

Why hadn't she noticed before that Asa had a scar on his forehead, running from his right eyebrow to his hairline? *Probably because he never had any reason to look up at you before, you ninny.*

He pointed at the sign. "Looking for that?"

The expression on his face was indecipherable, but if she didn't know better, Nell would have said that Asa was flirting with her.

"Yes," she said, taking it from him. "Thanks."

His crooked grin broadened as he backed up into the entryway. She held up the sign right where he had just moments before.

"Higher," he told her. After taking a few steps to the right, Asa added, "Lower. No, to the right a bit. Yes, there. That's it. No glare at all. Stay put while I fetch my hammer and a nail."

Keeping her balance on the counter required Nell to grip the edge of a shelf for balance. "Please hurry, Asa," she whispered. Precariously perched as she was, her knees ached and her arms shook.

When it dawned on her that she could just as easily reposition the sign once Asa returned, she hopped down. With the sign safely stowed on the registration counter, she picked up her cleaning rag, intent on using the extra time to dust. When Asa returned, she was on all fours, deep inside the lowest counter shelf.

"Now, where did she disappear to?" she heard him say.

In her hurry to stand, Nell tore her sleeve on a tack. As if that wasn't annoying enough, she thumped her head on the underside of the shelf. She hoped the hollow thud only seemed thunderous to her. Embarrassed, she held her breath and willed Asa to look elsewhere for her while she backed out of the cube.

She strained her ears for a few moments but heard nothing. Had he left the foyer? She hoped so, because he'd already witnessed her ungainliness far too many times.

Before she realized fully what was happening, Asa had gripped her by the waist and was gently tugging her out of the compartment.

"Are you all right?" he asked, drawing her close.

"I'm fine." Nell rubbed the back of her head, wincing when she touched the tender spot. "It'll take a lot more than a little thump to damage this thick skull."

The hint of a smile eased the concern etched into his brow. "Let me be the judge of that," he said, using his fingertips to comb through her hair. "I remember the way you pretended that the gash on the back of your hand was only a minor scrape."

Nell couldn't argue with him about that. It had taken weeks instead of days for that cut to heal, mostly because she couldn't keep the dressing clean and dry without letting the dishes and laundry pile up.

"I don't see any blood, but you'll have a good-sized bump by morning." He turned her to face him again. "Headache?"

Unable to find her voice, Nell shook her head.

"Feeling dizzy? Light-headed?"

Not because of a blow to the head, she thought, her heart hammering as she stared into his green eyes.

"Unless mortification qualifies as a symptom, I'm fine," she said.

Trapped between Asa and the wall, Nell considered her options. There wasn't room to go around him, and since he'd made no effort to move to the other side of the counter, she was, quite literally, stuck. Did she possess the strength and dexterity to climb over the cabinet?

Asa stooped, effectively putting himself at eye level with her. "I won't bite, you know."

Maybe not, but would he kiss her? He was certainly close enough!

Nell heard herself swallow. Had he heard it, too?

Asa raised his right hand. "As God is my witness, I would never hurt you." He lowered his hand and took a step back. "You believe that, don't you?"

"Yes." Despite his brooding silences and absent stares, she had no reason to doubt him. "But why would you say such a thing?"

A faint grunt passed his lips. "Maybe because you seem afraid, pressed against that wall that way. I'd wager you'll have a cross-hatch pattern etched into your back when you step away."

"If there was anyplace else to stand...."

His eyes widened, and so did his smile. Nell watched him pick up his hammer, then fish the nail out of his shirt pocket. With no announcement or fanfare, Asa reached over her head and drove the nail into the wall with one well-timed blow. He slid the hammer onto the counter, and when he'd finished hanging the sign, pressed both palms against the wall, one on either side of her head.

He was standing so close that Nell could see his pupils dilate. "If this is another test...."

"Test?"

"Like the one I had to pass the day I showed up here—all that cleaning and cooking—to prove that I had what it took to help turn this place into a functioning hotel."

"Ah, that."

She boldly lifted her chin. "So, again, if this is a test, have I passed it?"

His lips formed a taut line as he focused on the sign above her head, then used a fingertip to straighten it. "There," he said, stepping back. "If there's still a glare, then so be it."

He walked away but stopped when he reached the hall, as if he had something important to add. But he remained silent. Shaking his head and driving a hand through his hair, Asa started down the hall.

He looked miserable and lost, like a stranger in his own house. And it was her fault. If she'd simply asked him to allow her to pass, rather than standing there, expecting a kiss—and making that silly comment about a test—Asa would wouldn't have retreated, feeling awkward and inappropriate.

"I'll let you know when supper's ready," Nell called after him. "We're having roast chicken. And potatoes."

From what she'd observed of her father, grandfather, and brother, men would rather endure physical pain than acknowlededgment any sensitivity. They might not show it, but men felt things as keenly—if not more so—than women.

Asa, for the most part, behaved as though he believed himself to be forged him from cast iron. Yes, he was taller and stronger than any man Nell had ever known, but inside that broad, muscular chest beat the heart of a caring, thoughtful, *sensitive* man.

The beautiful room he'd provided for her was but one example of many she could list to prove it.

It didn't matter to her where he'd gone, or what he'd done in the time he'd spent away from Denver. In her experience, he was nothing but good and decent.

What would it take to make him believe it, too?

Chapter Twelve

Shaken to his core by the encounter with Nell, Asa decided to make a trip up Ragged Mountain to clear his mind. God willing, by the time he made his way back down again, he'd have a better idea why he'd behaved like a love-starved boor...and why Nell had reacted as she did.

It wouldn't be an easy journey, so he planned to spend the night there rather than make the trek back to Denver after dark. He hoped the trail markers left by his grandpa and brothers hadn't been washed away by melting snow or pounding rain, dislodged by clumsy bears, or hidden by years' worth of new growth.

He started out late in the afternoon, after leaving a piece of paper on the kitchen table with a single line of explanation for his temporary absence.

Thankfully, enough of the signs remained: a pyramid of flat stones, stacked by Chester. The giant west-pointing arrow Edgar had carved into the bark of a Lodgepole pine. The tepee-shaped structure he and Duncan had erected, using the branches of a giant fir.

Duncan.

Of all his brothers, he'd been closest to the brother who most resembled their mother in appearance and temperament.

It had been Duncan who put a toad in Chester's bed, who'd replaced the apple in Edgar's lunch bucket with a rock. Why couldn't the Cheyenne arrow have found Asa instead of the always-smiling Duncan?

Asa had been over that same tired ground too many times to count, and it hadn't brought his brother back. Besides, he'd come up here to reckon with his feelings for Nell, not to beat himself up yet again for failing to save his beloved brother.

He rode into what his grandfather had called Stone Camp. It lifted his spirits some, seeing the giant felled trees that formed its north border and the enormous boulder that kept them from rolling into the valley below. He dismounted, unsaddled his horse, and tethered it to a nearby silver buffaloberry shrub—exactly how Grandpa Stone had taught him—then drank in the sights and smells like a man stranded in the desert might suck at the wet lip of a canteen. A sense of peace always settled over him here, in the place where he used to come when trouble brewed.

Trouble. It was almost laughable that the things he'd considered problematic as a boy—a poor mark in school, a scolding for busting his ma's flower vase, even the loss of a faithful dog—seemed downright silly when compared to time spent with Chivington and the James-Younger gang. If he'd known then how easy he'd had it as a boy, he might have spent a lot more time giving thanks.

A hawk shrieked overhead, and he looked up in time to see the bird skim the cloudless blue. But he couldn't dillydally much longer. Up here, the world went from brilliantly sunny to black as pitch in a heartbeat. If he didn't set up camp soon, he wouldn't have enough light to do a proper job.

Using the side of his boot, Asa cleared a space for his fire. The wood was good and dry, and it didn't take long for the blaze to ignite. Any would-be predators that weren't discouraged by the fire would surely heed a round from his Springfield, leaning within reach against a nearby tree. Next, he constructed a make-shift tent—an oil tarp draped over sturdy rope that he'd tied around two trees. If it rained—and there was a good chance that it would—he'd sleep inside. If it didn't, he'd stretch out under the stars.

As a boy, the very notion that he shared this summit with mountain lions, wolves, coyotes, and black bears had terrified him. But his years on the road had taught him that nature couldn't hurt him any worse than life already had.

In minutes, it seemed, day gave way to night. Asa stirred the bright-glowing coals, squinting as a thousand sparks rose up hot and red before fading to yellow and dying like the flame of a turned-down lantern. After adding a few logs to the fire, he stretched out under the starry sky.

Reminders of his grandfather were all around, in the mournful song of the coyote, the sad notes of the night hawk, the scent of smoldering wood. Asa reflected on some of the most important lessons his grandfather had taught him, including "Not every question has an answer," and "There isn't a solution to every problem." He'd also passed along common-sense wisdom that had saved Asa's hide more than once during those hard years alone on the road: how to build a shelter from just about anything, where to find clean drinking water, how to identify berries and mushrooms that were safe to consume…and which could kill him—or make him wish he was dead.

If Silas were with him now, what advice would he impart regarding the situation with Nell? One thing was certain: Before sharing words of wisdom, he'd subject Asa to some good-natured ribbing, followed by a series of challenging questions, starting with "What do you see in the girl?" To have him back, even for one night, Asa would gladly endure the inquisition; and his answers could be summed up truthfully in one sentence: Nell Holstrom was even more beautiful inside than out—which was saying something; and if he thought for a minute that she'd have him, despite his dishonorable past, he wouldn't hesitate to make her his partner in life.

He pictured her as she'd looked with her back to the wall, stubbornly determined to stand her ground. When he'd taken her in her arms to inspect the bump on her head, she'd seemed small and fragile. But he'd seen her at work, and knew that when Nell set her mind on a task, she was anything *but* vulnerable.

He checked the Springfield, and satisfied it would protect him if he needed it, Asa wrapped himself in a dense brown blanket. Soothed by night sounds and the warmth of the fire, he closed his eyes. *Just a short nap,* he told himself.

Hours later, he woke cold and shivering. Wisps of smoke spiraled from the pitiful campfire. He sat up, yawned and stretched, knowing that if he wanted coffee, he'd have to stir the remaining coals and feed it enough kindling to boil the water.

While the pot hissed and spit, Asa breathed in the crisp scent of pine and spruce. He felt peaceful, in spite of the fact that the answers he'd come here to find eluded him, still.

His grandfather's lessons had served him well. He'd learned to live without the usual creature comforts, how to look a man in the eye and take his measure, when to thank God for each swallow of water and every morsel of food.

"Sure could use your advice right about now, Pop," he whispered.

Unfortunately, there hadn't been a lesson in surviving without *him.*

⌒

The low drone of conversation among the congregants the next Sunday made Nell feel a bit like a bee in a hive. The mental image made her laugh to herself, and she glanced around to see if anyone wondered what she found so funny.

Instead, she saw Janet coming up the aisle. Her friend sat down beside her.

"You look so pretty today, Nell," Janet said, giving her a sideways hug. "Is that a new dress?"

Nell smoothed the folds of the blue calico fabric. "As a matter of fact, it is." She wore a new hat and new shoes, too, thanks to the extra pay Asa had tucked into her envelope weeks ago. She'd tried giving it back, but he'd insisted she keep it, telling her that if she refused to accept it, he would be forced to buy her a dress himself—and wouldn't *that* get people talking!

"Looks lovely," Janet said.

"Why, thank you. And now it's my turn to admire your outfit. Pink is definitely your color," Nell told her. "Brings out the natural rosiness of your cheeks."

"Do you think so?" Janet smoothed her own skirt. "I wasn't at all sure what shade Godey's would deliver. It's difficult shopping from a catalog, with nothing more than the word *pink* and a pen-and-ink illustration to go by."

That was the reason Nell had chosen to make her dress. After she'd purchased the fabric and necessary notions, there had been money left over for yardage from a second bolt of pastel material, along with thread, buttons, and enough white rickrack to make three blouses. In addition to her old reliable gray skirt and cream-colored shirt, two new skirts and five new blouses now hung in her wardrobe. But, because the colors were all compatible, she could mix and match them, it was like having a dozen new outfits instead of just two.

"Is Asa coming to church today?" Janet asked.

Nell sighed. "I invited him, as usual, but he politely declined—as usual."

Janet's brow furrowed slightly. "That's a shame. I thought for sure he'd join us, now that the inn is open for business."

"That's the very reason he gives for staying at Stone Hill," Nell said. "Can't take the chance someone might want to rent a room!" She rolled her eyes.

Her friend looked taken aback for a moment, probably because she was unaccustomed to hearing Nell speak negatively about anyone. Nell decided then and there to surrender her attitude toward Asa to the Lord and let Him give her the compassion and patience required to deal with him.

"Well, if it isn't my friends Janet and Nell, looking pretty as a couple of catalog models."

At the familiar deep, resonant voice, Nell and Janet scooted to the left to make room in the pew for Dr. Amos Wilson, whose dedication to treating his patients made it next to impossible for him to attend Sunday services.

"It's good to see you, Amos," Nell said, looking around Janet. "Mighty thoughtful of your patients to hold their complaints until noon."

He shushed her. "My prayer this morning is that they'll hold off until after the social." Then he leaned forward and said with slightly raised voice, "I can't remember the last time I had a good home-cooked meal."

His sister, Elsie Fletcher, turned around and feigned a scowl. "Oh, stop your whining. You join Abe and me for dinner nearly every day."

Her husband turned around, too. "She's right," Abe said. "You know how the government has been working to enact a new statute to replace the one repealed in '72? Well, if they succeed, I might have to charge you a 'meals fee' to offset the tax!"

The doctor chuckled. "You're lucky we're in church, brother-in-law, or I'd tell you exactly what I think of your tax!"

While Janet, Amos, and Abe continued chatting, Elsie waved Nell closer. Cupping her beside her mouth, she whispered, "Are you seeing what I'm seeing?"

"That your brother never misses an opportunity to flirt with the young widow Sinclaire?"

Now, Elsie hid a giggle behind her hand. "If this keeps up, we may find ourselves helping her sew a wedding dress before long!"

Nell had noticed the pair exchanging furtive smiles now and then. As committed as Janet still was to her late husband, Nell hoped her heart would open fully to the prospect of a new romance. She deserved the love of a good man, and they didn't come much better than Amos Wilson.

"Look, Joe! It's Nell!"

She turned toward the familiar voice, and before she could offer a word of greeting, Michelle had leaned into the row to say, "Mama just *loves* the cottage. She can't stop talking about all the things you did to make it a homey place to live."

"It's good to hear she's happy."

"I know we introduced the two of you in the store, but she made meat-stuffed ravioli for dinner, and she wanted me to invite you to share it with us."

A beaming Maria peeked around Michelle's shoulder and waved a white-gloved hand, nodding enthusiastically.

Nell hesitated, not wanting to leave Asa to eat all by himself. He spent far too much time alone as it was.

"We stopped by the inn on our way here to invite Asa, so if that's why you're hesitating, there's no need. He said yes!" Grinning, Michelle added, "Believe me, we were just as surprised as you are that he said yes. We'll sit down between two and two thirty, so we'll see you then."

When she'd checked the registration book shortly after breakfast, Nell counted four guests, and all but Cooper Preston—their only long-term renter—would be gone by lunchtime. Letters in the inn's mailbox confirmed the arrival of two businessmen first thing tomorrow. If she didn't dawdle after the service, Nell could turn all the rooms before heading over to the DiMaggios'.

All conversation quieted with the first robust chords from Tillie Truett's piano. Everyone stood, waiting for her signal to begin "How Firm a Foundation," and after two verses, they slid straight into "Amazing Grace."

When the singing concluded, Reverend Truett moved to the center of the altar. "Morning, friends. As always, it's wonderful to see your bright-shining faces. I almost hated to signal Tillie to begin playing, because it did my heart good to hear you sharing God's love with your neighbors. You had no way of knowing it," he said, stepping behind the pulpit, "but you were living out the Scripture I'll be speaking on today: Ephesians, chapter four, verse thirty-two."

He waited for the flutter of pages as everyone opened their Bibles, then began to read: "'*Be ye kind one to another, tenderhearted....*'"

As Truett paused for emphasis, as he often did, Nell's mind wandered back to the day when Asa helped her hang the sign inviting guests to take breakfast at the inn. She hadn't meant to be unkind or overreact to his nearness; yet, despite the dozens of little extras she'd done in an effort to make up for it in the days since, a sense of guilt still weighed upon her heart. And all because of that note.

If she closed her eyes, Nell could still see it, anchored by the salt and pepper shakers on the kitchen table. "Headed to Ragged Mountain to think on a few things," it had said. "Be back in the morning." It hadn't started "Dear Nell," and he hadn't signed it. What she'd read between the lines had kept her up all night, pacing her room and peering out the windows, praying he would come home safe and sound.

"'...*forgiving one another,*'" Reverend Truett continued, "'*even as God for Christ's sake hath forgiven you.*'"

Many times after the mine collapse that had crushed her pa, Nell turned to the Good Book for solace, for help in understanding how a man could put something as elusive as gold ahead of the people who loved him, who relied on him. She'd come to understand that if she didn't get a handle on her anger, it could easily mutate into hatred. The passage that had given her an especially strong conviction in this regard was Colossians 3:12–13: "...*mercies, kindness, humbleness of mind, meekness, longsuffering; forbearing one another, and forgiving one another...as Christ forgave you, so also do ye.*"

Her fellow parishioners were singing again, this time "A Mighty Fortress Is Our God." Nell slid the hymnal from the pew rack in front of her, but she didn't sing. For the first time in recent memory, her heart just wasn't in it. And it wouldn't be, until she knew for certain that Asa had forgiven her.

Chapter Thirteen

"Nearly every room is booked for the weekend of July Fourth," Nell told the DiMaggios over supper that afternoon. "I don't remember Denver being quite so busy over that holiday, do you?"

"Not that I can recall," Joe said. "Say, Asa, pass the meatballs, will you? I'm ready for another round."

Maria beamed at her son-in-law, clearly glad to see he was enjoying his meal. "Joseph, you belly, she gonna 'splode," she said, forefinger wagging like a bony metronome. "Let Nell and Asa, and the *bambini*, they have-a more. Then you *mangia*, okay?"

Asa jabbed his fork into another one before passing the bowl down the table. "These are…how do you say 'delicious' in Italian?"

Asa's clumsy stab at an Italian accent provoked a round of boisterous laughter from everyone but Nell, who whispered, "It's such a relief to see that Sophia and Maria have bonded!" To that point, she'd been unusually quiet, and he wondered if it was due to fatigue—she'd cleaned every recently vacated guest room in just a few hours. But that couldn't be it. She pushed herself that hard every day.

Whatever it was, he hoped she would perk up for a discussion about the prospect of hiring the DiMaggios' children to help at the inn. "So, Joe, Michelle," he began, "there's something Nell and I have been meaning to run by you."

The jovial back-and-forth banter quieted as all eyes turned to him. One look at the three youthful, expectant faces told him this was not the time or place to talk jobs and hourly wages; if the parents said no, the children would be disappointed.

"I...uh, it's probably best if we discuss it later."

Nell emitted a sigh that sounded like one of relief, then sent him a sweet smile that made his mouth go dry.

"Oh, my," Michelle said. "This sounds serious."

"Oh, no," Nell assured her. "It's nothing to worry over."

She shot Asa another look, and this time, she winked! Asa held his breath, hoping to bring his heart rate back to normal.

After dessert, the DiMaggio youngsters were excused to go play outside.

"Carry your plates into the kitchen first," Joe said.

"Nonna will do," Maria said. "Okay?"

"Okay," he said, and facing his sons and daughter, added, "Stay out back, but only for half an hour or so."

"Your pa is right," Michelle put in. "Tomorrow is a school day. And you know the main rule...."

"Don't go near the road," they said together.

As they cleared the table, Asa silently agreed with their parents' rule. Denver's streets were rife with dangers far more serious than runaway wagons or drunks on horseback. It should have been expected that when the population grew by a factor of twenty—to 107,000—crime would grow, too. A sensible mayoral administration might have taken that into account, hiring more policemen and building a bigger jail to house those captured. But Asa suspected more than a few of Denver's elected officials participated in some of the illegal card games that led to fistfights and gunfights...and murders. Innocent people were often injured or killed in the crossfire. And then there were those who just went missing, like young Penny Daugherty. Her ma and pa found it less painful to accept the "She eloped with a sweet-talking salesman" story. Though weeks of searching turned up nothing, the sheriff still believed witnesses who'd seen her being carted off—kicking and crying, hogtied and gagged—by the notorious Bummer gang. Asa had grown up on a small farm just outside the city limits. There, his ma's worst fears consisted of him or his brothers falling out of their saddles or getting bellyaches from eating too many wild blackberries. If God ever saw fit to bless him with young'uns— an unlikely blessing considering the way he'd lived his life—Asa wouldn't want to raise them here in Denver! "Such good *bambini*," Maria said as the children ran from the room. Then she smiled at her daughter and said something in Italian.

"Grazie, Mama." Michelle smiled, then turned to her husband. "She says we've made her very happy, letting her spend her latter years here, watching them grow."

Then the older woman turned her smile on Nell and Asa. "So? When you make marriage, have *bambini* of your own?"

Asa nearly choked on a mouthful of water, and Nell's eyes widened to twice their normal size.

"Asa is my boss," she blurted out, "not my beau!"

Maria waved the comment away. "You no fool me. I see the way he—"

"Mama," Michelle cut in, "would you be a dear and check on the children?"

The older woman's face wrinkled with a mischievous smile. She slowly rose from her chair, wrapped her shawl around her shoulders, and shuffled to the door, muttering to herself.

"All right, Asa," Joe said when Maria had left. "Let's have it. What did those ruffians of mine do? Track mud onto your porch? Trample the flowers? Lose a ball in your rose garden?"

"What they've done," Nell began, "is behave so well that we're hoping you'll let them help out around the inn. Not hard labor, of course. Naturally, we'd pay them. Sophia could help me serve breakfast to the guests, and Joey could mind the vegetable and flower gardens, sweep the porches, and such. Dom's a bit young for official chores, but if you're amenable, he could gather eggs from the coop."

Joe and Michelle exchanged glances, then looked at Asa.

"You're in agreement with this idea?" Joe asked him.

Nell sat up straighter and folded her hands on the table, clearly offended by Joe's question. Asa, for his part, was puzzled. Given that Joe had tasked her with balancing his books, ordering goods, and paying the bills while she was in his employ, it seemed he should be more trusting of her business sense.

"Nell's come up with lots of great ideas," he put in, "not only for improving the inn, but for streamlining standard operations, as well."

He glanced over at her, hoping he hadn't offended her further by jumping to her defense. Instead, she looked surprised.

"I think it's a wonderful idea," Michelle exclaimed. "In fact, I can't think of a single reason to say no! Think of it, Joe—the children will learn to budget and to take orders from someone other than us, and they'll be close by. *And* they'll have less time for playing out there," she concluded, pointing toward the windows, "where all sorts of dangers lurk."

"Lurk." Joe grinned, then looked at Asa. "Reading too many of those dime novels we stock."

The children thundered into the room just then, laughing and shoving one another good-naturedly.

"What's a wonderful idea, Mama?" Sophia asked as she wrapped her arms around Nell.

"Well," Joe began, "Asa and Nell, here, were wondering if the three of you might like to go to work for them."

"You mean…we'd have real *jobs?*" Dom asked. "Besides helping out at the store?"

"Real jobs," Asa said.

The boy met Nell's eyes. "Is he joking?"

She shook her head. "He's one hundred percent serious."

Sophia looked up at her. "What sort of work would we do?"

"Well, Dom could gather eggs, for starters, and Joey could maintain the vegetable garden." She winked at Michelle. "That means fresh vegetables for your table, too." Gently cupping Sophia's face in her hands, she said, "And you, my little princess, would help me prepare and serve breakfast in the dining room."

Joey laid a hand on Asa's shoulder. "Does this mean we'd get a salary?"

"It does."

The boy moved to his father's side. "What do you say, Pa? Dom echoed the question as Sophia leaned against Joe. "It's like an answer to prayer, isn't it?"

A hush fell over the room for a moment, until Michelle explained, "With the new department store right up the street, we've lost quite a few of our regular customers."

Joe looked embarrassed, as though he worried Nell and Asa might be sitting in judgment of his business skills or questioning his ability to provide for his family. Later, Asa would ask Nell if she had any ideas as to how the DiMaggios might attract more shoppers to their store. He had no doubt she could come up with something.

"When can we start?" Dom wanted to know.

"As soon as you'd like—even tomorrow," Nell said. "*After* you've finished your homework and any chores your mother or father may have assigned to you."

"School will be out for the summer soon," Joey observed, "so the homework part won't be a problem." A crooked grin lit his face.

But Asa's gaze kept returning to Nell's face, which was radiant with obvious affection for the DiMaggio children.

He couldn't remember seeing a more beautiful sight. If only he could do something to inspire the same glow.

⌇

On the Fourth of July, the skies over Denver loomed gray and gloomy, but that didn't stop Denver's citizenry from making the most of the local festivities. All the guests at the inn had decided to participate in the events, making it possible for Asa to lock up and join them.

The day began with a parade featuring some retired soldiers in full dress uniform, most of the town officials, members of the Ladies Auxiliary, and a few stragglers whom Asa couldn't name. They marched down Front Street, crossing Cherry Creek by way of the two-lane wooden bridge; and after zigzagging up Larimer and down Holladay, the noisy procession made its way into a grove near the creek, where Mayor John Long Routt was scheduled to deliver a speech.

The address lasted all of five minutes, and then Routt announced his intention to recite the Declaration of Independence, in order to remind his constituents what Denver and Colorado—indeed, all of the United States of America—stood for.

"'When in the course of human events,'" he began, "'it becomes necessary for one people to dissolve the political bands which have connected them with another, and to assume among the powers of the earth, the separate and equal station to which the Laws of Nature and Nature's God entitle them, a decent respect to the opinions of mankind requires that they should declare the causes which impel them to the separation.'"

Good, Asa thought when the mayor paused. *He doesn't really intend to read the entire document.*

Sometimes, he quickly discovered, a pause is just that. A minute or two into the document, the crowd dispersed, preferring, it seemed, to engage in quiet conversation with their neighbors or partake of the baked goods provided by the ladies of several area churches.

If Routt noticed the thinning crowd or their lack of interest in his recitation, it didn't show. More than a few people perked up, though, when he announced the start of the boxed lunch auction. "I hope that all eligible bachelors will be generous in their bidding," he bellowed through his megaphone, "because, as you know, the money will help repair the recent flood damage."

There was a flurry of activity as the unwed women of Denver rushed the gazebo where they were to leave the sewing baskets, pails, bowls, and boxes they'd packed and decorated with bright satin bows, flowers, and checkered tablecloths in an effort to entice the local bachelors to bid high. They'd decorated *themselves*, too, for much the same reasons.

Asa hadn't intended to participate in the auction, but then he saw Nell climb the gazebo steps and set a plain wicker basket on the table. How like her not to let the contents speak for themselves, instead of embellishing it with beads and baubles. He emptied his pockets into one palm and poked through the coins. He could go as high as five dollars, if that's what it took to guarantee he could have her all to himself for a change. The inn had been booked solid for weeks, and while the DiMaggio children had proven themselves worth every penny he paid them, they had an uncanny knack for showing up just when he was hoping to compliment Nell on a culinary masterpiece, a skillful piano performance, or a new arrangement of furniture.

Homer Nelson, winner of the hog-calling contest, was the auctioneer. He sold a picnic basket and a lunch bucket before hoisting Nell's contribution into the air. "Who'll start the bidding at a quarter?" he said.

Asa raised his hand, and when Homer shouted out his name, all heads turned his way.

"That's Nell Holstrom's lunch," someone called out.

"He can't bid on that," a coarse female voice behind him whispered. "Bad enough they're livin' like they do. Must they flaunt it, too?"

Gus Anderson raised his hand. "Fifty cents!"

"I hear fifty," Homer said. "Do I hear seventy-five?"

"I'll bid two dollars," Gus shouted, outbidding himself. The Pinkerton did a slow turn, as if daring any man present to top the bid.

"Two dollars, going once," Homer said, auctioneer's hammer in the air, "going twice...*sold* to the man with the shiny silver badge!"

Grinning like a schoolboy, Gus made his way forward, paid for his lunch, then searched the crowd for Nell. Asa did the same, spotting her to the far right of the gazebo.

Gus had found her, too, and he promptly walked over, offered his arm, and led her to the area cordoned off by a sign that read "Boxed Lunch Auction Winners Only!" *Could be worse*, Asa told himself. Deputy Mort McCreery could have bid on Nell's lunch. Mort's clean-cut Irish looks and quick wit appealed to women of all ages, some old enough to be his grandma. Gus, on the other hand, was pleasant enough, but the things he'd seen and experienced as a Pinkerton agent must have jaded him, for it was rare to catch him smiling.

It wasn't likely that Gus and Nell would leave the cheerfully adorned picnic bench as more than friends, but he didn't intend to stand around, watching as they shared a meal. Lowering his head and pocketing his hands, he started back toward Sterling Street to seek solace in the solitude at the inn.

He'd gone only a few steps when someone grabbed his arm.

"You can't leave, Mr. Stone," Sophia DiMaggio pouted. "Nell promised to tell us a story after lunch."

"Is that so?"

Nodding, she looked up into his face. "Have you ever heard one of her stories?"

"Can't say I've had the pleasure," he admitted.

"Oh, then you just *have* to join us. Nell is the best storyteller in the whole wide world!"

"Is she, now?" Asa chuckled. "Well, that's all fine, but I think I need a treat to tide me over till then. I think I saw an ice cream booth over there," he said, pointing, "but I don't like eating alone. Won't you join me?"

An excited grin lit her face. "Of course!" she said, then grabbed Asa by the hand and raced toward the booth.

"Two ice creams, please," Asa told the boy behind the counter.

"Vanilla or chocolate, sir?"

Asa looked down at Sophia. "Well? What do you say?"

She clasped hands under her chin and made a pensive frown. "Oh, how to decide?"

Asa chuckled again. "We'd both like a scoop of each," he said, sliding the proper coinage on the counter.

They carried their bowls to a nearby bench and sat down to enjoy the treat. Asa immediately regretted the spot they'd chosen, for he had a direct line of sight to where Gus and Nell sat, fifty yards due north, munching fried chicken, corn bread, and apple slices.

"Why don't you like Mr. Anderson?" Sophia asked.

"What makes you think I don't like him?"

"You're scowling at him, that's why."

Asa pressed a fingertip against his brow. "Took too big a bite of ice cream," he said, "and about froze my brain."

She giggled, but it was clear by the look on her face that his explanation hadn't satisfied her.

"You know what I think?" She glanced around conspiratorially. "I think you're sweet on Nell." She shrugged. "That could've been you over there, if you hadn't quit bidding."

Asa sat quietly as Sophia tilted her head and studied his face. He braced himself for the next question in her inquisition.

"It's very good ice cream, don't you think?"

As she scraped the last of the treat from her bowl, Asa decided this girl would go far, because she'd already mastered one of life's most nuanced lessons: knowing when to change the subject.

"Oh, look," she said, pointing with her spoon. "Nell and Mr. Anderson are cleaning up." She got to her feet and held out one hand. "Will you join us for Nell's story?"

"Ought to get back and unlock the inn, in case one of the guests wants to get in." One look at her disappointed face was all it took for him to change his mind. "But I don't suppose it'll hurt to make them wait a few minutes more."

He let her lead him toward the bench where Nell now sat alone.

"Asa," Nell said, sounding surprised. "It's good to see you. I wasn't sure if you'd be joining us today."

"Having a good day?" he asked her.

"A wonderful day. And you?"

He tousled Sophia's hair. "Better now that my little friend is with me."

"Don't tell Joey and Dom," the girl whispered, "but Mr. Stone just bought me some ice cream."

"He did, did he?" Nell met his eyes.

"Chocolate *and* vanilla," she said, sitting on Nell's left. "But if the boys find out, they'll want some, too."

Nell's lips parted, no doubt to gently take the girl to task for the comment, but the boys' approach prevented it.

"Did we miss the story?" Dom asked.

"We're not too late, are we?" Joey put in.

"Listen to you, so out of breath, you can barely talk!" Nell laughed. "I'm happy to say that you're right on time."

The boys joined her on the bench, sitting to her right.

"Where will Mr. Stone sit?" Sophia asked.

Nell looked up at him. "*You* want to hear the story, too?"

"Sure, but I don't mind standing. We're ready when you are."

"All right, then." She cleared her throat. "This story is called 'The Astrologer,' and it goes like this: There once was an old man who believed he could read the future written in the stars. One night as he walked along, he saw that the whole village had gathered, and everyone was looking up at the sky. 'Oh, my,' he said to himself. 'It must be the end of the world!'"

The kids snickered at her rendition of the man's voice.

"He was so busy looking up that he didn't see the big hole in the road, and he fell right in. When he got to his feet, he saw that he was covered in mud, all the way up to his ears!"

"Was he hurt?" Sophia asked.

"No," Nell said, "but he was frightened, because the mud was slippery, and he couldn't climb out of the hole."

"What did he do?" Dom wanted to know.

"Bet he started caterwaulin' like a bull moose," Joey speculated. "'Help! Help!'"

"You're a funny boy, Joey," Nell said, laughing softly, "and you're also perceptive."

"Perceptive," Sophia echoed. "What does that mean?"

"It means your big brother understood what was going on, and had a pretty good hunch about what might happen next. So, as Joey predicted," Nell continued, "the old man called and called, and finally, the people in the town heard him. They went to the edge of the hole and looked in.

"'You pretend that you can predict the future,' one man said.

"'That's because I can!' the old man argued.

"'Then you would have known that this hole was here, and you could have avoided falling in!'"

"Those people were very perspective!" Sophia observed.

"Perceptive," Joey corrected.

"'Maybe you'll learn to pay attention to what's right in front of you,'" the people said, "'instead of looking to the sky to predict the future!'"

Nell reached into her apron pocket and withdrew a napkin-wrapped treat. "Sugar cookies, she said, tapping the bundle, "one for each child who can tell me the moral of the story."

One by one, the children licked their lips, then made their guesses.

"Watch where you're going," Sophia said, "and you won't fall in a hole!"

Dom blurted out, "Don't expect to find answers written in the sky!"

Joey piped up with, "If you take care of the things that are important, the things that aren't important will take care of themselves."

"I'm impressed!" Nell said, then unwrapped the napkin and handed a sugar cookie to each child.

They accepted the treats gratefully, giggling and chattering as they basked in the glow of her fondness for them.

Asa was impressed, and not just with the insightfulness of the DiMaggio children. It seemed a shame that a woman with as much love to give as Nell hadn't married, that she didn't have half a dozen children of her own. It seemed to him that what Denver needed was a whole mess of mothers like Nell, who'd raise children that grew into productive, respectful citizens with open hearts and perceptive minds.

He was so engrossed in their playful banter that he didn't notice the stranger, watching from behind the shaggy trunk of a Buckley oak.

Chapter Fourteen

Who is that man? I keep seeing him around town."

Joe and Michelle DiMaggio, and her pastor husband Meb looked in the direction Tillie had pointed.

"What man?" Nell asked, peeking out the window.

"I don't see anyone," Janet affirmed.

Tillie exhaled a groan of frustration. "That's because he's gone *now*. But I swear to you, he was there." She pointed. "Right *there* in the alleyway between the bank and the post office."

Asa had a feeling that everyone present shared the same concern—that Tillie might be drinking again. She'd held her own when Doc Wilson delivered the bleak diagnosis of terminal cancer to her only son. But after the young man chose to end his life rather than endure years of suffering, Tillie slipped deep into a pit of despair, and whiskey had become her only companion. A year or so ago, she'd fought the fiend, and won. One of the few lasting lessons Asa had learned, watching his pa battle the same demon, was that it took strength of mind and character to maintain control over an addiction.

"How many times have you seen him?" Meb asked.

"Six or seven, I'd say."

"And what does your mysterious stranger look like?"

Tillie shot him a heated glare. "He wears a flat-topped hat and long black duster," she said through clenched teeth, "even on the hottest of days."

Could be anyone, Asa thought.

"There's a black-handled pistol in his gun belt, and he wears it backward, so that the grip faces outward."

He changed his mind upon hearing that last bit of information.

"His boots are a pale leather, unlike anything I've seen. And he smokes. I saw the glow of his cigarette when—"

"But what does he *look* like?" Meb pressed. "Is he young or old? Dark hair or light? Mustache or beard?"

"Well, I…I'm afraid I can't say." Tillie shrugged. "I've never seen his face, because he keeps his collar turned up and wears the hat low on his forehead."

Nell slid an arm across Tillie's shoulders. "I'm sure it's very unsettling, seeing a man like that lurking about."

"I'd shake right out of my shoes!" Janet agreed.

Tillie searched the faces of those gathered in DiMaggio's store: her husband, Joe and Michelle, and Asa. Tears filled her eyes, and she wrung her hands. I know what you're all thinking," Tillie said, wringing her hands, "but, as God is my witness, I haven't so much as sniffed the cork of a bottle of whiskey—of liquor of any kind, for that matter."

No one spoke, but Nell drew the woman a little closer.

"So, not even one of you has seen him?" Desperation rang loud in her voice. "But how can that be?"

"I'm guessing we've all seen him, probably more than once," Nell said softly. "But, because this town is filled with unsavory characters—some new, some old—he just blended into the background."

Tillie thought about that for a moment. "Yes, I suppose that makes sense." She took a lace-edged handkerchief from her pocket, blotted her eyes, and managed a shaky smile. "Thank you,

Nell. You're a good friend." Just short of the door, she turned to Meb. "Can you manage all the groceries by yourself?"

Asa had seen that expression on the preacher's face only twice before...when he said a final prayer over his grandparents' graves. Tillie looked just as miserable. It must be pure torture, Asa decided, to have so little faith in your life mate.

Meb gathered up their purchases and, standing beside his wife, said, "We'll see all of you in church on Sunday."

Once they were out of sight, Michelle excused herself to sort and price the shipment of canned goods delivered that morning. Janet said it was time to open the library for business.

"Tell me, Nell," Joe said, "do you actually believe what you said to Tillie? Or were you just being your typically kind and protective self?"

"That Denver is so overrun with strangers that we might have seen the stranger, too?"

Joe nodded.

She blinked, then swallowed. "You have to admit, there's a very good chance."

Joe chuckled. "Very diplomatic. Pity you didn't go law school. You would have been an impressive lawyer." He looked at Asa and added, "A non-answer, yet accurate just the same. She's very clever, isn't she?"

"I wasn't trying to be clever," she insisted. "Tillie described him in such detail that I can't help but believe her. And, in case you're wondering, she was this far from my face."—Nell held her thumb and forefinger several inches apart. "And I can tell you for certain that she had *not* been drinking."

"All right, then, where is this guy bedding down? Taking his meals? Tillie said he smokes, so where's he buying his cigarettes? Not here, I tell you. I'd remember a guy in a black duster and flat-topped hat!"

An image from Asa's memory flashed through his mind.

"Now that we know what to look for," Nell was saying, "I'm sure we'll all get answers to our questions."

He'd seen boot prints—big ones—all around his campsite that night....

Michelle looked up from her work. "But even if we never spot him, it's a bad idea to badger Tillie about this."

For years now, Asa had told himself that the man in the black duster had been part of a weird dream, nothing more.

The store-keeper's wife continued, "Because I for one would hate to be the person who destroyed her precarious hold on sobriety."

Asa remembered the sense of foreboding Ambrose Brigham had felt the night he'd escorted him back to the Tivoli. He'd dismissed it as the ramblings of a superstitious old man, but he was almost certain he'd heard footsteps and smelled cigarette smoke all the way back to Stone Hill.

When he looked up, Asa realized Nell had been watching him. Though he could never admit it—especially not to her—he cared about her, and not just as an employee. If anything should happen to her....

He hadn't strapped on a gun since coming back to Denver—a personal decision that had nothing to do with the city's strict policy on firearms. Starting tomorrow, that would change.

〰️

On a Sunday morning several weeks later, a frosty wind blew down from the Rockies, making it cold enough that Asa decided to wear a jacket to church. Every other man seated in the sanctuary had worn a coat or duster, too, whether to keep out the chill or to conceal a sidearm, he couldn't say. Probably both, in many cases.

From his aisle seat in the last pew, he could see Nell, seated with Shaina and Sloan Remington, on the left, and Janet Sinclaire on her right. Even from this distance, he could hear the women laughing at something Sloan had said. He wondered if it had anything to do with the news Nell shared with him after returning from a grocery run at DiMaggios' yesterday. Shaina and Sloan were expecting their first child. When the Remingtons' carriage passed Stone Hill, she'd whispered, "But it's top secret, so you mustn't tell a soul." Excitement caused her to tremble from head to toe as she added, "Be honest now...have you ever seen a more beautiful mother-to-be!" *No,* he'd thought, *but only because I haven't seen you with child.*

It had been a mistake to let his brain go down that path, because thoughts of a life with Nell as his wife had kept him up half the night, planning how he'd close off a wing of the inn to afford his family some privacy from guests, and ensuring safety and security for his wife and children. Out back, beyond the vegetable garden and the chicken coop, he'd hang a rope swing from the fattest branch of the bur oak. Asa could almost hear the sound of utensils clicking against plates and the music of children's laughter as steaming bowls of food were passed up and down the dining room table.

He shook his head, diffusing the pleasant—if improbable—thoughts.

With his eyes on the cross adorning the pulpit, Asa prayed, *Lord, if I could go back in time, undo the things that make me unworthy of her....*

But prayers like that were a waste of time. And dreams were for wet-behind-the-ears boys, not men whose past deeds had hardened their hearts and blackened their souls. What better place to come to terms with that fact, once and for all, than in the house of God?

Asa watched as Reverend Truett approached the pew where Nell was seated, leaned over, and whispered something to her and Janet that prompted smiles and nods before they rose from their seats. The friends linked arms and walked to the altar, where Janet slid onto the piano bench, evidently filling in for Tillie. Beside her, Nell flipped through a book of sheet music.

After a few moments, Nell clasped her hands under her chin, lifted her shoulders, and nodded enthusiastically to Janet. He didn't know which hymn they'd chosen, but there wasn't a doubt in his mind that it would sound heavenly. He'd never heard Nell sing a solo in church, and he could hardly wait to hear that angelic voice of hers resound through the rafters.

Nell met his eyes just then, and several congregants turned around, likely to see who her smile was for.

Asa stared down at his boots and pretended not to have noticed, his heart swelling...then sinking. Without saying a word, Nell had told him that she cared for him, too—had been telling him almost from the first day, with her little kindnesses and gentle smiles. If only the good Lord would give her a reason to like him less—a whole lot less. Nell deserved someone like Gus Anderson, honest and true, without a blemish on his record. It would hurt like mad, seeing her with someone else; but Asa would handle it, because her happiness and well-being far outweighed his undeserving dreams of a future with her.

Truett signaled Janet to begin playing, and the congregation rose to sing the opening hymn, "Sweet Hour of Prayer." When the song ended, she touched a soft, subtle chord, and Nell stepped forward.

Hands folded at her waist, she took a deep breath, closed her eyes, and began to sing "All Things Are Possible to Him." The congregation joined in, but by the last line of the second verse, something—her sweet face? the clarity of her voice?—silenced them. Janet stopped playing, but Nell seemed too lost in the lyrics to notice she was singing a capella: "If nothing is too hard for Thee, all things are possible to me."

Why she chose that precise moment to open her eyes, or how she managed to single him out in the crowded church, Asa couldn't say. But the words that issued from her lips opened a long-forgotten place in his heart, the place where hope once dwelled. He warned himself not to read too much into it, but it wasn't easy. Not with her standing up there on the altar, backlit by the bright sunshine that streamed in through the windows, looking like an earthly angel, an angel whose heart could belong to him...if only he'd lived a different life.

When the hymn ended, Reverend Truett took his place at the pulpit and with trembling voice said, "Nell, that was just about the most beautiful song I think I've ever heard."

Blushing, she thanked him, then sat quickly in the chair beside the piano as he faced his flock.

"You know how often I've solicited your prayers on behalf of my mother," he began.

Dozens of heads nodded as murmurs of "Yes, Reverend" floated softly through the church.

"Well, I've received word that she's taken a turn for the worse. So, first thing tomorrow morning, Tillie and I will leave for Golden to care for her. I apologize for our sudden flight; you can be sure Tillie and I will miss you, and we'll certainly keep you all in our prayers. But you know that when duty calls...." He stopped to blot his eyes with a white handkerchief. "We have no way of knowing how long we'll be gone. That decision is in the hands of the Almighty. But I would never leave you without a godly man to minister to your souls. So, I wired a good friend from seminary, and he has graciously agreed to assume my duties here until I am able to return."

Truett extended his arm, and a man stood from his seat in the front pew and made his way forward to join him at the pulpit.

"This, dear ones, is Reverend Robert Crutchfield. And this," he told the preacher, "is your new flock."

Crutchfield thanked Truett, then briefly summarized his qualifications for the congregation. "My wife and daughters will join me in a few weeks," he then told them. "But right now, I believe it's important to tell you a little something about me, and it may or may not put you at ease: The length of my sermons has earned me something of a reputation…." He paused, smiling as the parishioners mulled that over. "Yes," he continued, "it's a well-documented fact that I deliver some of the shortest sermons on record."

When the wave of relieved laughter abated, the new preacher opened the Bible, already in place on the pulpit. "I had a sermon all prepared for you. Stayed up half the night writing it." He lifted a sheet of paper, both sides of which were filled with large, bold script, and tore it in half. "But this morning, as I sat listening to Meb share his sobering news, God put a different message on my heart. I have no idea which of you He intends these words for, only that I feel duty-bound to speak them."

Nell sat up straighter, and Janet turned away from the piano to face the preacher. Everyone, it seemed, had perked up, anxious to know what God might want him or her, in particular, to know.

"Our Christian faith is not meant to be a moment in our lives. Rather, it's a moment-by-moment relationship with the Almighty. We bring our daily burdens to the cross, trusting that He will answer our prayers. But, as most of you have probably learned from experience, God's answers do not always materialize immediately. And yet, we must continue to trust that He will answer when the time is best for us. One way we show Him our confidence is through perseverance. We stay the course. We hold fast to our faith. We don't walk away from Him, even when things are difficult."

The way you did, Asa thought, *when Pa and Duncan were killed?*

Crutchfield closed his eyes and nodded thoughtfully, as if receiving additional insights to share. When he opened them again, he continued, "David Livingstone, the great Scottish preacher, put it this way: 'I am prepared to go anywhere...provided it be forward. I am determined never to stop...until I have come to the end and achieved my purpose.'"

He made eye contact with a few people in the front row, making Asa especially glad he'd chosen to sit in the back. Crutchfield then paraphrased Ephesians 6:18: "Pray always in the Spirit, and *persevere*."

Beside him, Cooper Preston was snoring softly. Across the aisle, Michelle shushed young Dom. Two rows up, Ambrose said a craggy "Amen, Lawd, *Amen*" as Crutchfield's steady gaze settled on Asa.

The hairs on the back of Asa's neck stood up, and he clenched his hands into fists, feeling a strong sense of conviction for basically giving up on God. He also felt a powerful need to escape. But he couldn't leave, much as he wanted to, without calling even more attention to himself. So, he would suffer in silence...for now. When the next hymn began, and everyone was busy getting to their feet and finding the right page in their hymnals, he'd make his exit. Until then, he'd keep his head down. Exercise patience. He'd *persevere*.

Something moved to his right. If he had blinked, he wouldn't have seen it at all. The hem of a black duster brushed past. Pale leather boots paused for a fraction of a second beside his pew.

Forget lying low. If this was the stranger Tillie Truett described, someone needed to have words with him.

Asa started to rise, but the sound-sleeping Cooper Preston slumped against his shoulder. He propped the man upright and headed straight for the door.

Outside, he stood on the sidewalk, looking up and down the busy street. Two seconds sooner, and he could have had the man by the lapels. Could have demanded to know why he'd come to Denver, and what purpose was served by loitering in the alleyways at all hours of the day and night, terrifying good women like Tillie Truett.

A stray dog moseyed up to Asa and sat down beside him. It wasn't until he went to scratch the sad-eyed mutt behind the ears that he realized he'd wrapped his hand around the grip of his revolver and even pulled back the hammer.

The dog whimpered, no doubt hoping Asa had a crust of bread or a sliver of jerky to share. "Sorry, pal," he said, uncocking the pistol.

He started down the street, and the dog followed. Anybody else would have told it to scram, and not gently, either. But he'd spent enough years alone, afraid, and hungry to identify with the scruffy critter.

The skies had darkened with clouds, and the wind was kicking up. Crouching, he ruffled the dog's muddy, matted brown fur. "Why, you're shaking from head to tail. Guess you sense the coming storm, too, don't you, boy?"

A breathy bark was his answer.

"First order of business," he said, looking into copper-brown eyes that seemed to emanate gratitude, "is a bath. Can't introduce you to the lady of the house in the shape you're in."

Lady of the house, indeed. Asa groaned. "I'm not doing a very good job putting the brakes on this lonely heart of mine," he confessed to his furry friend.

In the distance, thunder pulsated across the mountaintops. Asa straightened and started walking again, the mutt trotting alongside him. "If we don't dawdle, we'll have you cleaned up before the storm hits." He looked down at the grinning pooch. "If you mind your p's and q's, you'll never spend another night looking for shelter from the rain."

When Asa introduced the dog to Nell, it was love at first sight. She wrapped her arms around his furry neck. "Don't you have the sweetest face ever?" she squealed.

Should have seen him an hour ago, Asa thought, grinning.

Nell looked up at him. "Have you named him yet?"

"Didn't dare do that without clearing it with the manager of Stone Hill," he said, nodding at her. "Wasn't sure how you'd feel about having another mouth to feed *and* another thing to take care of. Or if you even liked dogs."

Her lips slanted upwards in a mischievous grin. "*You* brought him home. That makes him your dog, not mine."

Asa laughed. "Good point, I suppose."

"Where did you find him?"

He didn't want to tell her how he'd left church early after getting a glimpse of Tillie's outsider.

"More like he found me. And followed me home. Near as I can figure, he's been sneaking into the livery stable to stay warm and dry. Couldn't decide if he smelled more like manure or sweaty socks."

"Well," she said, giving the dog a vigorous rub behind the ears, "he isn't smelly anymore, is he?" Nell went to the sideboard, and selected two delicate teacups. "I'm in the mood for a spot of tea," she said in an exaggerated British accent. "Care to join me for a cup? Perhaps we can come up with a name for our new tenant." She spooned some leaves into a metal infuser.

"Thanks, but I find the stuff to be a mite on the bland side."

She scoffed, then drowned her infuser with hot water. "You wouldn't say that if you'd ever had a properly brewed cup." He plucked a toothpick from the box on the stove's shelf and clamped down on it. "Oh, I've had strong tea! Got beat up pretty bad while I was with the Third Colorado Cavalry," he said, leaning against the door jamb. "An old squaw found me, delirious and near-frozen, and patched me up." He crossed one boot over the other. "Don't know if it was her tobacco and spit poultice or the cactus wine she forced down my gullet that saved me, but I'll never forget her."

"Cactus wine?"

"Equal parts peyote tea and tequila." Asa chuckled and walked the toothpick from one side of his mouth to the other. "Never understood a word she said. Except...she called me *navese'e*. It's Cheyenne for 'friend.'"

"Nah-*vis*-eh-ih," Nell said. And then she said it again. "Nah-*vis*-eh-ih. Is that right?"

"It's as near-to perfect. I'm impressed."

She carried her teacup to the table and sat. "Well, whatever we name him, I think our shaggy friend will make a fine mascot for the inn."

"He would at that." Asa sat down beside her.

The dog sat back on its haunches, looking from Nell to Asa and back again.

"If he's staying," Nell said, "he'll need a name."

"Yes, he will." Chuckling, Asa added, "He looks like a spectator at a badminton game."

Their eyes met, and together they said, "Birdie!"

"Not the most masculine of names," she said, "but I like it."

"I like it, too."

Nell smiled. "As my grandfather loved to say, 'Great minds think alike.'"

Coincidence? Asa wondered. *Or proof that we're more alike than I thought?* Either way, Asa couldn't afford to entertain that line of thinking, because *Nell* couldn't afford to bind herself to a man whose past was clouded by so many faults and failures.

"Every time my grandpa heard that old saw," he grumbled, "he followed it up with, 'And fools seldom differ.'" On his feet now, he headed for the door.

"Where are you going all of a sudden?"

"Some things need attention in my office."

She pressed her lips together, then looked at the dog. "Better go with him, Birdie. Maybe you can sweeten this brand new sour mood."

Asa made his way down the hall and up the stairs, listening to the sound of Birdie's toenails clicking on the hardwood behind him. He closed his office door behind him and got down on one knee.

"Seems you came along at just the right time, Birdie," he said. "'Cause I have a feeling this old place is going to feel mighty lonely once I manage to convince Nell that she'll be happier elsewhere."

⌒

That night, the storm raged for hours, and Nell wondered if everyone else in town was awake wandering from window to window to take its measure. Rain came down the windowpanes in sheets, giving an underwater appearance to Sterling Street, below.

She gathered her robe more tightly around her, wishing she'd thought to start a fire in her own room after making sure the guest room hearths glowed warm and bright. Unable to think of a single reason why she couldn't do so now, Nell slipped into the quiet hall and headed for the kitchen to borrow a few logs from the wood bin. Before loading her arms with kindling, she put the kettle onto the stove, thinking that a nice, hot mug of tea and a good book would help her ride out the storm.

As she laid the kindling onto the floor of the fireplace, she thought of her pa, of how much he'd loved storms. The brighter the lightning and the louder the thunder, the better. Nell had never understood his thirst for thrills, especially when they often went hand in hand with destruction. She'd had a lot of time to think on such things since his passing, and had come to believe that his greed for gold was rooted in a passion for excitement. But life could be so gritty and gruesome, all on its own, and Nell, for one, preferred to find her excitement in the pages of a book.

Now, with the fire popping and cracking and radiating warmth, she headed back to the kitchen for that cup of tea. This was her favorite time of the day, when the guests were sleeping and the demands of her day had ended. Despite the raging weather outside, she felt safe and secure in a way that she never had in the run-down old cabin near the Holstrom Mine. Long hours of hard work, and Asa's sometimes mercurial mood swings, were a small price to pay for peace of mind.

She carried the mug of tea into her room and placed it on the small table between her two matching chairs. With the lantern wick up high, she almost didn't notice the flash of lightning outside her curtained windows. Janet had recommended several books, and they sat in a tidy stack on the table. Nell picked up *Moods*, by Louisa May Alcott, and turned to the page she'd marked with a six-inch scrap of lace left over from the dresser scarf she'd sewn for one of the guest rooms. What would happen to Sylvia Yule, Nell wondered—a strong, willful young woman who married the wrong man?

With her slippered feet resting on the brocade ottoman, she read, so wrapped up in the story that she forgot all about her tea until it was too cool for her liking. Grumbling to herself, she marked the page once more, then tiptoed to the kitchen to warm it up.

A loud clatter outside startled her so badly that she sloshed a bit of the brew to the back of her hand. They received the occasional lodger late at night, but Nell somehow doubted that the noise had been caused by a hopeful guest. Even if a knock sounded on the door, she'd be hesitant to open it; for who but an outlaw would be out and about on a night as fierce and frightening as this?

Hearing the noise twice more, Nell was relieved to identify the sound as a shutter blown loose by the wind, banging against the side of the house. She dreaded going out there, but she didn't want the racket waking every guest—and Asa, who didn't get nearly enough sleep as it was.

She grabbed Asa's slicker from the row of hooks just inside the kitchen door and shrugged it on. He'd hung the hardware just that morning, and his screwdriver and hammer still lay on the bench beneath it. Nell tucked both tools in the front pocket, thinking she might need one or the other to secure the shutter...or defend herself against the outlaw who'd come looking for a room.

As it turned out, the hardest part about fixing she shutter was finding something to stand on so that she could reach it. By the time she'd silenced the noise, Nell was soaked to the skin. Teeth chattering, she dashed back inside, and nearly leaped out of her slippers when she saw Asa standing in the middle of the dimly lit kitchen.

"Have you lost your mind?"

Nell put the tools back where she'd found them, removed the slicker and gave it a good shake. "Not that I've noticed," she said, hanging it back on a hook. "Why? Have you found it?"

Backlit by the lantern as he was, she couldn't see his face clearly; but something about his stance told her he hadn't found her joke the least bit funny.

"What were you doing out there in this vicious weather?"

"There was a loose shutter. I went out to secure it before the commotion woke all the guests."

She followed his gaze to the puddle at her feet.

"Should have come for me. That's no job for a woman like you."

A woman like her? What did *that* mean?

"Just look at you, shaking from head to toe."

"That tends to happen when you've been out in the cold rain, and a well-intended employer's inquisition prevents you from changing into dry clothes."

Asa stepped aside. "When you've changed, why don't you join me in the kitchen again? I'll stoke the fire and put on some coffee."

She reached for the string mop, thinking to sop up the puddle, but he grabbed it from her. "I'll take care of that. Your only job right now is to get warm and dry."

Since she wasn't likely to get any more sleep tonight—after fighting the storm to refasten the shutter, then being greeted by a six-foot mountain of disapproval, Nell decided to put on tomorrow's work clothes: a simple gray skirt and a high-collared pink blouse. She towel dried her hair and, knowing it would dry faster if she didn't tie it up in braids or a bun, left it down, and to protect her shirt from the dampness, Nell draped her shoulders with a shawl.

As she sat on the edge of the bed to button her boots, the shawl slipped off and fell to the floor between her bed and the windows. When she lay on her stomach to fetch it, a wave of sleepiness swept over her. Maybe she ought to close her eyes for just a minute…or two….

Had Nell suffered a dizzy spell and fallen in her room? Asa wouldn't have been surprised, after the soaking she'd taken while fixing that shutter.

What other woman would brave the dark and a violent storm to ensure the sound sleep of others?

Only Nell, he decided, walking toward her room.

The door was slightly ajar, and he rapped softly, so as not to startle her. Hearing no answer, he used a fingertip to shove it farther open so that he could look inside and make sure she wasn't sprawled on the floor.

She was sprawled, all right, across her bed. He moved closer, to see if she'd fainted or had merely fallen asleep. Though how he'd tell the difference, Asa wasn't sure.

In the lamplight, her hair shimmered with golden waves. He couldn't help but stare for a moment, because he had no idea there was so much of it. Nell always wore it up, secured in a tidy, practical bun, or twined atop her head like a braided crown.

How small she looked atop the big mattress, like a little girl worn out after a day of frolicking. Nothing could have been farther from reality, of course, because Asa had never known a person—man or woman—who worked harder than Nell. That very diligence had been what had compelled her to venture outside into the pounding rain.

"Work" could have been her middle name, and he thought yet again of shirt buttons sewn on tight, of creases pressed into his shirts and handkerchiefs, his favorite foods served at every meal. She took such pleasure in the simplest things, like finishing the chicken coop or snipping a perfect rose from the shrubs she'd planted. She shared his pride at seeing Stone Hill succeed once again. And praised every one of his accomplishments, great or small. He'd warned himself not to take it too personally, but it was too late.

Still sleeping, Nell frowned and drew herself into a tight little ball.

Still cold, are you? A great wave of affection washed over him, and it took every bit of his self-control to keep from gathering her near to let her draw warmth from him.

Instead, Asa lifted the thick quilt from the foot of her bed, unfolded it, and draped it over her body. As he tucked the edge under her chin, she exhaled a soft sigh and snuggled beneath it, a look of peace easing her furrowed brow.

He gently brushed several wisps of hair away from her forehead, exposing eyelashes longer than any he'd ever seen. Then he bent down and pressed a light kiss to her temple, feeling the steady beat of her pulse against his lips.

"Ah, Nell," he whispered, "if only I'd lived a different life, so I might have half a chance that someday, you'd care for me, too."

Asa turned down the lamp, and on the way out of her room, he added a few logs to the fire.

"Rest well, lovely Nell," he said softly. "You've earned it."

There was no mistaking what she said on a sleepy sigh just before he clicked the door shut: "Sweet dreams, dear Asa. Sweet, sweet dreams."

As touching and tender as it was to hear, her loving wish nearly broke his heart.

Chapter Fifteen

Asa had spent most of the night alternately staring out at the driving rain and pacing the kitchen until early morning, when he'd slid into a fitful sleep on the parlor sofa. Now, he felt the cushions dip slightly, as if someone had sat down beside him.

"Asa?" Delicate hands gripped his shoulders. "Asa, wake up."

Ah, what a beautiful dream...having Nell close enough to gather in his arms.

"Asa! Please wake up," she repeated, shaking a little harder.

Hearing the fear in her usually sweet voice, he opened his eyes.

"There's something happening outside," she said. "Something awful!"

His first impulse was to hug her close, so that whatever was happening wouldn't harm her. But she was on her feet now, tugging at his arm, repeating the warning, again and again.

Fully awake now, he, too, heard the terrifying, telltale growl. He'd heard a similar sound years ago, while passing through Cimarron, Kansas. Asa remembered the aftermath of the tornado all too well—how it had razed a dozen homes and businesses. It was a miracle only two people had been killed.

All the guests of Stone Hill Inn thundered down the stairs, hair askew, wrapped in dressing robes and blankets. Cooper

Preston wore nothing but his red long underwear. He threw open the front door and, as if pulled outside by the whirling, groaning gusts, everyone huddled together on the covered porch.

"We can't stay here," Asa told them, glancing nervously at the creaking, groaning porch roof. "Isn't safe."

"I'll be right back," Nell told him, then dashed back inside before he could stop her.

"Where will we go?" Cooper asked, trembling in his underwear.

"Into the root cellar, all of you!" Asa shouted.

But everyone remained rooted in place, watching the storm clouds swirl round and round in the darkening sky.

"Don't just stand there!" he thundered. "Get a move on!"

As they scrambled along the walkway to the root cellar, Nell rejoined them, a lantern in one hand, a stack of blankets pressed to her chest.

Cooper yanked the doors open, and Asa held them as, one by one, the guests descended the stone steps.

When he motioned for Nell to follow, she squinted up at him, rain streaking down her face. "What about you?" she shouted.

"Need to check the rooms one last time," he yelled. "Make sure everybody got out." He nodded toward the cellar. "Latch the doors behind you. I'll join you as soon as I can."

"No, Asa," she said, grabbing his forearm. "Don't go back inside. Everyone is already down there, except for—"

"Birdie," they said together.

"I have to go back," Asa said. "He's in my room, and the door is closed." He turned to leave, but remembering the devastation in Cimarron, realized this could be the last time he saw Nell. Gripping her upper arms, he drew her near and gave her a gentle shake. "No matter what happens, I want you to know that I—"

An empty buggy came bouncing down the street as if it weighed no more than a child's scooter.

"Go," she said, giving him a gentle shove. "Hurry back!"

He'd never forget the look on her face—a mix of apprehension and affection, as tears filled her huge blue eyes. As he rushed back toward the inn, he heard the cellar doors slam shut, and he felt a degree of relief knowing that Nell and the others were safe.

Why he chose that moment to look to the end of Sterling Street, where the first light of day was just beginning to dawn on the horizon, Asa would never know; but what he saw struck him dumb: not one but *three* twisters grinding closer, closer.

The tail of the largest dragged along the ground, flapping like the tail of a furious dragon. Within seconds, it was directly overhead. Asa threw himself on his stomach, wrapped his arms around the trunk of the nearest tree, and held on as if his life depended on it—because it did.

He squinted as a cloud of dust and dirt stung his face and hands. And then, suddenly, everything grew deathly still. Was it his stark terror that made it difficult to breathe, or the strange, pungent odor that filled the air?

Asa looked up—right into the eye of the storm cloud. He blinked as bright flashes of lightning bounced against the funnel's interior walls. He saw his grandmother's piano whirl by. Guests' empty suitcases. His pa's favorite rocking chair and his ma's Bible. Linens from the beds billowed like great white sails catching an ocean gale. Nell's sewing machine rolled end over end, and his grandfather's pipe hovered so close that if he had reached out, Asa probably could have plucked it from the revolving cloud.

And then, like the silence that follows the grand finale of a fireworks display, the earsplitting roar calmed to a mild purr as the cloud shrank and then vanished into the charged air.

At first, he was afraid to let go of the tree, for fear that one of the two remaining twisters might pick up speed or grow in size. On his knees, he chanced a glance behind him, thanking the Almighty that they, too, had fizzled.

Asa stood and turned in a slow circle, his heart hammering. What he saw next put him right back on his knees.

His beloved Stone Hill Inn had been reduced to rubble.

The once-sturdy house—home to three generations of Stones, and longtime refuge for road-weary guests—had collapsed in on itself, leaving nothing but a mountain of sodden lumber that resembled a pile of matchsticks. The tornado had scattered chimney bricks and fireplace stones as if they weighed no more than the grains of chicken feed Nell sprinkled throughout the coop every day.

People had started milling about on the road below, some crying, others calling the names of loved ones or lost pets. Here on Sterling Street, shards of glass from the inn's windows covered the ground, glittering like diamonds in the early morning sunshine.

One by one, his guests stumbled from the root cellar, arms crooked over their eyes. They looked bedraggled and bewildered, and no wonder. His heart went out to them, for he'd been in their position only minutes ago, coming to the painful realization of what had happened. Those who'd planned to travel by train or stagecoach would have to wait for someone from back home to wire them money, because their tickets, like everything they'd stuffed into suitcases and steamer trunks, were gone.

But where was Nell? Asa scanned the property, his gaze settling on the large plank leaning against the side of his shed. It looked an awful lot like one of the root cellar doors, torn right off its hinges.

Panic seized him, and he sprinted forward, praying with every step that she was all right. He wouldn't have put it past her to insist on going out first, to make sure it was safe for the rest of them to exit.

When he got that first glimpse of her windblown hair, he doubled over with gratitude. For a moment, he stood, breathing heavily, palms pressed to his knees, thanking God.

The instant their eyes met, Asa read relief in her big, teary eyes. He held out his arms, and she fell into them as though she'd been doing it all her life. Gratitude, joy, and relief churned inside him as he buried his face in her soft curls.

That's when he noticed she was bleeding. Asa reached into his back pocket, removed one of the countless white handkerchiefs she had laundered and pressed for him, and dabbed lightly at tiny cuts—above her right eyebrow, across her left cheekbone, below her bottom lip. "Oh, Asa," she sobbed. "When you didn't come back, I thought—"

He kissed her worry-lined brow. "Shhh," he whispered, drawing her nearer. "You're all right, and so am I. This...." He took a quick look around the yard and somehow found the gumption to say, "We'll be all right, somehow."

Nell pressed her palms against his chest and turned slightly, surveying the damage.

"How strange," she said, "that it seemed to pick and choose which houses and businesses to destroy." She met his eyes to add, "Almost as if it had a mind of its own."

She'd made a good point. From what he could see, the storm hadn't touched the DiMaggios' store or Held's blacksmith shop. Farther down the road, the Remington Hotel stood undamaged, and across from it, the bank and the Windsor looked none the worse for wear. In Cimarron, the path cut by the tornado had been wider, but its pattern of annihilation had seemed just as haphazard.

Nell inhaled a deep, shaky breath, then let it out slowly. "It appears that Janet's house and the library were left unscathed. Thank the good Lord for that." Then she patted his chest and looked up at him. "You probably have a hundred things on your mind, things you want to look into. Why don't I walk down to the Remington and see if they can accommodate our guests? We have no idea how many others were hit by this monstrous storm. Hotel rooms are likely to be a rare commodity."

He nodded. "Excellent idea." One of the things he intended to look into was whether Janet would agree to let Nell stay with her for a while. He'd pay her for any extra expenses, of course. Then he spotted Priscilla, who owned the dress shop on the other side of the grocery store. She looked dazed, clinging tight to her little boy, but physically unharmed. So far, Asa hadn't seen anyone else who'd lost everything, as he had. No doubt she, too, was wondering where to begin picking up the pieces.

"Oh Asa," Nell said again, "just look at her. What will she do now? That shop was her sole means of support for herself and Reggie."

"While you're at Remington's, I'll take her to the church. I'm sure by now the new pastor is busy setting up cots for those who need 'em."

She nodded. And then she bit her lower lip, as if to still its trembling. "Have you seen Birdie?"

Asa shook his head. "No, but he's a survivor. I'm sure he found a safe place to hole up."

"Yes, of course." She giggled nervously and wiped her eyes. "How silly am I, blubbering like a baby over a stray mutt that walked into our lives just days ago!"

"Not the least bit silly," he told her. And when he reached out to tuck a stray wisp of hair behind her ears, she leaned her cheek against his palm.

As she did, he felt a twinge of guilt for his self-centeredness. Because, given the chance, he'd ask her to be his woman, now and forever. And, judging by the way she stood in his arms, she'd say yes.

"I just don't understand," she murmured. "What, Nell? What don't you understand?" he asked, pocketing the offending hand.

"Why did this terrible thing happen, just when things were going so well for us? Of course, other establishments were damaged—I'm sorry for all those who will have to rebuild their lives—but…." She'd always exhibited such strong faith, so nothing could have surprised him more than when she said, "Sometimes, God is so unfair!"

It was pretty much what Asa had said just months after his mother's death, when the bill collectors began hounding his pa. Instead of admitting he'd spent every dollar on whiskey, Daniel shook his fist and snarled a distorted version of 2 Thessalonians 1:6: "God will recompense tribulation to them that trouble you!"

Yes, it did appear that the tornado had targeted Stone Hill. Was it possible that because Asa had been too weak to do the right thing by Nell, the Almighty had stepped into give her a reason to leave? With Stone Hill demolished, she would need to go elsewhere to start over. And he had to let her go. Had to find the strength to do so.

Frustrated with the depths of his selfishness, Asa took a deliberate step away from her.

"You'd better go," he said. "Have that talk with Sloan. If he has space for my guests, tell him I'll reimburse him for the cost of the rooms."

For a moment, she looked surprised by his brusque tone. But then, true to form, Nell sent him an understanding smile, and Asa could almost read her mind. She blamed the catastrophe—not his flawed character—for his sudden change of attitude.

As he watched her walk away, Asa's heart ached at the bitter irony. Nell was, by far, the best thing that had ever happened to him—which was precisely why he could never have her.

Chapter Sixteen

When Nell reached the Remington Hotel, she found a dozen families gathered in the lobby, sipping tea and clutching blankets around their shoulders.

As she approached the registration desk, she thought that it didn't look good for the guests from Stone Hill. She was glad she hadn't brought them with her, because the walk back to Stone Hill would seem ten times as long, especially since there hadn't been time to finish buttoning up her boots when she dozed off.

"Goodness, me," said Caitlin Sweeny when she saw Nell. "Yer face, girl! Did y'get all cut up that way in the storm?"

She'd always loved listening to the lilting Irish brogue of Sloan's staff. But not today.

"It's nothing," she said. "Some flying glass, is all. It'll heal by the end of the week."

"Fergus Sweeny!" the woman summoned her husband. "Fetch a clean rag, and a bowl o' warm water, too." She wagged her forefinger at Nell. "I feel it only fair to warn you, girl, t'isn't wise to disagree wit' me this mornin', 'cause I'm not in a very agreeable mood."

Nell glanced over her shoulder at the people who'd taken shelter in the lobby. "I appreciate the offer, but it's plain to see that you already have your hands full. I'll clean myself up just as soon as I get back to…."

She'd almost said "back to Stone Hill." Nell swallowed, unable to admit that the inn no longer existed. Neither did her tidy rows of gauze and Merthiolate, and other items she would have used to disinfect her cuts and scrapes.

"I came here to see if perhaps there's room for our guests," she said instead.

Shaina stepped up at that very moment. "Your guests? Oh, Nell, don't tell me the inn was damaged."

She turned to her friend. "You could say that." She wasn't ready to admit that it was gone. "Asa and I…we were wondering if our guests could stay here, just until they make other arrangements. He said to tell you he'll take care of the charges."

Shaina opened the registration book. "We have four vacant rooms." She nodded toward the lobby, then met Nell's eyes. "They'll have to double up, though. And let's not worry about room rates and such. People have to pull together at times like these."

The front doors opened, and Sloan joined them at the counter.

"Are you all right?" he said, frowning as he inspected Nell's face.

"I'm fine. Just a few little cuts. Nothing a little Mercurochrome won't fix."

He looked skeptical. "Are you sure? Because I was just up there on Sterling Street, and…." He met his wife's eyes and shook his head. "The tornado flattened Stone Hill," he told Shaina. "Nothing left but a pile of splinters. Reminds me of what that fire did to Sterling Hall."

Nell had heard about the blaze that leveled the grand old mansion. According to the rumor mill, Sloan had taken Shaina home to his ranch outside of town, on the pretext of helping his housekeeper, who'd broken her leg. That catastrophe that had resulted in something beautiful and lasting. Was it too much to hope that the same happy ending was possible for her and Asa?

"Flattened," Shaina repeated. "Oh, how dreadful!" She grasped Nell's hand. "What about you? Where will you and Asa stay? You're both welcome here. I know it'll be crowded, but it's only temporary." She looked to Sloan. "We'll work something out, won't we, dear?"

"Of course." He grasped Nell's other hand. "Let me take you back to...." He licked his lips and started over. "Give me a few minutes to fetch the wagon, then I'll drive you back to Sterling Street, and we'll bring the guests back here. Asa, too."

Sloan left by way of the back door as Caitlin returned, her daughter Bridget close on her heels.

"Take this poor girl aside," the Irishwoman said, "and get her cleaned up, will you, darlin'?"

"Happy to, Ma." Bridget led Nell to an empty chair, then dragged an end table over. "'Tis awful, what that storm did to the town, ain't it?"

Nell nodded as Bridget dabbed her cuts with a damp cloth. "No one here at the Remington was harmed, I hope."

"Would y'believe it didn't so much as muss a hair on our heads? But I threw open the window and heard some terrifying things: glass shattering, wood splintering, people screaming and running all about." The girl shivered. "Heard a child, calling to his ma, 'We're not gonna die, are we?' And his ma said, 'Course not.' But you could tell by the way she said it, she wasn't at all sure 'twas the truth."

"Can't control the weather," said the elderly woman seated on a nearby divan.

The gentleman beside her nodded. "You know what I always say...keep your doorstep swept clean, 'cause you never know when the Lord will decide to call you home."

Bridget rolled her eyes as the hint of a smile lifted the corners of her mouth. "Was anyone hurt bad at Stone Hill?"

Nell pictured Asa's troubled face. "Not physically. But the chickens are missing, and so's the dog." She lowered her voice to whisper, "I just don't understand. Where was the Lord during that terrifying tornado?"

Bridget only offered a sympathetic shrug. Too young, Nell decided, to wonder such things.

A young man near the door did his best to comfort his weeping wife, but she slapped his hand away.

"Stop it," she snapped. "Just give me a few minutes to clear my head."

He looked past the elderly couple, a sheepish smile on his face. "We thought we was safe down there in the cellar. Had us a jug of water and a lantern, so we thought we was safe, even though we could hear that monster, roaring like a lion up there. Then the doors started rattlin', and we sat there watchin' the screws fall out of the latch. Next thing we know, them doors flew off—first one, then the other—and there we was, like sittin' ducks just waitin' for that beast to chew us up and spit us out, same as it done to them doors." He wrapped both arms around his wife and buried his face in the crook of her neck.

Bridget leaned close to Nell's ear and whispered, "Is he…is he *cryin'*?"

"Yes, and I have to admit, he has every right to." *So does Asa*, she thought. But it wasn't likely her stoic employer would break down. At least, not where anyone else could see or hear him.

Her young nurse gathered her supplies and got to her feet. "There now, nothing left to do but heal."

Truer words were never spoken, Nell thought. "Thank you, Bridget."

Sloan appeared in the doorway. "Wagon's out front, if you're ready." Meeting his wife's gaze, he added, "I shouldn't be long." He blew her a kiss.

"Asa won't be expecting you," Nell said as the wagon lurched forward, "so if he seems…." She didn't want to send the wrong message and leave Sloan with the impression that Asa was an ungrateful brute. "If he seems reluctant to accompany the guests, it's only because he lost a lot last night."

Sloan eased back on the reins, slowing the horses to a walk. "Not just last night," he said. "Lost his mama when he was a boy, and, in some ways, lost his pa at the same time. Lost the only home he ever knew, and the grandparents who loved him like their own, when Daniel dragged him and the other boys away from Denver."

It felt strangely reassuring to hear these things from someone who'd known Asa before he'd left Denver.

"But he survived, became a man who's easy to respect and admire, despite it all. Granted, what happened to Stone Hill is a big loss, but he'll survive this, too."

Nell wanted to believe him. But Sloan hadn't seen Asa's shoulders slump under the weight of it all.

When they arrived at the site where Stone Hill Inn had once stood, Asa was nowhere to be found. Nell rounded up the guests and led them to the wagon.

"First order of business," she told them, "is getting you a hot meal. And then, while you're resting, I'll scrounge up some dry clothes and shoes. After that, we'll see about wiring your kinfolk."

"That's good of you, Nell, real good," Cooper said as Sloan helped the women into the wagon, "but you needn't worry about me. There's a change of clothes and a cot in the back room at my store."

"Thank you, Nell," one of the ladies said, grabbing her hand. "You're a dear, dear girl."

Nell smiled up at her. "Try to get some rest, now, and I'll see you soon."

Sloan climbed into the driver's seat. "You're not coming with us?"

"No. I'm going to find Asa and let him know that, thanks to you, our guests have someplace to stay."

"Again, you're welcome to join them for as long as you need to," Sloan said as he released the brake.

"You're a good friend, Sloan. Thank you."

As Sloan's wagon turned onto Front Street, Janet ran up and hugged her.

"Aren't *you* a sight for sore eyes! I was so worried when I saw what the tornado did to the inn. Thank God you're all right."

"It's a relief to see that you're fine, too," Nell admitted. "Was there any damage at your place?"

"Nothing that a rake and a broom and some elbow grease won't fix." Janet looked toward the ruins of the house. "Where is Asa?"

"Off somewhere torturing himself, I expect. There are half a dozen outbuildings on the property from when his grandparents ran the place, so he's bound to be in one of them—if they're still standing, that is."

She'd probably find him in one of two places: the family cemetery or the big shed where he stored his ladders and carpentry tools.

Janet grabbed Nell's hand. "Let's go back to my house. We'll get you out of those damp clothes and into something warm and dry—we're about the same size, after all—then move you into the parlor. You can sleep on the sofa. And I won't take no for an answer."

"Thank you, Janet." Nell smiled gratefully. "But would you mind very much if I met up with you in a few minutes? I'd like to check on Asa."

"Of course," Janet said, squeezing her hand. "Oh, before you go—not that you want to hear this right now, but, given that the inn is no longer and you'll likely need a place to work—I understand that Dorothy Forbes, who's been filling in for the grammar school teacher, is going to have a baby."

Meaning that the school needed a teacher every bit as much as Nell now needed a job. "Then I suppose I'd best pay the principal a visit as soon as possible."

Janet smiled, then pointed over Nell's shoulder toward the shed. "There's Asa. Oh, my. He looks so sad. Go to him, Nell. He needs you, I think."

Nell thanked her friend again, then lifted her skirts and started up the hill.

Asa stood as still as a statue in the doorway of the shed.

"Sloan came with his wagon," she said, stepping up beside him. "He took the guests back to the Remington."

"Good."

"A few of the guests will have to share rooms, but at least they'll have a warm, dry place to sleep until they make other arrangements."

"Remingtons are good people."

"Yes, they most certainly are."

Something had changed since she'd left him earlier. Had he discovered something while she was gone—something that compounded his already devastating loss?

Nell peered into the shed and saw a narrow cot pushed up against a side wall. "Are you planning to stay here awhile?"

Asa grunted. "A long while, I expect."

She walked past him into the shed and planted her hands on her hips and assessed the space. "I'll help you move your tools into one of the other outbuildings," she said, "and see about finding you sheets and blankets. And a pillow, of course. I'm sure we can secure at least one usable chair out there somewhere. And, look," she added, pointing at the back wall. "Lanterns on the shelf. I can polish them up, and clean the windows, and—"

"Stop worrying about me," he growled, "and start worrying about where *you'll* sleep."

She ignored his terse tone. "Janet has invited me to stay with her. Told me about a job opening, too."

He frowned slightly, then raised an eyebrow. "Oh?"

"It sounds as if they're in need of a teacher at the school. I don't have a teaching certificate, but perhaps Principal Blakeley will hire me as a substitute until he finds someone with suitable credentials."

Asa scoffed. "You're the smartest woman I know, with or without suitable credentials. Those young'uns would be lucky to have you. If Blakeley doesn't see that, he's a fool."

"Why...thank you." While she appreciated the compliment, time wasn't on their side. It would be dark in five or six hours, and they needed to make this long-neglected place habitable, not only because it would be Asa's home for an indefinite length of time, but also because he'd never rest properly, surrounded by rakes, hoes, and cobwebs!

Nell took hold of a stepladder and started lugging it out the door. "Better step aside," she told him, "because we're burnin' daylight!"

Asa cooperated, probably just to shut her up. But it didn't really matter why, as long as the job got done.

They emptied the shed of yard and carpentry tools, ladders, sawhorses, and a wheelbarrow. Then, while Asa busied himself arranging the items in a smaller shed nearby, Nell inspected the big cedar trunk she'd noticed earlier across the yard. She nearly wept with relief when she opened the lid and found clean feather pillows, blankets, and sheets.

After a quick trip to the Helds' house to borrow some supplies, Nell was ready to clean and set up housekeeping. Once the windows were gleaming, she strung baling wire above them to serve as makeshift curtain rods. Then she went back for a few pieces of intact furniture she'd spotted at the far end of the yard. Finally, she rescued the rug from her bedroom, which, by some miracle, had ended up draped over a tree branch.

When she was finished, Nell stood in the doorway to take stock of the newly decorated space.

Asa had not one but two upholstered chairs to choose from, should he decide to read his newspaper by the light of a hobnail lantern. Why, he could even prop his feet on the ottoman she'd uncovered while digging out the mahogany end table. The bed was made up, there was ample firewood in the stove, and plenty more in the crate beside it. It was nowhere near as grand as his room at the inn, but at least he'd have a roof over his head—one that didn't leak, even after being subject to the force of a tornado.

"I left you alone for just a few hours," Asa said when he returned. "How'd you accomplish all this in such a short time?"

"I must confess, my motives were purely selfish."

Asa grunted. "If this is your definition of selfish, we're reading different dictionaries."

"But it's true. How could I expect to get a good night's sleep, picturing you trying to get comfortable in this sty?"

A sad little smile lifted the right corner of his mouth as he studied her face.

"You're unlike anyone I've ever known, Nell Holstrom."

She thought she saw tears in his eyes as he dropped into the nearest chair and ran his fingers through his hair. "I could sell the land, I suppose...."

She scooted the ottoman closer and sat down facing him. "Sell? But *why*, Asa? I would have bet anything that you'd rebuild."

He shook his head, and for a long, agonizing moment, Nell thought he might not say anything more.

"I just stopped by the bank to see exactly how much I could put toward rebuilding." He hung his head. "The simple truth is, I can't afford to rebuild."

It hadn't dawned on her until just now how very angry she was with God. He'd allowed so many things to be taken from her, and from Asa, too, and hadn't given a hint as to *why*. A month, a week ago—yesterday, even!—she might have asked for His help in choosing the words Asa needed to hear. But why waste her breath and the time it took to pray when it seemed He had no intention of answering?

"Should have let you balance the Stone Hill books," Asa said with a sigh. "Seems I can't even do *that* right."

"Asa, you can't blame yourself for an act of nature." Then she remembered what Sloan had said, and she quoted him: "You've survived many crushing disappointments, and you'll survive this one, too. You pulled through those other tragedies all on your own; but this time, you have—" Nell fell silent at a distant sound that grew louder with every passing second. She leaped to her feet and ran to the door. "Listen," she said, pointing her finger at the ceiling.

Asa sat up straighter, cocking his head toward the sound. "Your chickens?"

"Not *my* chickens, silly—*our* chickens!"

He stood, crossed the shed in three long strides, and looked over her shoulder out the window. "Well, I'll be. They found their way home."

She faced him. "Did you hear yourself just now?"

A confused frown drew his eyebrows together.

"You just said 'home.'" She grasped his hands gave them a gentle shake. "You know what that means, don't you?"

Oh, Asa, she thought as he looked down at her, sadness and seriousness battling for control of his facial features. *Have a little faith, why don't you?*

It felt as though the hand of God had reached down to gently smack a little sense into her. She had to smile at His infinite patience and understanding.

"It means," she explained, "that you want to rebuild every bit as much as I do."

"Dear, sweet, innocent Nell," he said, shaking his head. "It has nothing to do with what I want, and everything to do with what's possible."

"Then we'll just have to believe *everything* is possible, won't we?"

As if on cue, Birdie trotted through the door and nuzzled Asa's hand. He crouched down to look the dog in the eye. "So, you found your way home, too, did you?" He glanced up at Nell. "I know you're relieved that the critters came back. Just don't let yourself be fooled. They operate purely on instinct. They don't see this as home; so much as the place where there's food and shelter."

Nell thought she understood his point of view. Asa had been let down one too many times in life, and he hadn't been taught to trust, to have faith. But it was all right. Everything was going to be all right! Maybe not today, or next month; but God had finally given her a sign that He heard her prayers—even those she hadn't yet put into words. She didn't deserve it, having given in to immaturity, selfishness, and anger; and yet He had delivered tangible proof, and it was right here, clucking and panting around her and Asa's feet.

Then, an idea she could only describe as heaven-sent began forming in her mind. Filled with overwhelming joy, Nell reached up and touched Asa's cheek.

"Don't you worry, dear Asa," she said. "I have faith enough for both of us."

Chapter Seventeen

I f she didn't want to waste an entire day walking to and from the mine, Nell had no choice but to tell Shaina why she wanted to borrow a horse. And although she wasn't obliged to do it, she also shared her plan to ask Asa to become her partner in the Holstrom Mine venture.

Now, arm in arm, the women walked the path connecting the Remington Hotel to the horse barn out back.

Nell slid the heavy barn door open along its iron track. "I can't tell you how much I appreciate this. I promise to find a way to repay you, soon."

Shaina shook her head. "You don't owe me a thing. Not payment, not a favor, and certainly not an explanation. And, just so you know, I think you're just about the most generous, kind-hearted person I've ever met."

"What a coincidence," she said, grinning. "I feel the same way about you and Sloan."

Shaina continued as if Nell hadn't said a word. "You're not only securing your financial future, you're assuring Asa's—if he's wise enough to accept your offer—and preserving his self-esteem, to boot."

"My," she said, stepping inside, "I don't think I've ever seen a more beautiful barn." Nell hoped the compliment would take the focus off herself.

Unfortunately, it did not.

"In your shoes, I wouldn't want to return to that horrible mine at all—not on foot *or* riding horseback." Shaina stepped up to the first stall and opened the gate. "You're actually doing me a favor," she went on, resting a hand on her slightly-rounded abdomen. "Poor Flame, here, hasn't had a long ride since we found out about the baby. It'll make me feel good, knowing he's getting some much-needed fresh air and exercise." Then she pointed to the tack bench behind them. "That big black saddle is his favorite, but it's fairly heavy. Let me get Sloan to harness him for you."

Nell believed she could harness a horse and hitch it to a wagon in her sleep. But saddle a beast as big as Flame?

"Let me at least give it a try before you bother him." Nell eased into the stall and stroked Flame's cheeks. "Listen here, you big, handsome thing, you. If you promise not to trample my feet, I promise to give you the best rubbing-down of your life when we get back."

Flame's ears swiveled forward, and he nickered quietly.

"Well, I'll be," Shaina exclaimed. "He likes you, Nell...not that I'm surprised."

Laughing, she slid an arm around the horse's neck, and as she did, he nuzzled her arm.

She led him closer to the tack bench, where she climbed on a stool and draped a soft blanket over his back. Then, hefting the saddle, Nell held her breath, steadied herself, and dropped it into place. When she hopped down from the stool, Flame looked over his shoulder and watched patiently as she tugged the cinches and dropped the stirrups into place.

"I'm impressed," Shaina said. "You did that in record time. I wouldn't share this with just anyone, but I couldn't lift that saddle, even before the baby. You're quite a woman, Nell Holstrom! I can see why Asa admires you so."

"What do you mean?" Had Asa spoken of her to his friends? Nell didn't know what to make of that.

"Oh, Nell. Surely, you've noticed the way he looks at you. As if you personally placed every star in the sky or something. If you asked me, I'd say he's in awe of you. Seeing what you did at Stone Hill, then turned that ugly old shed into a place he can call home? I'd like to meet just one person who in town *isn't* in awe of you!"

"Yes, well, anyway...." Nell buttoned her coat and wrapped a warm scarf around her neck, both articles on loan from Janet. Then, shoving her left boot into the stirrup, she reached up and took hold of the saddle horn. A moment later, she was on Flame's back. "We'd better be on our way if we want to get there and back before dark."

"Just promise me you'll be careful."

Outside again, they heard a low whistle.

"You saddled him all by yourself?" Sloan asked as he strode toward them.

"I'm stronger than I look." The polite conversation was pleasant enough, but it wasn't getting Nell any closer to the cabin. "See you before dark, God willing."

"Do you have a sidearm?" Sloan wanted to know.

"No."

"You know how to use one?"

"Of course."

"Then take this." He handed up a Peacemaker revolver, butt first. When she hesitated, he added, "Take it, or I'll have to ride along with you. And we both know you'll only feel guilty if I leave my pregnant wife here alone because you wouldn't—"

Nell accepted the Colt and tucked it into her waistband.

"Thank you, both of you," she said, then clicked her tongue at Flame.

"I'm worried," she heard Shaina say. "She's so tiny. Think she'll be all right, alone out there on the road?"

Nell nearly laughed out loud at Sloan's reply: "If I were you, I wouldn't worry about Nell; I'd worry about anyone who crosses her path."

"Well, Flame," Nell said, leaning forward to pat his sleek neck, "it's just you and me now. How do you feel about the upcoming election?"

The horse snorted, inspiring a chuckle. "Not a big fan of politics, I see. How about weather? Is that subject more to your liking?"

She chattered incessantly for more than an hour about things she'd never shared with any two-legged creature: bitter parental disputes, sparked by her father's tendency to fritter away the food money; Grandfather scuffling with her father when the elder Holstrom demanded an accounting of a series of suspiciously small gold-for-cash exchanges; the time she'd finished her walk through town earlier than expected and found her father at the saloon, kissing a dance-hall girl like she'd never seen him kiss her mother.

"Despite it all, he was my pa," she said, "and I loved him."

Flame snorted.

Nell laughed to herself. "You sure don't *look* judgmental. But then, I can't blame you. Nothing I've said so far gives you reason to think he had any redeeming qualities."

A rabbit raced across the road ahead. The horse's ears stood straight up, yet his pace remained steady. This stretch of rarely traveled road had never been noisy, but she couldn't remember its ever being this quiet, either. Nell scrutinized the landscape, looking for anything that seemed out of place. It was mating season, after all, and running into a bull moose might not end well. The hairs stood up on the back of her neck as she realized it was also the time of year when bears were relentless about fattening up in preparation for months of hibernation. It was the reason she'd decided not to pack a lunch. One of her most terrifying childhood memories was of the day she witnessed a neighboring miner being dragged into the woods by a big sow. Hours later, the expressions on the faces of the search party said what words needn't: The man would never return to his family, not even for a funeral.

All of a sudden, the leaves of the skunkbrush to the left of the road began to rustle, causing Nell to tense. There wasn't so much as a breeze blowing on this warm, sunny morning. Had the memory of the bear attack fired up her overactive imagination? No; Flame had heard it, too, as evidenced by the direction of his ever-alert ears. Nell held her breath and slipped her fingertips around the grip of the Peacemaker, Tillie Truett's report about the mysterious stranger echoing in her mind.

After several minutes passed without incident, Nell shook off the chill that had snaked up her spine. "Stop looking for trouble," she muttered, fixing her gaze on the road ahead.

Why was it so quiet? This close to the Rockies' Front Range, it could snow at any time. But it was still October—too early for every cricket and locust to have holed up already. Why hadn't she seen a mischievous magpie, or heard the steady knock-knock of a red-headed woodpecker? If the story about hidden treasures turned out to be another of her pa's tall tales, and she'd taken this nerve-wracking trip for nothing, she'd never forgive him.

She saw the old oak up ahead, the bulbous growth on its trunk far bigger than she remembered it. If lightning or wind ever knocked it down, could she find her way back here? Nell wasn't at all sure that she could. It had stood right there for as long as she could remember, like a giant sentry whose only duty was pointing weary travelers in the right direction.

The chimney of the old cabin came into view first. The vines clinging to the craggy stonework had grown thicker, but, for the most part, the building looked much as it had the last time she'd come here...to lead Doc Wilson and the undertaker to her father's body.

One quick glance at the entrance to the mine was all she could bear, but it was long enough for her to notice that the hand-hewn sign reading "The Holstrom Mine" now dangled from one rusty chain instead of two. Another beam had fallen and now blocked the opening. Just as well, because she had no intention of going into the dark, musty place that held nothing but heartache and hard memories.

Nell dismounted and tethered Flame to the sprawling branches of a piñon pine.

"I won't be long," she said, stroking his silky neck. "Trust me, this is the last place I want to be."

The horse nosed her, propelling her forward.

"All right, all right," she said, laughing as she headed up the weedy path. "I can take a hint."

The corroded hinges squealed when she pushed open the door and stepped into the dank, dusty darkness. Cringing, she ducked under a hanging cobweb and made her way to the back wall, where a row of cots stood side by side, each piled high with wadded-up quilts and holey work clothes. The one nearest the door had been her father's, and somewhere beneath it, he'd squirreled away a small treasure.

Or so he'd said.

To find out for sure, Nell had to slide the cot aside and get onto her hands and knees. But now that she was down here, which plank should she choose?

Oh, Pa, she thought, *still playing games, even from the grave?*

Crawling a bit to the left erased her shadow from the floor, and in the light pouring in through the open door, she saw what appeared to be gouge in the wood.

"Of all the fools on God's earth," Nell complained. Why hadn't she thought to bring a tool to pry up the board? Her pa had a whole bag of tools—which he'd kept in the mine.

There didn't seem to be any way around it. If she wanted to find out whether her father had been telling the truth or simply toying with her, Nell would have to go out there and hope to find a crowbar. With a groan, she got to her feet and trudged toward the door, stopping when something shiny glinted in the sunlight. Knuckling her eyes, she moved closer. No, her eyes weren't playing tricks on her. It was a screwdriver.

Nell rushed back to the floorboard. It came up so easily that she let out a little whoop and tossed the wood aside. Down in the hole, she saw a gray metal box covered with dirt and sheathed in spider webs. She lifted it gingerly and placed it beside her on the floor. Would it be empty, save a few beetles and bugs?

"Only one way to find out," she whispered, and raised the creaking lid.

And there inside, in three-inch thick stacks, each tied with twine, five hundred dollar treasury notes. Dozens and *dozens* of them.

They looked genuine enough, and yet Nell couldn't allow herself to believe it just yet. Wouldn't it be just like her pa to leave a box full of counterfeit bills, one last practical joke to remember him by?

He'd told her about a sack of gold, said she'd find it behind a knothole in the front wall of the cabin. Nell crawled over to it, the barrel of Sloan's Peacemaker thumping along the floor, keeping time with her heartbeat. Using the screwdriver as a poker, she jabbed at every knot within reach until she found one that jiggled slightly. She broke a fingernail, unplugging it from the log, but sight of burlap threads peeking from the hole made it easy to ignore the discomfort. The money might be forged, but Nell knew real gold when she saw it. Was it too much to hope that since the gold was real, the bonds would be, too?

"Only one way to find out," she said again. And that meant getting right back to town, where a bank official could tell her, one way or the other.

Nell stuffed the small sack inside the metal box, which she then tucked into Flame's left saddlebag. She returned to the cabin to gather all the maps and charts she could find, then headed outside once more, pulling the door shut behind her. It seemed so final when the latch clicked into place, like closing the book on a fantastical story.

She tied the long paper tube behind the cantle and climbed into the saddle.

"It's probably the last time I'll see this place," she told Flame. "Funny, but I always expected saying that would make me happy."

She led the big horse back onto the road, and tempting as it was to let him run full-out, Nell held him to the same steady pace that had brought them there.

Her father hadn't been the most reliable man, but the treasures had been right where he'd said they'd be. Maybe, just maybe, she could believe his final words, as well: "I know you've heard it before, but this time, I swear it's true. I'm *this close*, Nellie-girl. *This close* to the big one."

If he was right, her life was about to change in a big way.

And so was Asa's.

Once she returned to the Remington, it wasn't easy to take her time rubbing Flame down; but a promise was a promise, even when made to a horse. And the task helped distract her from the enormous favor she was about to ask of Asa.

After filling the horse's water bucket and sneaking him a few handfuls of oats, she tidied the tack bench, tucked the tube of drawings and maps under her arm, and headed straight for the shed Asa now called home. It would be dark soon, so she expected to find him there, unless he'd gone to the Windsor for supper. Knowing Asa, he hadn't had a bite to eat since breakfast—if he'd even eaten that. Hopefully, he'd found the note she'd left him, along with the eggs she'd found in the chicken coop.

Lard + eggs + hot woodstove = breakfast. Thanks for repairing the chicken coop...I found these inside!

See you soon,
Nell

Birdie was there, smiling up at her, but it appeared Asa was not; no one answered her knock on the door.

"Oh, how disappointing," she said to the dog. "Now I'll have to wait until morning." She started back down the walk, the mutt trotting along beside her. "Guess that means no sleep for me tonight, Birdie, ol' boy." But on the bright side, she could use the time to draft the speech that, God willing, would convince Asa to help her out.

"Do you think he found the note I left this morning?" she asked the pup.

The door jerked open, startling her enough that she nearly dropped the tube.

"I found it," he said, looking left and then right. "But...what brings you here at this hour?"

How like him to worry about her reputation at a time like this.

"I have something to show you," she said, barging past him, "that's far more important than my good name."

"Well," he said, closing the door, "won't you please come in? There's coffee on the stove."

"I'd love some." She spread the charts on the table. "But, first, come see what I've brought."

Asa stepped up beside her. "Thanks for the eggs, by the way. And the skillet. Where did you find it?"

"Out there," she said, nodding toward the yard. "Saw the handle poking out from under a shrub, and thought it would be a shame to waste those eggs. I never would have looked for them if you hadn't repaired the coop. And the enclosure."

"Didn't have time to fry them up. Maybe when we're finished here, you'll share them with me." Asa leaned forward and propped one hand on the table. "What is this? The Holstrom Mine?"

Nell slid the top page aside so that he could see her grandfather's original pencil drawing detailing the shafts and tunnels. Then she moved that aside to show him the equipment inventory and, behind that, a detailed log citing dates, weights, and which vein had produced the gold. Finally came the deed to the land where the Holstrom Mine land, purchased to protect the family from claim jumpers. Nell put the log back on top and drew Asa's attention to an entry near the bottom of the list. "This is what I'd like to talk to you about," she said, looking up at him.

"But…there's nothing there. Line's blank."

"It's blank because, instead of entering the number of ounces that would be refined and smelted, my father hid a small bag of ore in one of the walls of our cabin. And he hid the treasury bonds from his last sale in a box under a floorboard." She told him how much the two secret stashes represented. Then, turning to the first map again, she used a fingertip to underline a hand-drawn arrow. "He was certain *this* deposit would salvage his reputation and make him rich."

"His reputation…?" Asa poured them each a mug of coffee.

"Long after all the other mines were tapped out, Pa kept the Holstrom running. Now and then, he'd find a nugget or two— just enough to keep his hopes afloat—and when he brought them to town, well, he became something of a laughingstock."

Nell pulled a chair to the table and invited Asa to sit, then scooted the second chair closer and seated herself beside him.

"You're going to reopen the operation?"

"I'd like to."

"What's stopping you?"

"I need a foreman. Someone I trust. Someone the crew will respect."

"Got anybody in mind?"

She could tell from the grin forming on his face that Asa already knew what she was about to say.

"You."

After clearing a space on the table, Nell handed him the list of tools and equipment they were likely to need. She assured him that she would subsidize the operation, including salaries, until the mine started turning a profit. She'd also have a contract drawn up naming Asa an equal partner of the Holstrom Mine.

"An equal partner? But, Nell—"

"I can't be part of the day-to-day operations," she interrupted him. "Not if I want to keep teaching, and I do. So, you're in charge. What you say goes, from hiring a crew to lining up the equipment to setting the pace for the work, itself."

"But, Nell," he repeated, "I don't know the first thing about mining."

"So? Tomorrow is Saturday. We'll borrow a couple of horses and ride out there. We'll see how much work it'll take to shore up those falling-down support beams and clear out the mud and muck that've collected over the years. We'll have a look at the equipment, too, see if any of it still works or, at the very least, might be salvaged." She gave him a playful jab in the ribs. "Oh, stop looking so worried. I practically grew up in that mine, working alongside my grandfather and father. When they were in town on business, I ran things. If I can do it, so can you."

"Wish I had your confidence."

"I foresee just one possible problem."

"That I know nothing about mining?" he ventured.

"No. It's that…well, you've always been in charge, made all the decisions. But until you learn the ropes…." She shrugged one shoulder, then watched him process her comment. "So, what do you think? Can you take orders from a woman? Just for a while, anyway?"

"I'd say no...."

Nell's heart sank. She hadn't considered what to do if Asa said no.

"...if it was any other woman making this offer." He met her eyes. "But since it's you...."

Nell all but threw herself into his lap, nearly overturning their mugs of coffee. "Oh, Asa! You don't know what a relief it is to hear you say that."

"Easy," he said, holding up his hands and leaning back in his chair. "We don't know what we'll find out there tomorrow. Broken-down equipment can be repaired or replaced, but if that last cave-in was bad enough...." This time, it was Asa who let a shrug end his sentence.

She got to her feet and began gathering the papers. "I'm going home," she said, tucking them under her arm, "but I'll be back first thing in the morning."

"Sleep well, then," Asa said, opening the door. "We'll both need to be clearheaded if we hope to make sensible decisions tomorrow."

With his final words to keep her company as she made her way to Janet's, Nell believed she *would* sleep well...if she managed to contain her excitement.

As she approached Janet's house, she saw a figure silhouetted on the porch. Even without the benefit of lantern light, she recognized Doc Wilson's long-legged stride. She hurried her footsteps out of concern that her good friend might have fallen ill or injured herself.

Once inside, it took just one look at the dreamy expression on Janet's face to calm her fears. For a few minutes, the women chatted quietly about the events of the day. Janet didn't mention the doctor's visit, and Nell didn't tell Janet that she'd come within a hair's breadth of kissing Asa Stone.

Chapter Eighteen

R an into your new pastor this morning," Asa said to Nell as they journeyed to the mine the next morning.

"*My* new pastor?" Nell looked over at him. "If the prospect—pardon the pun—of reopening the mine makes me important enough to own a church, I can hardly wait to see what will happen once it starts producing."

"I just meant, since I'm not a regular parishioner...." It was small talk, and that teasing grin of hers told him she knew it as well as he did. What was it about this woman that made him feel the need to explain even the simplest things?

"Said he had a letter from the Truetts."

"I was thinking about them the other day—Tillie, in particular. Every little thing had me spooked."

"The man in the shadows, eh?"

"I didn't pay it much mind before she mentioned him, but her description reminded me that I'd seen someone like that, too. Half the town has, I imagine, but there are so many newcomers and people just passing through that no one thinks twice about such things."

He recalled again the night Ambrose had warned him to be careful traveling back to the inn. Even a blind man believed he'd "seen" Tillie's stranger.

"What about you?" she prodded. "Have you seen him?"

Not in so many words, Asa thought. But if he admitted how often he'd had the sense that somebody was watching him, she was likely to wonder about his sanity.

"If I had a dollar for every man I've seen in a black duster and a flat hat, I could retire in style," he said instead. It was a slight exaggeration, but it saved him from having to relive those hair-raising moments beside the campfire all those years ago.

After they'd ridden in silence for a few minutes, the methodical beat of the horses' hooves lulling him into a near stupor, Nell broke the silence. "I'm guessing that, to start, you'll need just two men for your crew."

"If you're right, and there's gold, I'll want at least three." Nell had said she didn't want to be involved with the day-to-day operations. This was as good a time as any to see if she'd meant it. "Soon as word gets out that we're open for business, scoundrels will come crawling out of the ground like worms after a storm. We'll work in shifts, with one man always standing guard."

"For years, Pa was the butt of a hundred jokes," she said dismissively. "Folks will likely think I inherited his foolhardy nature."

Asa saw no point in stating the obvious: For every Denver resident who would call her crazy, there was a down-on-his-luck man who would view the venture as an opportunity to line his pockets with gold someone else had worked for.

"Maybe, but we'll still have a guard—if the Holstrom isn't too far gone." *Dismiss that,* he thought.

"You know, I don't remember my grandfather or my pa ever having to unholster their pistols. I grabbed Pa's once, to shoot a snake." She shrugged. "I guess being a laughingstock isn't *all* bad."

Asa wondered what she'd been like as a girl. No doubt scrappy and hardworking, despite being barely bigger than a minute. But it couldn't have been easy, spending hour upon hour down in a dark, dank hole in the ground, swinging hammers and axes and hoping to expose something shiny. He thought of Priscilla MacMillan, the bustled, nose-in-the-air socialite to whom a few hairs blown out of place by the wind constituted a great hardship. He doubted her velvet-gloved hands had ever wielded anything heavier than a silver fork. The comparison made Nell all the more admirable and beautiful in his eyes.

When they were studying her father's papers the night before, she'd rolled up her sleeves, determined to confirm the man's belief that the Holstrom wasn't tapped out just yet. *Who's she trying to convince—me or herself?* he'd thought at the time. And while watching her point out the tunnels that had proven productive in the past, he'd noticed a long raised scar on the inside of her right forearm. Her enthusiasm hadn't left him a moment to ask about it.

But they had plenty of time now. He decided to be blunt. "How'd you come by that scar on your arm? Noticed it last night while we were talking."

"Oh, that little thing? Would you believe I don't remember, exactly? Near as I can figure, it happened when I tried to heave that cracked beam off Pa's chest. Or when I fell, hurrying to get into the wagon to fetch help." She sighed. "It was Doc Wilson who first brought it to my attention, when he asked how I'd bloodied my fingers. 'That's bound to happen,' I told him, 'digging through rocks and dirt.' He cleaned me up—wasn't much he could do for Pa—and warned me to keep it covered, so it would heal properly." She grunted. "For someone like me, that's easier said than done, as you've seen."

Asa nodded as she briefly held up the hand she'd scraped while trying to prove herself worthy of a job that first day at Stone Hill. She'd wear that scar for the rest of her life, too.

Nell pointed at a giant oak tree. "We're close," she said. "The mine is just around this bend in the road."

Road? It may have been a thoroughfare of some sort when the mine was in operation, but now, it was now a game trail, at best.

If the old place hadn't sustained too much damage, he and a crew would reestablish it as they traveled back and forth to Denver with wagonloads of supplies.

"Your people use horses or mules?"

Nell sighed. "One old horse, and they treated her horribly. She always did what they asked of her, and then some. I think Betsy was the only one who truly loved those miserable old men, even as they were working her to death."

He knew a little something about fathers who hadn't earned love and respect. Just about the time he was getting ready to ask how they moved the gold after the horse died, he saw the cabin up ahead.

After they had tethered the horses, Nell grabbed the tube of maps and led him inside. While she spread the papers on a long trestle table, he checked out the place. He counted six cots against the back wall and two rocking chairs in the opposite corner. He walked to the side counter and worked the pump handle. Amazingly, water splashed into the tin pan beneath it. The stuff was gritty and brown, but that was to be expected after so many years of disuse. The cookstove door squealed when he opened it, but if nothing had fallen into the stovepipe, it would do the job of warming the space.

Getting ahead of yourself a mite, aren't you? He hadn't even seen the mine yet.

"If things look good," Nell said as she led the way outside, "I'll give this place a thorough cleaning. Bring in some canned goods, linens, lantern oil, and maybe some books."

If, Asa thought, *biggest little word in the English language.*

"You wait out here," he said, stepping into the mine. And when it appeared she was about to protest, he added, "Somebody needs to go for help if this thing collapses again."

A collection of rusty tools leaned against the side wall, and he grabbed a pickax. After poking it here and there, he moved deeper into the mine, tapping the walls and the ceiling, too. He couldn't say what had caused the beam that had killed her father to give way, but unless he was mistaken, the mine could be shored up again. Whether or not they'd find gold, well, he couldn't say that, either. But with some sturdy timbers for reinforcement—and they were in ample supply in the woods surrounding the place—chances were fair to middling that they could look for it without being buried alive.

Next, he inspected the water flumes and sluice box, the wagon and wheelbarrows. Everything, like the mine itself, needed a good overhaul, but from what he could see, the most important equipment wouldn't need to be replaced.

"Well," Nell said, walking with him back to the cabin, "don't keep me in suspense. What do you think?"

Asa started rolling up the charts and maps. "I think," he said, stuffing them into the cardboard tube, "we need to get back to town, the sooner, the better."

To say that she looked let down would have been an understatement. But, true to form, Nell didn't grumble or whine. He would have paid a fine sum to know what was going on in that pretty head as she fastened the tube behind the cantle of her saddle.

They'd traveled about half a mile when he said, "I hope you have plenty of paper and pencils."

"Why?" she growled. "So I can write down all the disappointments of my life?"

She didn't sound like herself at all, and Asa felt guilty for leading her to believe the mine was unworkable.

"We need to start a list of everything we'll need: mules, crew, and axle grease—lots and lots of axle grease."

He couldn't have been more than ten when his grandmother told him he was the easiest-to-please human being she'd ever come across. When Nell smiled, and it lifted his spirits still more, Asa thought maybe Gran had been right.

"Speaking of the crew," she said, "do you have anyone in mind?"

"Haven't had a chance to put much thought into it." He thumbed his hat to the back of his head. "Wish I knew where my brothers were. They're just the kind of men I'd hire."

"Tall, broad-shouldered, and hardworking, like you?"

He grinned, trying not to feel overly flattered. "All the men in my family are over six feet tall."

"And you have how many brothers?"

"Had three. Chester and Edgar are still alive, as far as I know, but Duncan was killed. Had a sister for a few hours— Bernadette—but you saw where she is buried."

Nell nodded gravely. After a few moments, she smiled and asked, "Was it deliberate, the way your mother named you alphabetically, or just a coincidence?"

He thought about that for a moment. "Seems she would have kept the letters in order, if it was deliberate."

"What was your mother's name?"

"Hanna," he said on a sigh.

Asa pictured her in the doorway, handing out kisses and lunch buckets as she sent him and his brothers off to school. "She had long dark hair and big brown eyes. Little slip of a thing with a heart of gold and the voice of an angel." Looking over at Nell, he added, "You remind me of her in many ways."

Nell blushed when he said that, and they let the subject drop.

For the rest of the ride, they talked about the weather, how Denver had changed and grown in the past few years, and whether or not Tillie's sinister-looking stranger was a figment of her imagination. There were long periods of silence between topics, too, but rather than feeling awkward or uneasy, it felt comfortable, the way Asa imagined a happily married couple might behave.

At that thought, Asa fixed his gaze on the pommel and exhaled a sigh. When would he learn to stop picturing a future with Nell?

⌒

Who would come out on a night like this? Asa wondered in response to the pounding at his door.

"Ambrose, have you lost your mind?" Asa asked as the old man stepped aside. "Get on in here and sit by the fire."

Asa led him to a chair near the woodstove, relieved him of the big sack he carried, and hung his dripping slicker on an iron peg that had once held a garden spade.

"I heard you got yourself a place to hang your hat," Ambrose said, "so I brung some things I thought you'd need."

"Mighty kind of you, but you shouldn't have. Especially in weather like this."

"Aw, never mind that. There's a coffeepot in the bag," Ambrose said, pointing a gnarled forefinger. "Ground beans, too. I'll tell you how you can show your 'preciation—by boilin' up some coffee to warm these old bones."

Asa draped a quilt around his friend's shoulders, then stoked the fire and got some coffee brewing. While it perked, he inspected the remaining contents of the bag: bread, apples, butter, jam, bacon, and two of everything—shirts, trousers, and socks. Why, he'd even brought shaving supplies and a comb.

"What, no horse and carriage to turn me into a proper gentleman?"

Chuckling, Ambrose waved the joke away. "Man needs to look tidy when his boss is a lady, 'specially when that lady done stole his heart."

It was a good thing the old man couldn't see the frown his comment had inspired. "How about if I fry up some of this bacon?" he asked, rather than respond. "Just so happens I found a few eggs in Nell's chicken coop."

"Naw, but thanks. Had my supper already. If you're hungry, you go right ahead and eat. I promise not to watch."

While Ambrose laughed at his own joke, Asa admitted that he, too, had already eaten supper. He filled two mugs with coffee and hoped to find enough topics of conversation to keep his friend seated until the rain stopped.

"Sounds like the Truetts might be in Golden to stay," he said.

"I heard the same. Good thing Meb brought in a new preacher before he left. If there's one thing this town needs, it's God's Word!" He took a sip of his coffee. "Well, doggies, I don't believe I've ever tasted *good* coffee in all my life."

Asa smiled. "Glad you like it. But I can't take any credit. Nell taught me how to brew it properly."

"That's one good woman." Ambrose nodded. "I'm sure you have your reasons, but *I* can't figure out why you haven't made her your bride."

Asa exhaled a sigh. "I'll give you the only reason that matters: She's too good for the likes of me."

Ambrose faced him squarely, and if Asa hadn't known he was blind, he would have sworn the man was looking him straight in the eye as he said, "Self-pity is a mighty unbecoming trait in a man. It's a liar, too, makes you believe things about yourself that just ain't true." He took a long, slow sip of the coffee, then set his cup on the table between them. "I don't much like it when somebody runs down a man I respect," Ambrose continued. "Not even when that somebody is the man, himself." He held up one hand. "I can count my friends on these knobby old fingers, and still have a few left over. That's 'cause I choose my friends wisely. Men I can respect, who ain't always lookin' after their own best interests. That li'l gal needs somebody to look out for her, somebody she can trust, 'specially now that she's got a few dollars hid under her mattress. Who in this town fits that bill, Asa Stone? You tell me that!"

"I'm sure he's out there somewhere," Asa muttered.

"Who? That fool Pinkerton who talks through his nose?" Ambrose huffed. "He ain't no outlaw, I'll give you that, but he still ain't good enough to polish her boots."

Not knowing what else to say, Asa finished his coffee. "Thanks for all you brought over. I'll repay you for everything, soon as I get my first pay envelope."

"Now, is that any way to talk? You don't owe me nothin', son. Are you forgetting that it's thanks to you I have a job at the Tivoli and a room at the Remington?"

"You just needed a hand, that's all. Would have pulled yourself up all on your own, eventually."

"We both know that ain't true."

Ambrose lifted his chin, and yet again, Asa had the unsettling sense that the old fellow was looking deep into his eyes, searching his soul.

"You never did tell me how it was you came to give up the drink."

And he wouldn't have agreed to tell it now, except that the rain was still pouring down, and he would use any method to give his friend reason to tarry.

"I was down in Abilene, not a penny to my name, when I wandered up to an old farmhouse. Asked the lady of the house if she had any odd jobs I could do in exchange for a hot meal and a place to spend the night. That widow woman looked me over like nobody else ever had. And even though I reeked of Old Grand-Dad and hadn't had a bath or a shave in weeks, said she'd do more than feed me and give me a place to sleep. Said she'd hire me on a permanent basis—plus give me two meals a day and clean sheets on my cot in the bunkhouse—on the condition I didn't so much as look at a bottle of whiskey. About a year later, she took another husband, and when he moved his young'uns in, they couldn't afford to keep me on. When she handed me my last pay envelope, she made me promise to keep my nose clean."

"She had no way o' knowin' if you went back on your word."

"But I'd know." And the last thing Asa wanted was to end up like his pa, an angry, hateful old drunk.

Ambrose chuckled. "That don't surprise me none."

"What about you? Working for Soapy Smith, surrounded by dance-hall girls and Old Crow, couldn't have made it easy to clean up your act."

"I have Doc Wilson and the Lord above to thank for my sobriety. Started vomiting blood one day, and Doc said I had to make a choice—the bottle or hell—'cause no way God would let me into heaven smellin' like Old Overholt, even if it was Abe Lincoln's favorite brew."

The men shared a quiet laugh, then Ambrose rose to leave. "Sounds like the rain stopped," he said. "Think I'll get movin' 'fore it starts up again."

Asa fetched his slicker, then reached for his own. "I'll walk you back."

"If it's all the same to you, I'd rather go it alone. Got some important things to think on."

"Might sink to your knees in mud, the way it was coming down."

"If that was gonna happen, it would have been on the way over here, whilst I was bogged down with that heavy sack."

Ambrose held out his hand, and Asa shook it. "Take care, my friend. We both know danger lurks in the dark."

"Darkness don't scare me none," Ambrose said, shuffling down the path. "It's the only world I've ever known."

Asa watched until the old man disappeared from sight, then bolted the door. It was a blessing to have a steadfast friend he could trust with one of his most shameful secrets.

He blew out the lantern flame, then sat on the edge of his cot and toed off his boots. Lying back on the crisp sheets Nell had stretched taut across the mattress, he pictured the notes she'd written, drawing his attention to one thoughtful gesture or another. He liked the last one best, because she'd signed it "Sweet dreams."

He closes his eyes, knowing those were exactly what he'd have tonight.

⌒

She hadn't been their teacher for long, but it didn't surprise him to see that Nell had the students eating out of her hand.

She was in the middle of an arithmetic lesson, and he didn't want to interrupt Craig Held's youngest son, who'd made it halfway through the multiplication tables without a single error. Asa leaned against the doorjamb, arms crossed and smiling as he watched Nell's lips move with every number the boy recited.

A little girl at the front of the class turned around and saw him standing there. "Miss Holstrom!" she said, her voice loud enough to rattle the windows. "Is that your beau back there?"

With all eyes on him, Asa thought he knew how the mannequins in Cooper Preston's haberdashery felt when folks lined up outside the window to inspect the latest styles in suits and hats.

"Class," Nell said, "I'm sure most of you know Mr. Stone."

"He owned the inn on Sterling Street," the little girl said, "before the tornado blew it away."

Nell's gaze locked on his. "That's right, Emily, he did. Lots of our neighbors lost things that day, didn't they?"

"Uh-huh." Emily faced the back of the classroom again, this time looking Asa right in the eyes. "So, are you? Her beau, I mean."

"We're...Nell—Miss Holstrom, that is—we're...."

"He's a friend," Nell said. "Now then, Emily, would you like to go next and recite your multiplication tables?"

Emily's eyes widened. "No, ma'am, I sure would not." She turned around and sat up straight, hands folded neatly on her desk.

Nell reached into her apron pocket and withdrew her father's watch. The quiet *ping* as the case popped open echoed in the big classroom. "It's nearly time for recess," she announced. "Single file, now, and be sure to listen for the bell, so I won't have to count you tardy when it's over."

The children filed quietly past him in a tidy row, and the instant they stepped outside, they exploded into happy laughter and squeals of joy.

Hands pocketed, he walked to the front of the class. "She cooks, she sews, she can put a shine on the dullest wood, and she can emulate the Pied Piper without even playing a flute." He picked up a piece of chalk from the blackboard ledge, tossing and catching it several times before putting it back. "But I'm sure if she had a mind to, she could do that, too."

"Goodness," she said, blushing prettily. "If you keep that up, I'll get a swollen head."

Nell stepped up to the sink to the right of her desk and pumped water into a big ladle. She took a sip and held it out to him. "Thirsty?"

"Don't mind if I do."

Their fingers touched ever so briefly as he accepted the dipper, and the pink in her cheeks intensified.

"So, the reason I stopped by," he said, returning the ladle, "was to let you know I might have assembled a crew. Young, able-bodied men who won't pocket any nuggets they might find."

Her eyebrows rose. "Oh? Would I recognize their names if you shared them?"

"Shaina Remington's brothers, Earl and Ben Stewart. They've been working for Sloan, splitting their time between the hotel and the ranch, but he told me the other day that he feels guilty that there isn't more for them to do. So, I made them the offer, and they accepted."

Nell clasped her hands under her chin. "That's perfect. And did you find a third, to stand guard while you work?"

"It'll just be the three of us for now. Once we get the shaft cleared and shored up, we'll revisit the issue."

"And you were worried about being a good manager." She perched on the corner of her desk. "I can't tell you how excited I am. How *relieved*! Finally, I can stop slaving for the basic necessities of life, all without ever really getting ahead. I have two things to call my own," she said, palming the pocket watch. "This, and my mother's cameo." She took hold of the ribbon she'd threaded through the clasp. "And don't look at me that way, as if you think I'm setting myself up for a big disappointment. If I am, well, I'll deal with it when it happens. But, thanks to you, I have hope. For the first time since I was a young girl, I'm not afraid to dream!"

"What do you dream of, Nell?"

She got up and walked around to the front of her desk. "People are always saying that I have an eye for design. I could offer my opinions to Denver's rich and famous...."

"Opinions?"

"On upholstery, drapery fabrics, paint colors, furniture placement.... Wealthy people rarely have time to spend on such mundane decisions and are willing to pay someone else to make them. I'd be my own boss." Nell glanced toward to the window. "I could buy a house." Peering into the schoolyard, she added, "Maybe have a few children of my own."

"I can't think of anyone more suited for motherhood," he said without thinking.

Nell faced him. She held his gaze for a long moment, then opened the top drawer of her desk. "This is just a first draft," she said, handing him a packet of papers. "If you see anything that you disagree with or that seems unfair, we can make amendments."

It was the contract, naming him full partner in the Holstrom Mining Company.

"Nell, this really isn't necessary. I trust you."

Then it hit him like a slap to the face: Maybe Nell didn't fully trust *him*. If his signature would provide the assurance she needed.... "Where do I sign?"

"There are three copies, one for you, one for me, one to file at the courthouse. But you can't sign yet. Not without reading the document first. Besides, the attorney said we need a witness to sign, as well."

Asa stepped into the hall and saw Will Benson, the assistant principal. He waved him over.

"Can you keep a secret, Will?" he asked, leading him to Nell's desk.

"I suppose," the young man said. "Why? What's going on here...?"

"Nell and I are entering into a business arrangement, and we need a witness to our signatures on that contract, there."

"A business?" He looked at Nell. "You don't mean to say you're leaving us already!"

"No, of course not," she said, laughing softly. "I've decided to reopen my father's mine. Take one last chance at giving him back his good name, and Asa, here, has graciously agreed to help by running the day-to-day operations."

"I see. Well, in that case, where do I sign?"

Nell opened the copies to the last page and signed her name three times, then held the pen out to Asa. "I really wish you'd read it first."

"Don't need to. As I said, I trust you." He took hold of the pen, dipped it into the inkwell, and scratched the nib across the proper lines.

The principal followed suit, then excused himself. "Don't worry," he told Nell. "Your secret's safe with me."

When he was gone, Nell extended her right hand to Asa.

The ink was still glistening on the pages when he took it.

"Well," she said, shaking his hand, "it's official. We're partners now."

He nodded. "Guess I'd better head out, too," he said, releasing her. "I'll pull a list together of things we'll need to start the cleanup, and show you the invoices."

She followed him into the hall, the fingers of one hand wrapped around the handle of an enormous brass bell, the others tucked into the bell to keep the clapper quiet. He opened the door, but she stepped in front of him, blocking his path.

"Thank you, Asa. *Thank you.*" Then she faced the playground and rang that bell for all it was worth.

Asa hurried down the schoolhouse steps, wishing that they could be more than just friends. They were partners now, too, but he wanted to be partners in a different sense.

Chapter Nineteen

Nell could scarcely believe she'd been teaching for nearly two months. Under normal circumstances, the town council and school board never would have hired someone without a teaching certificate. It boggled her mind that in a town as populous as Denver, no one with the proper credentials had responded to their search for a new teacher. Not that she minded. She'd found teaching to be one of the most fulfilling jobs she'd ever held. Every morning and every afternoon on her walk to and from school, Nell thanked God for putting the opportunity in her path.

She thanked Him for putting Asa in her life, too, and not just because his dedication to the Holstrom Mine was beginning to pay off. Her father had been right—there *was* gold in the vein he'd located just before his death. His tarnished reputation had now been restored, and it couldn't have happened without Asa.

Christmas was still nearly two months off, but already, Nell was planning his gift. He deserved something better than a hat or a sweater. She wanted to give him something memorable and meaningful that would prove her gratitude. What she had in mind, if it was possible at all, would take time. Hopefully, she hadn't waited too long to get started.

The minute school let out, Nell headed for the local Pinkerton agency. With any luck, Gus Anderson would be at his desk, because she didn't know any of the other agents well enough to outline her plan…without sounding like a silly, love-struck female.

Thankfully, she found Gus alone in the office. "Gus," she said, "I'm so sorry to barge in without an appointment."

"That isn't necessary," he said, gesturing toward the chair beside his desk. "We're friends, and friends are welcome any time."

She sat down and tidied the folds of her skirt.

"Uh-oh." He frowned. "Something tells me this isn't a social call."

"I'm not sure how to approach this, but I'd like to hire you to find someone for me. Two someones, actually. And since this isn't company business, I'm guessing you'll have to look for them in your spare time. If you decide to take the job, that is."

Grinning, Gus sat back and linked his fingers over his stomach. "Whoa. Let's not get ahead of ourselves. Tell me, why are you looking for these…someones?"

"I've written everything down," she told him, sliding an envelope out of her purse. "Names, approximate ages, vague descriptions." She rolled her eyes. "I know it isn't much to go on, but—"

"Wait." Gus looked up from the paper. "Chester and Edgar Stone? Asa's brothers?"

Nell nodded. "I'd like to surprise him with a living, breathing Christmas gift, to thank him for all he's doing at the mine."

"Everybody's talking about what a surprise that is," he admitted. "Must feel good, thumbing your nose at all those people who called your father crazy."

"Well, we can't gloat just yet. At this point, we're barely making a profit."

Gus tapped the paper. "I'll do what I can," he said, "but things like this take time. It could be next Christmas before I find them. *If* I find them."

After the Pinkerton named his price, Nell counted out half the amount and placed it on his desk.

"I've written letters to them," she added, handing him two more envelopes, "explaining why I'm extending this invitation."

"And?"

"And if you locate them, I'd like you to deliver them."

"In person?"

"Well, you can't very well wire them if you don't know where to find them, and there may not be time to send them by way of the post office."

"I know some people," he said. "A few well-placed telegrams might just turn up some information."

"Have I paid you enough to cover your expenses? I'll pay the other half once they arrive in town, naturally."

He pocketed the money. "More than enough. If I hear back from my contacts, I may need some traveling money, though."

Nell got to her feet and held out a hand. "Thank you, Gus."

He shook her hand. "Don't thank me yet. There's a good chance we've just begun a wild goose chase."

"But you're going to try, which is more than I could do on my own. So, thank you for that."

"I'll get started this afternoon," Gus said, patting the pocket that held the money.

She started for the door, then faced him again. "I'll be praying for you!"

That evening, Nell turned up the lamp and snuggled into the cushiony chair beside the sofa in Janet's living room, then picked up the copy she'd made of the identical letters she'd written to Edgar and Chester. She'd done her best to explain who she was and why she wanted to find them. With any luck, they'd take her seriously instead of prejudging her as an escapee from an asylum!

She'd stuck with the facts: Asa had returned to Stone Hill in time to care for their grandparents before their deaths, and that he'd refurbished Stone Hill after they had passed. He was just beginning to turn a profit, she'd written, when a tornado flattened the inn and destroyed everything in it. He was now managing the Holstrom Mine, and doing a fine job. So fine, in fact, that he'd soon need to expand his crew. If they were interested in steady work and a place to live, plus a reunion with their brother, they need only reply, and she would wire train fare and spending money to get them here. It was a calculated risk—Nell realized that. If Gus found them, one or both of them might very well pretend to be interested, only to take the money and run. But it was a risk she was willing to take for Asa's sake.

Nell tucked the letter into her purse, along with the exchange and deposit receipts for the gold and treasury notes her father had left her. It felt good to have a reason to remember him fondly instead of with disdain.

She turned down the lamp and got on her knees to pray, just as she'd done every night since childhood:

"Lord," she whispered, "I thank You for bringing me safely through yet another day and for meeting my every need. If I have offended You during these daylight hours, I ask Your forgiveness. Hear my prayers now, O Father, for everyone I hold dear...the students in my care, and Janet, who generously opened her home to me. Help Gus in his search for Asa's brothers, and inspire a complete healing in the Stone family."

The image of Asa, getting his first look at Chester and Edgar, encouraged a smile and tears of joy.

"Watch over Asa—dear, sweet Asa—and Shaina's brothers as they work in the mine. And, if it is Your will, let them find enough gold to provide well for us all. I ask these blessings in Your name, amen."

Nell climbed into bed, burrowed deep into the covers and quickly fell asleep.

The sun was just peeking above the horizon when she woke. Sometime during the night, the parlor fire had all but died out.

She stirred the coals and added a few logs, then tiptoed into the kitchen to make some coffee. While she waited for it to percolate, she slid three fat hens into the oven—a special treat for her students' lunch during today's outing at the library.

She sat with her back to the cookstove and her feet propped on a nearby chair, sipping coffee and writing down all the things she wanted to serve at Thanksgiving, which she would help Janet host this year: Bowls of hearty chicken soup, followed by thick slices of stuffed roasted goose, giblet sauce, mashed potatoes, buttered beans, sweet potatoes, and crusty bread, and finally, mince and apple pies for dessert.

Janet had invited twenty or so people to dinner. The dining table sat only a dozen comfortably, so they'd have to improvise. Nell thought some planks—and she knew right where to find them—held up by sawhorses, would work perfectly. And hidden under a tablecloth, no one would be the wiser.

"I'm *so* going to miss you when you move into a place of your own," Janet said, padding into the room on slippered feet.

Nell got her friend a mug of coffee. "You say that so often, I'm beginning to wonder if it's a hint that I should do that sooner than later!"

"Most certainly not! I love having you here. I'm only sorry I can't provide a room of your own." She sat across from Nell, reached across the table and took hold of her friend's hand. "Promise me something?"

"Of course!"

"Will you wait until summer to move out? Because it's such a joy waking to the aroma of fresh coffee in a nice warm house."

The women laughed.

"Speaking of a nice warm house, I've started on our Thanksgiving menu." Nell handed the paper to Janet. "Can you think of anything I've forgotten?"

Janet scanned the list. "It looks like you've thought of everything." She sighed. "How can it be mid-November already?"

"I know. That old Roman poet Virgil was right when he wrote, 'Tempus fugit.' Time really does fly, doesn't it?" She paused to add, "The Truetts have been gone for several months now. Any idea whether they'll be back in time to join us for the meal?"

Janet was still looking at Nell's list. "Mmm" was her distracted reply. She looked across at Nell and said, "So what's this I hear about you paying a visit to Gus Anderson yesterday?"

"Oh, my goodness. Who told you?"

Janet winked. "A little bird."

"'*A bird of the air shall carry the voice, and that which hath wings shall tell the matter.*'" Nell quoted Ecclesiastes 10:20.

"I also talked with Pastor Crutchfield yesterday. Seems he heard from the Truetts, and they're staying in Golden longer than expected."

"I guess I'm not surprised," Nell admitted. "On the one hand, it's wonderful that they can be there for Meb's mother. But it sounds like Tillie is miserable." She sighed. "We can continue writing to her, of course, and hope our correspondence doesn't just make her *more* homesick."

"You know what I think? I think Meb is going to stay, even after his poor mother dies."

"You could be right. As his mother's only heir, he'll inherit the family farm. Makes no sense, really, to come back here."

"Unless Tillie talks him into selling it...."

"It's a wonder she wouldn't rather stay there, after all the rumors that she was drinking again."

"People were pretty hard on her after she told that story about the stranger, lurking about." Nell sighed again. "I almost wish I'd seen him, too, if for no other reason than to back Tillie up."

"Not me!" Janet said. "He sounded scary." She sniffed the air. "Those hens smell delicious, by the way. Your students are going to wish you could adopt all of them, so they could enjoy your cooking every day!"

Nell smiled. "They've been talking of this outing all week."

Today, in lieu of morning recess, she and the children would visit the library, where Janet would read them a story, then give them a proper tour, so they'd have no trouble finding titles on the subjects that interested them. Wouldn't they be amazed to learn there was a shelf filled with nothing but books about art!

"It's bound to be another cold and blustery day," Janet said, "but at least the sun is shining."

"If all the children have bundled up properly, I might just take them on a quick side trip through the park to feed the ducks."

"Oh, that'll be such fun! Unless someone spies Tillie's scary stranger...."

Nell grabbed her umbrella from the hook beside the door and wielded it like a club. "If so, he'd better hope he can run faster than me!"

"See there? Just one more reason I hope you never, ever leave. You always know what to say to make me laugh!" She stood, and quickly grabbed the back of her chair. "Oh my, not another dizzy spell."

Janet *had* been looking more pale than usual lately. Not enough time in the sunshine, Nell had thought, thanks to the rainy weather and her duties at the library. But Janet had complained of headaches, too, and blamed them on reading at night with her lantern turned down too low. Her excuses had all made sense at the time, but with dizzy spells, too? Nell didn't know what to make of it, but she didn't want to upset Janet, either.

"Do you have time for a short nap before you go to the library?"

"A nap? Silly Nell. I just got up!"

Yes, she had. But she hadn't slept well. Nell heard her tiptoeing back and forth in her room all hours of the night, and it wasn't the first time. *One more symptom,* she decided, *and I'm having a talk with Amos Wilson!*

Chapter Twenty

Michelle DiMaggio's mother wasn't a large woman, but her hugs certainly were, Nell thought, smiling as she set her groceries on the counter.

"So, you shopping for T'anksgiving today?"

"Yes. I'm helping Janet. My way of thanking her for opening her home to me after the tornado destroyed the inn."

Maria nodded. "A good thing. That girl, she look-a pale as a ghost."

And it was true. With each passing day, Janet's symptoms were growing in number and severity. Just as soon as she'd put away her purchases in the pantry at Janet's, she intended to pay a visit to Doc Wilson. "You too busy all the time," the older woman said. "I try say thank you for the *molto bella* house you make for me, but you no stand still long enough!"

"I'm so happy it's working out for you."

"I have just one complaint."

Nell saw the twinkle in Maria's eye and waited for the joke that would surely follow.

"If I could stay there all day and all night, *then* what a happy old lady I would be!"

"It's a lovely little place," Nell admitted—not as lovely as the room Asa had set aside for her, but lovely all the same. "I'm sure you enjoy having the grandchildren around you."

"Oh, yes, I love them *molto*, but they are much like you...go, go, go. 'Get me this' and 'Help with that.'" Maria exhaled an exaggerated sigh. "My smile, she is *big* when the door close behind me in the little house!"

It had been a while since Maria spent time with children of any age. And the DiMaggio youngsters were some of the most intelligent and energetic Nell had ever encountered.

"I'm sure it's a big adjustment," she said, "but they're growing more independent every day. Before you know it, they'll be grown and gone, with homes of their own!"

Maria shrugged and turned her attention to the groceries Nell had placed on the counter.

Half an hour later, Nell walked into the clinic and whispered to Amos's nurse, Cora, "I have a quick question for the doctor, unless he's with a patient."

"Oh, dear," Cora said. "You're not feeling poorly, I hope?"

"No, I'm here on behalf of...a mutual friend."

Cora's wary smile betrayed her skepticism. "As a matter of fact, he's eating lunch. Let me just tell him you're here."

Moments later, the doctor appeared in the doorway to his office. "Nell Holstrom. Please, come in."

He shook her hand and invited her to sit in one of the big leather chairs facing his desk, then settled into the matching chair beside it. "What brings you here today?"

"Please, feel free to continue with your lunch," she told him, nodding at the plate on his desk. "I'm sure a man with your schedule needs to take full advantage of every opportunity to grab a bite to eat."

"Thank you." He took a bite of cheese. "Cora says you're here about a friend?"

"Yes," she said. "I'm worried about Janet."

He stopped chewing. "Janet?"

Nell nodded, noting that he looked concerned but not entirely surprised. Had he noticed some of the symptoms, too? She started to describe them: "She hasn't been sleeping well. I can hear her pacing the floor upstairs at all hours of the night. At first, I thought that her sleeplessness was a reasonable explanation for her chronic fatigue, even for her unusually pale complexion. But then she started having dizzy spells and headaches. And she gets out of breath just from climbing the porch steps. I've told her to come and see you, but you know how she is about doctor visits."

"Yes. Unfortunately, I do." He frowned slightly. "She once limped around on a sprained ankle for a week before I convinced her to let me wrap it up and got her to agree to stay off it until it healed."

"And I'm sure that's just one example. I'm sure you can find a creative way to ask her about it all."

He promised to do some careful investigating.

"Thanks for bringing this to my attention," he said as she rose and started for the door. "Janet is a good...friend."

Friend, indeed, she thought, smiling as she walked back to Janet's house. She saw more evidence of her suspicions two days later, as Amos and Janet ogled one another across the table all though Thanksgiving dinner. Nell hoped that they would act on their obvious attraction sooner rather than later. Amos had dedicated most of his adult life to caring for others, and he was more than deserving of the care of a loving wife. And Janet, who'd grieved her husband more than long enough, was just the woman for the job. They would be good for each other, if only they'd admit it!

The meal they'd prepared was well received by all. As laughter and steaming bowls of food traveled up and down the table, and Nell smiled. Except for church socials, she'd never shared a meal with so many people. Those gathered included Sloan and Shaina, and even James, foreman at Remington Ranch, Doc Wilson's sister Elsie and her husband, Abe, the Sweeny family, Reverend Crutchfield, Ambrose Brigham, and, of course, Asa. These were more than her friends. Over the months, they'd become family.

Asa looked exceptionally handsome today in a bright white shirt and black string tie. It took concerted effort to avoid staring, because either his eyes seemed greener than usual, or she was imagining things.

After dinner, they took a brief pause to let their food digest before Janet and Nell served dessert. Just as Janet handed Asa a plate of pie, she fainted. At the hospital an hour later, Amos shook his head. "Just as I suspected," he said. "She's severely anemic."

Janet looked so small and frail against the white linens on her hospital bed.

"But she'll be all right, won't she?" Nell asked.

"Yes, provided she gets plenty of rest. I'm relieved that you're staying with her. You can make sure she doesn't overexert herself. She'll need to drink plenty of water and increase her consumption of red meat and green vegetables."

"I have a feeling Janet doesn't know what she's in for," Asa said, "having such an industrious nurse at her side."

"I can take care of myself," Janet said, frowning as she tried to sit up.

The doctor stopped her with a gentle hand on her shoulder. "You're not going anywhere tonight. If you follow orders, I might let you return home tomorrow." He unscrewed the cap of a rectangular brown bottle, pouring until its contents filled a big spoon. "And you'll need to take three doses of this daily," he said, guiding the spoon into her mouth.

Janet swallowed the elixir, then immediately winced and shook her head. "Three times a day? But it tastes awful!"

"If you're diligent about taking it, you'll only need to endure it for a couple of weeks." Amos put the bottle on the bedside table, then tucked the covers under her chin. He looked over at Nell. "You'll see to it she follows doctor's orders, won't you, Nell?"

A statement, Nell noticed, not a question. "Of course I will," she said. "Even if I have to call on Asa, here, to help me!"

The foursome shared a moment of companionable laughter, and then Amos said, "I hate to be a spoilsport, but she needs her rest...."

"We can take a hint," Nell said, kissing Janet's cheek. "And aren't you clever," she teased, "collapsing before it was time to wash up all those pots and pans!"

Janet sent her a sleepy smile and squeezed her hand. "I'm sure if you ask nicely, Asa will help you."

Nell opened her mouth to say that wouldn't be necessary when he said, "I insist."

The walk from the clinic to Janet's house took all of five minutes. When they came upon a huge muddy puddle, Nell stopped, wondering which way around it was best. But before she could decide, Asa scooped her up in his arms and plodded right through it.

"Don't look so horrified," he said, grinning, "I promise to take off my boots at the door."

"That never crossed my mind," she admitted.

He set her down on the other side of the puddle and said, "So, what do you think? Were there sparks between Janet and Amos, or was I seeing things?"

"I've been asking myself that same question for weeks now." But if he noticed that, Nell wondered, had her own behavior raised similar questions regarding how *she* felt about *him*?

He sat on Janet's top porch step, and true to his word, tugged off his boots. Once inside, they saw that the dining room table had been cleared of dishes; everything was now stacked in the kitchen, ready for washing.

Asa hung his jacket on a peg near the door. "I'll wash," he said, rolling up his sleeves, "and you dry." To silence her protest, he added, "It'll save time, since you know where things go."

She put on an apron. "I suppose you're right. But at least let me get the wash pan set up for you."

They made quick work of the job, and once the last pot was put away, Nell poured them each a cup of coffee. "I could use some fresh air. It's been a long, peculiar day," she said, shrugging into her coat. "Won't you join me on the porch?"

Asa slung his jacket over his shoulder, picked up his mug, and followed her outside.

Side by side on the wide porch swing, they balanced their coffee mugs on their knees, quietly identifying neighbors across the way that shuttered their windows for the night. Asa named a few of the moonlit mountaintops: Gray's Peak, Mount Evans, Silverheels, and Twin Sisters. He stood and moved to the railing and leaned over slightly, to see past the porch roof.

"Look at this," he said, waving her over. And when she joined him, he pointed out Pegasus, and beneath it, Pisces. "That's Orion," he said, "one of my favorites, because it's bigger and brighter than most other constellations, and easier to see." Orion, he explained, was known as the mythical hunter. "Some say he's facing Taurus the bull, others believe he's chasing Lepus and his hunting dogs." His fingertip followed the curve of Orion's belt. "And that's the Trapezium cluster."

"And just where did you learn all of that?"

He shrugged. "Wasn't much to do out there on the road, so I read. Every chance I got. Books were hard to come by, though, and harder to carry," he said, returning to the swing. "For a while, I lugged *Crime and Punishment*. Read it three times before I left it behind."

A pang of guilt flashed in Nell, because if she'd ever had a book to call her own, she couldn't imagine leaving it behind.

"Spent a few months in Kansas farm once, doing odd jobs for a young widow-woman in exchange for food and a place to sleep. When she saw the book, she offered a trade. *Elements of Astronomy* by John Wilkins." He chuckled quietly. "Nearly caught it on fire a couple of times, leaning close to the fire to compare the diagrams to what I saw in the sky."

Her life at the mine hadn't been easy, but at least she'd had one place to call home. She tried to imagine what it must have been like for Asa, never knowing from one day to the next if he'd have food or shelter. No wonder his behavior sometimes seemed standoffish and brooding! The realization made her shiver slightly.

"Cold?" he asked.

"No. It feels good out here." Nell turned a bit so that she could see his face. "Did you always travel alone?"

"For the most part," he said, staring straight ahead, "yes."

"It must have been terrifying, especially at night. I remember how I jumped at every little thing getting from here to the mine the other day—in the daylight!"

She felt him shrug. Heard him exhale a heavy sigh.

"Did you get any sleep at all when you were roaming around? I know I wouldn't have. Why, I'd probably have slept with one eye open, all the time."

He chuckled softly. "Man gets used to it after a while."

Nell had no idea how anyone ever got used to a thing like that. "Rumor has it you fought in the Indian wars. At a very young age, I might add."

"Rumor, eh?"

"Oh, yes. You'd be surprised how often DiMaggio's buzzes like a hive, and occasionally, you were the main bee."

"Maybe I should have looked for a book about insects."

She looked over at him as he continued, "I thought the main bee was female."

Nell laughed quietly, not wanting to draw attention from the few townsfolk still milling about on Sterling Street, below. "So it's true, then? You fought in the Indian wars?"

"Only a few battles during my teens."

"But you were too young for such things!"

"I wasn't the only boy out there."

His tone, his posture, even the set of his jaw had changed with his answer.

Nell was searching her mind for a lighter topic of conversation when he said, "But I doubt I'd remember it differently, even if I'd been older."

He went on to describe the earsplitting gunfire. The caustic smoke that filled the air, bodies, strewn across the blood-soaked, snow-covered ground, the haunting cries of the wounded…and the moans of the dying.

"It's where I last saw my pa and brothers," he said, his voice a craggy whisper.

Nell could hardly believe how he'd opened up to her. She felt an odd urge to thank him, for she suspected he hadn't shared these dark memories with many others. "It's late," he said, standing, "and the crew will be at the mine at first light. How would it look if I showed up late?"

Nell walked with him to the gate, more aware than ever that Asa Stone was a good and decent man. When she'd worked for him, he had treated her with respect, and that didn't change once the roles were reversed. He'd experienced more loss and heartache than anyone she could name. Something truly awful must have happened during his years away from Denver, something he'd done out of dire necessity. She believed that as strongly as she believed in God.

"Sleep well, Nell."

Until that moment, she hadn't realized they were holding hands. Had she initiated it, or had he? *It doesn't matter*, she decided. Because they'd connected, finally, in a very real way.

"You, too." Was she imagining things, or did he intend to kiss her goodnight?

She'd never know, because Birdie ran between them, nearly knocking Asa off his feet.

For the first time since the dog entered their lives, he earned a scowl from his mistress.

⁓

He'd said more tonight than he wanted to. Fortunately, he'd stopped short of telling her about his months with the James-Younger Gang, and the atrocities he'd witnessed the day after the massacre at Sand Creek. Why put those grisly images in her mind when he could barely stand thinking about them, himself?

Asa walked through the gate, closed it behind him, and stood there, facing her. She looked lovelier than any woman had a right to. Somehow, he would learn to settle for friendship with her, despite the fact that he wanted more—so much more. Nell wasn't making it easy, though, blinking at him with those big, innocent blue eyes. If she kept it up, he might just give in to the urge to kiss those perfectly shaped pink lips. What would they feel like, pressed to his? Dozens of times since the first day she'd answered his ad, he'd dreamed of a moment like this. If he pretended that *almost* baring his soul was as good as confessing everything, would it be dishonest to lean in and find out, once and for all?

The atmosphere changed suddenly, reminding him of the sizzle and buzz that hang heavy in the air right before a storm. Swathed in moonlight, Nell's hair took on a delicate glow, like the halos of angels he'd seen in art books. He felt her soft breath puffing against his cheek, and he inhaled the delicate scent of rosewater wafting from her skin.

Asa leaned in, and just as he was about to make contact, Birdie ran between him and the gate, nearly knocking him on his backside.

Nell laughed softly and shivered. "You should get inside, warm up by the fire."

She seemed as reluctant to leave as he was to let her go, but, a moment later, she turned and hurried up the porch steps. He waited until he heard the reassuring *clunk* of the lock sliding into place, assuring him that she was tucked in, safe and sound. The curtains parted, she pressed the heels of both palms on either side of her face, peering outside. When she saw him, Nell wiggled the fingers of one hand, sending his heart into overdrive.

He'd set himself up for a powerful heartache, and when it happened, he'd have no one but himself to blame. Turning on his heel, Asa started walking toward Stone Hill. "Biggest fool this side of the Mississippi," he muttered.

But head down and hands pocketed, he smiled despite himself…

…unaware that just a few yards away, someone was watching.

Chapter Twenty-one

I can't believe how quickly you settled in!" Janet said. "Why, if I didn't know better, I'd say you'd been in your new place for a year instead of only a week!"

As Nell looked around her new home, she could barely contain her delight. Some of the furniture had come with the house, and she'd filled in the rest with a handful of new pieces, along with a few she'd restored.

Her father's hard work and stubborn determination had made all this possible. A twinge of guilt, born of the bitterness and resentment she'd harbored for so many years, dampened her excitement. The best she could hope for now was to keep moving forward to salvage his reputation, once and for all.

Without Asa, she wouldn't have the chance, and not even splitting the mine's profits right down the middle could repay him for that.

"You're looking so much better," Nell told her friend. "Obviously, you're following the doctor's orders to the letter."

"Amos—I mean Doc Wilson has been very attentive," Janet remarked. "So much so that I'm worried his other patients will suspect he's sweet on me."

"Well, they'd be right," Nell said. "And I think you know it, too."

Janet blushed. "Do you really think so?"

"Let me answer this way," Nell began. "If he doesn't ask you to marry him by Christmas, I'll be very surprised." She studied her friend's face. "If he does, will you say yes?"

A deep sigh was her answer.

"Surely you know that Brad would want you to be happy and cared for, and never alone again."

"I suppose."

"Do you love Amos, Janet?"

"Yes. Yes, I do. Very much."

"Then you have to say yes."

The librarian put on her coat. "We're getting ahead of ourselves, don't you think? He hasn't so much as held my hand!"

"Oh, he will. I'm sure of it."

"What about you and Asa? Do you think he'll ever propose?"

Nell laughed. "What makes you say a thing like that?"

Janet rolled her eyes. "You're not the only one who notices the way people look at each other, you know."

Asa had come close to kissing her on Thanksgiving night, until Birdie had pranced up to the gate and spoiled everything. Nell grinned to herself, picturing the look on Asa's face when he looked down at the dog.

"See?" Janet said. "*That* look!" She laughed. "But all right, I won't press the issue…for now." She glanced around. "Your house is lovely, Nell, truly lovely. I'm very happy for you, even if I miss having you around."

"You live just two doors down," Nell said, hugging her. "We'll probably see more of each other now than we did when I was staying with you. And don't forget—until that beau of yours gives you a clean bill of health, I still need to check on you several times a day!"

"Beau indeed." Janet clucked her tongue. "And if I see that beau of *yours* on my way home, I'll be sure to tell him he needs to stop by for a tour of your new house. I'm sure he'll be as impressed as I am."

"Beau indeed," Nell echoed. "The only way that's going to happen is if you ride all the way out to the mine. He and the crew have been out there for two straight weeks." She clasped her hands. "I'm heading out there this weekend to deliver some supplies. They're sure to be out of staples by now. I'd invite you along, but I think the trip would be too much for you."

"Next time, then," Janet said, "because I'd love to see it." Nell opened the door, and much to her surprise, there stood Gus Anderson, arm raised as if to knock.

"Hello, ladies," he said, removing his hat. "It's good to see some pink in your cheeks, Miz Sinclaire. I heard you've been under the weather."

"Oh, it was nothing," Janet said, waving the comment away. "And thanks to Nell's excellent nursing skills, I'm much better now." She gave Nell another hug. "I'll be at the library for an hour or so, and then I'm heading home."

Nell nodded. "I'll join you there in a bit, make sure you get a healthy meal and take your medicine."

"Ugh," Janet said, wincing as she headed down the porch steps, "thank you for the reminder."

Nell stepped aside and invited Gus in. "Do you come bearing news about Asa's brothers?"

He smiled. "As a matter of fact, I do."

"Wonderful. Would you like some coffee? I have a pot on the stove."

"Don't mind if I do," he said, following her to the kitchen. "Nice place. You sure settled in fast."

"I can't relax when I'm surrounded by chaos." She shrugged. "Besides, it wasn't as if I had much to unpack, thanks to that awful tornado. But they say God works in mysterious ways, and it's true. Look what a few little losses gained me! Mr. Zimmerman was nice enough to sell the place furnished."

"I wouldn't exactly call your losses 'little,'" Gus said, sitting on a kitchen chair, "but...." He placed a large envelope on the table.

"Did you find them?" Her hands were shaking so badly, she could barely open the flap.

"I did. Another example of God working in mysterious ways. I contacted a friend who works for General Ainsworth at the Department of the Army. He did some checking and found them working together on a farm in Kansas. You can wire them in Dodge City, but, from what I've gathered based on telegrams from my contact, they're keen to make a new start."

By her calculations, she had less than three weeks to get in touch with them and bring them to Denver in time for Christmas. *Look on the bright side*, she told herself. *If things don't work out for Christmas, what better way to start the New Year than by bringing the brothers together again?*

"I get the impression that the Stone brothers weren't on the best of terms when they parted," Gus said slowly. "Have you given any thought as to what you'll do if they arrive, and Asa wants nothing to do with them?"

Not in so many words, Nell thought, but from what little he'd said about them, it seemed to Nell that Asa would take advantage of any opportunity to reunite with them.

"I suppose I'll have to cross that bridge *if* we get to it." Then, smiling, she added, "You must have spent every spare minute on this investigation. I can't tell you how much I appreciate all you've done."

He pulled a slip of paper out of his shirt pocket and set it on the table. It was an invoice.

"I can," he said.

Nell didn't even glance at the total. "I'll make a withdrawal first thing in the morning and bring it by your office."

Gus got up and held out his hand. "Pleasure doing business with you, Nell. I hope things work out for you two."

For you two? She walked him to the door.

"I hope he knows what a lucky man he is." Gus put on his hat, snapped off a smart salute, and hurried down the stairs.

Janet had relayed similar sentiments, moments ago.

Leaning against the door, she closed her eyes. "Lord," she prayed, "if it's Your will...."

What you ought to be praying for is strength, she thought. Because, if it wasn't God's will, she'd need it as never before.

$$\backsim$$

"There isn't a question in my mind that all of this was a miracle," Nell said as the train chugged into the station.

Gus shook his head. "Don't get your hopes up too high. Just because I didn't find any wanted posters on 'em doesn't mean they're good men."

Steam from the engine puffed around their ankles like a thick cloud. She'd thought about that, more times than she cared to remember. How much more heartbreaking would it be for Asa if she brought him and his brothers back together only to discover they were outlaws? Why, it would be more painful than coping with the years of separation!

"I have no choice but to trust God. He wouldn't have taken us this far in such a short time only to break Asa's heart." She met the Pinkerton's dark gaze. "He hasn't let us down so far, has He?"

Gus shook his head again. "Well, li'l lady," he said as passengers began disembarking, "I hope you're right."

"So many people...." Why hadn't she thought to ask the brothers what they might wear, to make identifying them easier? An unnecessary concern, as it turned out. She would have recognized them even in a crowd ten times this size. Like Asa,·the brothers stood head and shoulders taller than everyone else, with thick dark hair and strides·that made it clear that it would take a great force to alter their course.

She approached them with a smile. "I'm Nell Holstrom," she said. "How was your trip?"

"Fine, just fine, ma'am," said the one on the left. And with a hand to his hat, he added, "Chester Stone."

"Long and bumpy, but otherwise all right," the other agreed. "You can call me Ed."

"I can't tell you how good it is to meet you." After introducing them to Gus, she said, "Are you hungry? Let's have a bite to eat, and then we'll get you settled in at the Remington Hotel. I imagine you could both use a nice long nap."

The four sat at a round table near the window, and by the time the meal ended, Nell was more certain than ever that sending for the brothers had been the right thing to do, especially considering how grateful they seemed about the opportunity to reconcile with Asa.

"Well," Chester said, pushing back from the table, "that was a fine meal. Can we see Asa now?"

"You'll probably think I'm a silly female, but—"

"But the two of you are a Christmas present," Gus put in. "Just be thankful she has no plans to wrap you up in a big ribboned box for Asa to unwrap on Christmas morning."

The men exchanged a quizzical glance, and then Edgar snorted. "A present. Us?"

"More like a surprise," she said, "to thank him for helping me reopen the mine. That's why I booked you a room at the Remington, so you'll have a chance to rest up until the twenty-fifth."

"You've paid our way long enough. I'd just as soon as to work, start earning my own way," Chester said.

"Then look at it this way, Mr. Stone." Nell looked from Chester to Edgar and back again. "What if your cooperation was a job, in and of itself? We'll say...we'll call it probation, and on Christmas Day, you'll get a promotion. And a raise." *And you'll get your brother back,* she added silently. "Would that make you feel more comfortable?"

Edgar shoved back from the table, too. "Told you she was smart."

Chester fixed his green-eyed gaze on Nell. "What he actually said was, it'd take a real special woman to keep Asa in one place all this time." One side of his mouth lifted in that same teasing grin she loved to see on Asa's face.

Nell didn't want to leave them with the impression that she and Asa were anything more than friends, but before she could conjure an explanation for their peculiar relationship, the brothers pushed in their chairs.

"Thank you kindly for lunch, ma'am," Edgar said.

Chester echoed the sentiment. "It's a true pleasure meeting you." He focused on Gus. "You'll let us know what time to show up on Christmas, then?"

"You'll see us—me, anyway—before that," Nell put in. "I'm planning to bring supper by every evening, if that's all right with you."

"See there?" Winking, Edgar tapped his temple. "If she feeds us well, we have no reason to gallivant around town," he said to his brother, "and risk spoiling Asa's surprise." Facing Nell, he said, "It'll be good to see if you're a good cook, too."

The "too" wasn't lost on Nell. Learning that the Stone brothers were perceptive should have been comforting. Instead, Gus's warning that they might not be as upstanding and reliable as their brother pinged in her head.

Nell paid the tab, then walked with them to the Remington. Sloan and Shaina were in on the secret, and as they checked the brothers in, they gave their word to make the Stones feel right at home.

"Don't know what I expected," Gus said as they left the hotel, "but that sure wasn't it."

"What do you mean?"

"I'm not sure, exactly." He moved to the outside of the walk-way to protect Nell from mud splattered by wagon wheels and horses' hooves. "They're a whole lot more like Asa than I thought they'd be."

A good thing, Nell thought, a very good thing, since they were all the family Asa had…and she'd have to trust them not to help themselves to any gold they might find in the mine.

Nell stopped at the gate in front of her house. "Thanks for walking me home, Gus. For staying with me all morning, too. Having you there made what could have been a very awkward meeting a whole lot easier to bear."

"Only too happy to do it," he said, bowing slightly.

He hadn't been gone two minutes when the doorbell rang. Had Gus forgotten something?

But instead of Gus Anderson, Maria stood on her porch.

"Oh, goodness," Nell said, drawing her into a hug. "How lovely to see you, Maria! Please, come in." And once the door clicked shut behind them, she added, "I thought you were someone else."

"Ah, yes. I saw him go away. Nice young man," Maria said, "but he is no Asa Stone!"

Was Asa the only person in town who didn't see them as a couple?

"I was just about to start supper. Won't you keep me company in the kitchen?"

"Ah, such a nice *cucina*. Like the one in my New York flat."

Nell assembled the ingredients she'd need for a beef roast as Maria commented on the curtains, the big black kettle, even the apron hanging near the stove. Nell had overheard Michelle and

Joe talking about how much happier Maria seemed, now that she'd had time to settle in. She was working hard to adjust, Nell would concede that fact. But Maria was anything but happy. She missed her house, her homeland, and most of all, the man who still held her heart, and it showed in her dark eyes. Her sadness didn't seem the least bit unusual, or difficult to understand. Nell barely knew Asa, but if he was suddenly taken from her....

"Once I get everything into the pot," Nell said, "would you like a little tour?"

"I thought you would never ask!" Maria helped herself to a mug from the drainboard, and as she filled it with coffee, the front bell rang again.

"Now who could that be?" But the moment Nell rounded the corner and saw the tall, broad-shouldered silhouette, backlit by the setting sun, she knew.

"What a lovely surprise," she said, opening the door wide. "Have you come for a tour of the new house, too?"

"Too?" He glanced toward the kitchen. "No, that isn't why I'm here, but I wouldn't mind having a look around."

"We're in the kitchen, Maria and me. I'm just making a roast. Have some coffee and talk with us while I work."

She poured him some coffee, and as he sat, Maria said, "This place, she like the train station...people in, people out." Laughing at her own joke, she added, "Tell me, Nell, when you get time to sleep?"

"It does seem that way, doesn't it? But I assure you, this has never happened before, and I'm sure it won't happen again."

"Until Christmas, you mean," Asa gently corrected, "when you'll feed that same crew who crowded into Janet's house on Thanksgiving."

Fortunately, she'd just put the pot back on the stove, because with her back to him, Nell had a chance to gather her thoughts and hide any secret-keeping thoughts that might register on her face.

"I think this can wait," she said, turning. "I can't wait another minute to show off my new house."

Maria and Asa followed her from the kitchen to the dining room and the parlor, and two small bedrooms. "My pride and joy," she said, opening a door at the end of the hall, "an indoor outhouse!"

"She so spoiled!" Maria said, laughing as she gave Asa a playful shove.

"She deserves a castle." And when Maria clapped a hand over her mouth, he quickly added, "It's a nice place, Nell. Real nice. I'm happy for you."

He seemed out of place and ill at ease. If they'd been alone, Nell might have teased that worried look from his face.

"He's a-right," Maria said with a wink. "I go now, make the supper for that crazy bunch of mine."

Asa walked with them to the door. He'd said himself that he hadn't stopped by just to see her house. The minute Maria left, she'd invite him to supper. What could be more appropriate than to discuss mine business over a hearty meal?

The door had no sooner closed behind the older woman when Asa reached inside his coat pocket and produced a small package, wrapped in butcher's paper and tied with twine. "It's not much. Just a little housewarming gift I made you."

His hands were shaking slightly as he passed it to her. Nell wondered if Asa noticed that hers trembled, too, as she read the tag.

"To Nell, from Asa," it said.

"Go ahead," he urged her. "Open it."

After watching her struggle to undo the knot, Asa took the package and untied it for her. "Sorry," he said, handing it back. "Sometimes I don't know my own strength."

Nell peeled away the wrapper and let it fall to the floor, her full focus on the small but meaningful gift in her hands.

He'd woodburned windows onto a house-shaped slab of wood no bigger than a dime novel. "YOUR DREAM, FINALLY COME TRUE" said the sign on its door. In place of a doorknob, she noticed, a small red heart. Of everyone who knew her, only Asa truly understood her longtime yearning for a home of her own—and not just because she'd blurted out her girlish dream in a moment of weakness.

She pressed the gift to her chest and met his eyes. He didn't understand her tears—that much was evident in the worried expression on his handsome face. Nell worked hard to find her voice, wanting to ease his concerns. "It's…it's lovely, Asa, and so very thoughtful."

The worry lines faded from his brow. "There's a wire on the back, so you can hang it. I'll drive the nail if you show me where you want it. Or maybe you'd rather use this…." He took a tiny wooden easel—also handmade—from his other pocket and held it out to her.

Nell carried both items into the parlor, moved aside the candles on the mantel, and put the plaque in their place. She waved him closer, and when he stepped up beside her, Nell said, "What do you think? A little to the left?"

"Looks good right where it is," he said, pocketing his hands. "Unless you think there's a glare." He grinned.

Nell grinned, too, at the reminder of those wonderful moments in the inn's lobby.

"Well, I'd better hit the road before—"

"If you can wait a while, I'll send you home with some supper. I was just about to put a roast into the oven. With potatoes and carrots. And bread. Oh, and pie for dessert."

Asa stood in the open door and said, "Thanks, but don't go to all that bother."

She hurried to catch up with him. "It's no bother. Really. I was going to borrow the Helds' wagon and bring it out to you, anyway." Nell pointed toward the kitchen. "Along with some flour and coffee. Lard. Sugar." She shrugged. "You know, staples you and the boys need at the mine?"

"Much as I hate to pass on a meal like that, I need to get back."

He was halfway down the flagstone path when she called out, "Thank you again for the plaque."

Asa waved and kept walking.

"I love it. And I'll treasure it always."

She closed the door, hoping he hadn't heard that last bit...and wondering why he'd been in such a hurry to leave.

~

"What time did you tell him to get here?" Edgar asked, peering through the parlor curtains.

"Relax," Chester said, looking over his brother's shoulder. "He'll be here at two, isn't that right, Nell?"

"Yes, and he's always punctual." If they were a little nervous, well, who could blame them? Her nerves were all a-jangle, too, and years and miles hadn't separated her from Asa!

She'd done her best to distract herself from the big moment by decorating, baking, cooking, and cleaning—anything to keep her mind off Gus Anderson's warning. Still, she wondered: If old resentments precluded a warm reunion, would Asa resent her for arranging it?

Nell had deliberately put the goose in the oven late, to give the Stone brothers time for an unhurried greeting before they sat down to eat. But she must have put too much muscle into stoking the fire, because the last time she'd lifted the lid on the roaster, the bird already appeared golden and crisp. From the looks of things, she hadn't done any better planning for Asa's arrival. Despite her nervousness, Nell had to smile at the way Chester and Edgar kept battling for a spot at the window, so they could sneak a peek outside.

"Would you like some bread and cheese?" she asked, hoping to lure them away from the door and windows.

Janet laughed. "And spoil our appetites for the meal you've been working on since dawn? You must be joking!"

"She's right," Doc Wilson said. "I'm half tempted to find Asa and drag him down here early. Everything smells delicious."

Nell checked every pot and pan on the stove, then tidied the place settings on the dining room table for the tenth time. She must have forgotten to wind the clock above the fireplace. Why else did the filigreed hands seem stuck on eleven and nine? Upon closer inspection, she heard the steady *tick-tick-tick*…and saw Asa's caring gift. It would have been meaningful if he sat at a desk all day, like a banker or an accountant. But she knew firsthand how long and hard he worked in the mine. The only way he could have found time to make the plaque was to sacrifice much-deserved sleep. That he'd do such a thing for her made it all the more precious to her.

The quiet conversation out in the parlor doubled in volume just before the brass doorknocker banged against the front door. Heavy footsteps thudded across the wooden porch.

"Asa Stone!" a deep baritone bellowed.

Another said, "You're a sight for sore eyes!"

And then…complete and utter silence.

Nell hurried into the parlor. Gus must have read the anxiety on her face, for he stepped aside to give her a clear view of the front walk. She was almost afraid to look, and when she did, her heartbeat doubled.

There, all three brothers, bound by arms and hearts, laughter and tears…

…as a solitary stranger, dressed all in black, watched through the window…unnoticed by all.

Chapter Twenty-two

It had been years since anyone had seen Edgar and Chester, and those gathered around Nell's dining room table were keen to hear where they'd been all this time.

None more so than Asa.

He hated rushing off before everyone had finished their pie and coffee, but he wanted time alone with his brothers. It seemed they wanted it just as much, because when he suggested they check out Stone Hill, the brothers were only too eager to take a walk with him.

Asa thought he'd prepared them for the shock of seeing the inn reduced to little more than its original foundation.

He'd been wrong.

Both men stood stone-still and silent under the cloudy sky, staring at the bleak landscape. It was good that he'd made time to clear away most of the debris, because the good Lord knew it was hard enough to look at, even in this condition.

He was about to walk away, give them a moment to take it all in, when Chester said, "Where do you think you're going?"

Asa half expected him to finish with "coward," as he had that night so many years ago.

Instead, his brother said, "Where were you when the tornado hit?"

"Just outside. I'd helped get the guests into the root cellar and wanted to go back for the dog."

"And Nell?" Edgar wanted to know.

"She was in the cellar."

Asa vividly recalled the terrified look on her beautiful face when she'd roused him from sleep when the tornado struck. Remembered, too, that from the moment she'd walked through the front door of Stone Hill Inn, he'd wanted to save her from life's sharp edges. How ironic that she'd saved him, instead.

"If it hadn't been for Nell," he admitted, "many of us might not have survived."

They scanned the grounds for a hushed moment.

"Then thank God for Nell."

Edgar loosed a grating sigh. "So, are you going to rebuild?"

They didn't need to know that his grandparents' wills named him sole proprietor of the estate. As far as Asa was concerned, the piece of paper merely protected the property from greedy developers. If the elder Stones were here now, he was sure they would gladly alter the document to include all three brothers, equally.

"I'm hoping *we'll* rebuild," he told them. "The place belongs to both of you as much as it does to me."

That invited a chuckle from Edgar. "The Holstrom Mine is doing that well, is it?"

"A month from now, maybe two, we'll be turning a profit. Right now, we're buying supplies and paying salaries from the money Nell's pa left behind."

The wind picked up, and a driving sleet began to fall.

"Let's go inside," Asa said, nodding to the shed he called home. "I'll put on some coffee, and we can dig up old skeletons."

They passed the next several hours reminiscing about fishing trips and horseback rides, and commiserating over past mishaps: Edgar's broken arm, sustained when he mistimed a jump from the loft into a haystack. Chester's bout of consumption. Asa's shoulder, dislocated when he got into a scuffle with a bigger, older boy over a pigtailed girl whose name they couldn't remember. The time Duncan fell down a well and they thought for sure he was a goner.

The mood darkened at the mention of his name. It would be a good time to leave, Asa thought…if he had anywhere to go.

"We were fools," Chester said. "What happened that night wasn't your fault."

"It was wrong of us to put that at your feet," Edgar agreed. "If anyone was to blame, it was Pa."

"Wonder whatever became of him," Chester mused.

Asa nearly dropped his coffee mug. "What do you mean?"

Chester glanced briefly at Edgar. "Half an hour or so after you lit out, a medic came by. Said Pa was out cold, but he wasn't dead. They loaded him onto a wagon with a bunch of other men, took the lot of them to the infirmary. It was a couple of days before he came around, and when he did…."

Edgar picked up where Chester left off. "Said he was seein' double and needed to sleep, so we left him alone." He shrugged. "Next morning, he was gone. We spent a few months looking for him. Then, 'round plantin' time, we ran out of money, so we signed on with a farmer up north."

He understood something about being short of cash, taking just about any job if it meant a biscuit in his belly and someplace to bed down. The difference? Asa had been alone, and believed himself at least partly to blame for what had happened to his pa and Duncan.

"What about Duncan? Did he vanish into thin air like Caesar's ghost, too?"

"'Fraid not," Chester said. "We watched 'em pull three Cherokee arrows outta that boy before they buried him, right there in the field where we fought."

On his feet now, Asa paced the six-foot rectangle between the door and the table where his brothers sat. "You knew Pa was alive, yet you let me carry that around all these years?"

Chester held up one hand. "Don't get your neck hairs bristlin', now, brother. We looked for you, too."

"Seems you inherited *one* thing from Pa," Edgar agreed. "Never known anybody to vanish the way you both did."

Asa hadn't felt any ill will toward his brothers, not once in all these years. The way he figured it, he'd earned their contempt. But now, finding out that the guilt and shame he'd hauled around so long had been uncalled-for—the guilt and shame that had nearly turned him into a coldblooded outlaw, too foul to deserve a woman like Nell....

Raw fury roiled in his gut.

He picked up his mug, thinking to take a sip of coffee to mask his outrage. But it was empty. So was the coffeepot. He threw the pot first, and as it clattered to the floor, he pitched the cup.

Both brothers jumped up, dodging shattered pottery.

"Now, see here, Asa," Edgar said. "There's no call for—"

"There *is* call for it," he growled.

"We tried to find you," Chester said again, "to say we were sorry, and—"

He flung open the door. "Go back to your hotel room. Need some solitude to sort things out."

"We'll go," Edgar said as he started for the door, "but we ain't leavin'."

"That's right," Chester put in. "We come out here to help you make a go of that mine. We ain't leavin' until...." He looked at Edgar. "How was it he put it?"

"Till the mine is turnin' a profit."

Chester nodded. "That's right. Meet you for breakfast at the Windsor," he said. "Six o'clock sharp. And if you're not there, we'll come get you."

As he watched them lumber down the sidewalk, he thought it funny how time and distance could draw lines on a man's face and put scars on his hands, while things like the way he walked, smiled, and looked when he was about to say something bullheaded remained the same.

He closed the door and frowned at the dented coffeepot and broken mug. Crouching, he picked up the shards, piece by piece, wondering if he'd ever reach a point in life when he didn't have to clean up a mess of his own making.

Chapter Twenty-three

Everywhere she went, Nell heard warnings about the upcoming storm, and yet she continued loading the wagon with supplies for the mine. When she finished, she went inside the blacksmith shop to thank Craig and Aleta for the loan of the horse and wagon.

Aleta looked up. "Are you sure this is a good idea?"

"All it takes is one puffy cloud and temperatures in the thirties, and the self-appointed weather experts predict a blizzard," Nell said, grinning.

"Well, all the same, you take care, all right? I'd hate to think of you stuck in a snowdrift or something. And did you pack plenty of warm clothes to change into, just in case?"

She didn't expect measurable snowfall, but by the looks of the sky, rain was a distinct possibility, so Nell had wrapped dry clothes for herself, as well as those she'd bought for the mining crew.

"I promise to be careful."

When she was several miles outside of town, fat snowflakes began floating to the ground. Soon, they were falling so fast that Nell could barely see the rump of the horse in front of her. And by the time she arrived at the mining cabin, the roads and fields were covered by a blanket of white.

Asa exited the mine and dusted his hat against his thigh as he marched up to the wagon. "Are you out of your mind? What were you thinking, coming all the way out here in weather like this?"

With Aleta's warning ringing loud in her ears, Nell said, "I've been stockpiling provisions for you and the crew, and I got tired of tripping over the boxes and bags and tins. Besides, I made a huge pot of soup and three loaves of bread—some pies, too—and you know how I hate wasting food."

He began unhitching the horse. "You ever considered cooking *less?*"

She climbed down from the wagon. "Is everyone else in the mine?"

Asa shook his head. "When I realized what the weather was about to do, I sent them home. His tone said even more than his words: *Where you'd be, if you had a lick of sense.*

"I'm surprised you didn't pass them going the other way."

They must not have wasted a moment getting back to town, because Nell hadn't seen so much as a hoof print on the snowy road. "The only living thing I saw was a squirrel, racing around the branches of the old oak."

After dropping her bundle of dry clothes in the cabin, Nell returned to the wagon and filled her arms with all she could carry: a basket of eggs, another of bread, and a tin of butter. By the time Asa had stabled the horse in her father's old barn, she'd moved most of the supplies inside.

"Those flimsy boots of yours are soaking wet," Asa remarked.

And her feet were freezing from trudging back and forth in the ankle-deep snow. "It's all right," she assured him. "I noticed a nice warm fire glowing in the cookstove. They'll dry in no time, tucked up close beside it. Besides, I brought another pair."

He shook his head and muttered as he hoisted sacks of flour, sugar, and cornmeal over one shoulder.

He'd added a row of hooks near the stove, she noticed, to give his crew a place to dry damp hats and socks when they came in from outside. She would avail herself of them once she'd changed into dry clothes—which she would do as soon as she'd put away the provisions she'd brought.

"You're shaking, Nell," Asa said, grabbing a big metal bowl from the shelf under the dry sink. "Don't worry about unpacking until you've peeled off those wet clothes."

"Where are you going with that?" she asked, nodding at the bowl.

"The well pump is frozen shut," he said, turning up his jacket collar, "so I'm going to fetch some snow to melt for wash water. And coffee."

"Oh. Yes. Of course," she said as he closed the door behind him. Had she really grown so accustomed to having heat and water right at her fingertips that she'd forgotten the years, right here in this cabin, when scrounging for basic necessities was an everyday occurrence? Yesterday, if asked to make a list of her traits, soft, spoiled, and pampered would not be on it. If asked to make that list today...

Nell hung up her coat and made quick work of arranging her gloves and hat on the hearth. Then she hopped on her right foot as she tugged at her left boot. "Why, oh why," she grunted, "is wet leather so difficult to remove when it's wet?" Asa returned, bringing icy wind and frosty snow with him. He kicked the door shut, startling her enough that she lost her balance...

...and fell right into him.

The now-empty bowl bobbled right and left and rolled into the wall with a hollow *bonk* as they sat facing each other on the floor, covered in white.

"Sorry," they said at the same time.

"Why are you sorry?"

"Because," she said, "I knocked you right onto your backside. Why are *you* sorry?"

"Because I scared you. Again." On his knees, he started scooping up snow.

"You're soaked to the skin," she said, following suit. "Why don't you change into something warm and dry while I clean this up?"

"First, we'll need more snow." He stood, picked up the bowl and headed back outside. One hand on the doorknob, he said, "What were you doing, anyway, hopping around on one foot like a wounded rabbit?"

Nell pictured herself as he must have seen her, and the image made her giggle. "Trying to get out of these boots. They're so stubborn when they're wet."

He turned the knob. "Just sit there by the fire, and when I get back, I'll help you."

While she waited for his return, she put the kettle of soup on the burner to warm. Kneeling in front of the open stove, she raked the poker back and forth through the coals. This time when the wind blew the door open, it banged against the wall, making her jump and bump her head on the edge of the cookstove.

Asa put the pan of snow beside the soup pot. "If I believed in such things," he said, helping her up, "I'd say this is a pretty clear sign you should have stayed home." He grinned.

"What, and deprive you of all this merriment?"

Lines of concern creased his brow. "Is that blood on your forehead?"

Nell touched the tender spot, then inspected her fingers. "No, it's only rust." She grabbed a blanket from the foot of one of the cots.

"I think I remember seeing a rope around here somewhere. If we could stretch it between a couple of nails, we could take turns changing behind it," he said, lifting a coil of rope from the nail behind his head. He made quick work of stringing it between the two middle cots, then relieved her of the blanket and draped it over the rope.

"There," he said, giving it a final tug. "Not the most fashionable room divider, but it'll do."

"It'll do quite nicely." Nell opened the oilcloth of fresh clothes, only to find they were damp. "So much for thinking I'd wrapped them well," she said. Asa plucked a pair of trousers and a plaid shirt from one of the hooks. "These will have to do until those things dry," he said, tossing them onto her cot. He added a pair of thick socks. "Well? What are you waiting for?"

Nell ducked behind the divider and decided that Asa had been right. "Not the most fashionable outfit for a lady," she said, "but at least it's clean and dry. As soon as I've changed, I'll check to see if the soup is warm enough to eat. I'm famished!"

"Don't change too much," she heard him say.

Oh, what a perplexing man he was—scolding her one minute, teasing her the next!

"You should change, too," she said, "before you catch a chill."

Standing, Nell looked down at her feet. The trousers were at least a foot too long, the tail of the shirt reached her knees, and its sleeves nearly dragged the floor. So she rolled the cuffs of the shirt and pants—three times each—and tugged on the socks, then left her cubby to hang the damp garments near the fire. She found a ladle and stirred the soup, and knowing Asa preferred his piping hot, Nell got down on one knee and opened the firebox. "Let's try this one more time," she muttered, reaching for the bellows.

Asa reached for it at the same time. "You've already done enough. Let me do that."

They traded places, and as he worked on the fire, she stirred the soup again.

"Smells good," he said.

"I made enough for a small army."

"Looks like we may need it, considering the blizzard." "Oh, my," she whispered, following his gaze to the window. "Looks like we're stuck here for the duration." Nell inhaled the warm, charred-wood-scented air. There were worse places to wait out a storm, she supposed. *And worse people to be stuck with.*

～

When they finished eating, Nell stepped outside, just far enough to scoop up another bowl of snow.

"For the dishes," she said, kicking the door shut. "And tea before bed."

"Hate to disappoint you," Asa said, "but there isn't any—"

Nell held up a squatty round tin of tea leaves, and smiled.

How he loved that smile. He'd probably never need another ounce of lantern oil to light life's dark corners, if only he could have that smile to look forward to, every day of living he had left.

"Should've known you'd come prepared," he said. "If there's enough for two cups in that little thing, I might just have a cup with you later."

And so it went for the next several hours, Nell talking—about her students and class work, her house, Janet's health—Asa listening. He'd happily do that for the rest of his days, too, if he thought for a moment God would allow it.

Outside, the wind howled like a banshee, snapping dry tree limbs and rattling the door and windows. But there she sat, feet tucked under her on the hard wood chair, calm as a purring cat.

She must have sensed that he had something on his mind, for she quieted and studied him for a moment before saying, "What are you thinking about?"

"Oh, just…things."

"I'm a good listener, they say."

"Don't I know it." He chuckled quietly. "You already know more about me than anyone."

"And can also keep a secret."

That simple phrase was all it took to pry the lid from his proverbial can of worms.

"Seems my pa isn't dead, after all."

Nell leaned forward. She was close enough to touch, but Asa didn't dare.

The story of the massacre at Sand Creek poured forth, and this time, he didn't leave out a single detail. His throat was dry and his eyes damp when all the details were out.

"Asa, you were barely more than a boy," Nell finally said. "No one could hold you accountable for decisions made by men who were two and three times your age."

Pretty much what his brothers had said, Asa recalled.

"For a long time, I blamed myself for every bad thing that happened to my family," Nell went on: If she'd taken better care of her grandfather, maybe he wouldn't have died. If she'd been more attentive to her grandmother afterward, the woman might not have mourned herself to death. If she'd shared watery soup and dry bread with her mother, instead of devouring them after working long hours in the mine, or gave up a few hours' sleep to help with the washing and cleaning, maybe her mother would have been strong enough to survive when dysentery struck her down. If she hadn't been so angry with her pa, blaming every other calamity to befall the family on his lust for gold, would she have realized he wasn't sober enough to protect Teo from a fatal accident? And if she hadn't fed that anger with bitter resentment after they were all dead and gone, could she have convinced him to walk away from the mine, or, at the very least, made him promise not to drink while he worked?

"If," Asa said. "Biggest little word in the English language."

Nell exhaled a shaky sigh. "I don't blame myself anymore, because someone made me realize I had no control over such those things."

"Who?"

"God."

She said it with such certainty that Asa had to tamp down the jolt of envy that coursed through him. Of course, God had helped her see that those things would have happened regardless of her actions, because Nell was as untainted as the fresh-fallen snow outside. But considering the choices he'd made, he had no right to expect the same from the Almighty.

Asa walked to the door and slid the bolt into place. "Soup was good, and so was the tea. But it made me drowsy. Think I'll turn in."

Nell blinked up at him, looking every bit as confused as she had a right to be. She surely wondered at his behavior—friendly one minute, withdrawn the next. If only he understood it, himself, he'd gladly explain.

"I think I'll finish up in here and do the same."

She got up and carried the mugs to the sink—first his, then hers, because she needed one hand to hold up the baggy trousers.

An extra length of rope dangled from their makeshift room divider, and Asa used the bread knife to cut it off. After returning the blade to the carving board, he went over to Nell. "Arms up," he said. And when she hesitated, he added, "Could be here two or three days. You don't want to spend the whole time doing things one-handed so you can hold up your trousers, do you?" She smiled. "I suppose you're right."

Asa reached behind her and wrapped the rope around her waist, then tied it in a huge, clumsy bow in front. "There. That oughta do it."

She blinked up at him, and he got the distinct impression she had something more to tell him.

"Yes?"

"I…um, I asked the Helds' boy, Clint, to mind Birdie until I… until you…." She inhaled a huge breath and started over. "Birdie is in good hands."

Ever since the dog became part of their lives, it had stayed with Nell whenever Asa was at the mine. He'd grown so comfortable with the arrangement that he'd naturally assumed she'd seen to Birdie's care before leaving town.

"Good to know. Thanks." It wasn't easy, but he walked to his side of the blanket and climbed under the covers.

He heard the faint squeal of the knob that controlled the lantern light, followed by the soft shuffling of her white-socked feet as she made her way to her cot. There was a thud, followed by a soft moan. *Ah, Nell*, he thought, *there's not another like you*. If she'd given her eyes a second a chance to adjust to the sudden darkness, she might not have stubbed her toe on the leg of her cot.

He linked his fingers behind his head and smiled contentedly. "'Night, Nell."

"Good night, Asa."

I love you, Nell.

If only he were brave enough—and deserving enough—to say those words out loud.

Chapter Twenty-four

Can you believe Easter is right around the corner?" Michelle DiMaggio asked Asa during a routine grocery stop.

To be truthful, he hadn't been paying much attention to anything on the calendar besides mine work, appointments to make exchanges, or trips to DiMaggios' or the hardware store for supplies.

"Will you be at the sunrise service?" Michelle prattled on.

"The what?" He plopped a sack of cornmeal on the counter.

Michelle laughed. "Out behind the church, at dawn on Sunday!"

"Ah," he said again. "Do you have any cornstarch? Didn't see any on the shelf."

"I don't see any, either. Let me check the storeroom."

She'd just left the counter when Nell entered the store, looking prettier than usual in a lace-collared pink frock. She'd braided her long curls, and a pink bow bobbed over her shoulder as she walked toward him.

"Asa. It's good to see you."

Not as good as it is to see you, he thought.

Michelle came back with the cornstarch and added it to his other purchases.

"Oh, no," Nell said when she saw it. "I should have brought some when—"

Asa knew why she'd stopped herself mid-sentence. People had been whispering about the days they'd spent snowed in at the mining cabin, and Nell didn't want to add fuel to the fire.

"You did bring some," he said, "but what we didn't use got spilled when Chester dropped the tin."

"I'm happy to hear your brothers are still with the crew."

Asa had no desire to talk about the rift that had almost sent his brothers packing, but he owed it to her to bite the bullet.

"Same here. They're hard workers."

Things had been rocky between the brothers until Chester had gotten his fill of Asa's gruff behavior and decided to speak up. "I suppose you've got a right to be mad that we gave up so easy on trying to find you. But you didn't even *try* looking for us, so get down off your high horse and be thankful we're together now... thanks to Nell!" There hadn't been any arguing with that. Ever since then, the bond they had shared had reminded him of those carefree days before their mother died.

"Have you finished your Easter dress yet, Nell?" Michelle asked.

Nell turned to her, clearly grateful for the distraction; and while the women chattered about ribbon trim and eyehooks, Asa's mind wandered.

He'd kept his distance from Nell since returning to town, thinking to silence the vicious rumors. But it didn't seem to have helped. He didn't believe for one minute that the school board had hired a replacement for Nell because the students' parents were suddenly demanding a certified teacher. Miss Kimball might have earned her certification, but even he could see that she knew nothing about children.

Craig Held had told him that after the principal let Nell go, she'd made herself scarce. And who could blame her, when, according to the blacksmith, folks barely spoke to her, even at church? It seemed to Asa that Nell's behavior *before* the storm should have made it clear she was innocent of all charges. He didn't know how—yet—but he intended to stop those self-righteous, judgmental hypocrites in their tracks, once and for all.

"Will that be all, Asa?"

He looked at Michelle, who'd loaded his purchases into boxes and written up a sales slip. "I believe so, yes."

Janet came into the store and immediately threw her arms around Nell. "You were right. *You were right!*"

Laughing, Nell held her at arm's length. "I'm so happy to see you looking bright-eyed and healthy again. See what following doctor's orders can do?" She let go of her friend to add, "Now maybe you'll explain what I was right about *this* time," she teased.

"You said he loves me, and it turns out, he does!" Janet held out her left hand to show off the bright ruby flashing in its setting on a gold band. "We've already talked to Reverend Crutchfield, and he's going to marry us next Saturday in the chapel. Nothing elaborate; just us, Elsie and Abe, and"—she took Nell's hand, then reached for Asa's—"the two of you."

Nell's eyes widened when she looked at him, and he could almost hear the concerns tumbling in her head—concerns of the stigma their presence might cast on their friends' nuptials.

"I know exactly what you're thinking, both of you," Janet said, "and you can just stop it. Stop it right now. Anyone who knows and loves you realizes there isn't a shred of truth in those nasty stories."

Tears filled Nell's eyes, and her lower lip quivered. "I'm so happy for you, Janet, and I'd be honored to come."

She glanced at Asa, an apologetic look on her face. He could tell that she didn't want to pressure him into agreeing to be there.

He gave Janet's hand a squeeze. "What time on Saturday?"

She beamed. "Nine o'clock."

The smile Nell sent him was even wider, if that was possible. "Does this mean I'll have to buy a tie?"

The women laughed—Michelle included. Then the shop keep's wife came out from behind the counter to hug Janet. Soon, the women were involved in happy chatter about dresses and bouquets, whether they'd take a honeymoon, and whose house they'd live in afterward. Chuckling to himself, Asa laid down enough money to pay for his goods, picked up his box, and headed for the door. It wasn't until he put it down again in his shed-turned-home that he realized Michelle had added a black string tie to his purchases.

Now all he needed was a new shirt, and trousers and boots that weren't coated with mine dust and road grit. "As good an excuse as any to see how ol' Cooper Preston is doing," he said to himself.

After the wedding on Saturday, Asa was in no particular hurry to reach his destination, but he wasted no time getting out of town.

He'd attended more than a few weddings, but, for some reason, watching Janet and Amos exchange vows hit him like a punch to the gut.

Despite their plans to keep things simple and private, the chapel pews had been filled with well-wishers—Sloan and Shaina Remington, and even Mayor John Routt and his wife. When the ceremony ended, the Remingtons invited everyone to the hotel, where the banquet room had been reserved for a special celebratory lunch.

As everyone set out for The Remington, Asa had pulled Nell aside and asked her to deliver the envelope containing his wedding present, since he wouldn't be able to make it.

She'd tucked it into her purse and looked up at him. Asa could still see the spark of disappointment in her big eyes as she whispered, "You'll be missed. How long will you be gone?"

How had she known he was leaving…and not for the Holstrom Mine?

"Not long," he'd said. "But don't worry. The boys know what to do."

A shining blonde curl had escaped her bun when she'd nodded.

"You look beautiful today," he'd said, tucking it behind her ear. "Yellow brings out the blue of your eyes and the pink in your cheeks."

Most women would have thanked him or waved off the compliment, but Nell? Asa's heart ached as he remembered her response: "I pray for you every day," she'd said, pressing a palm to his chest, "but I'm going to double up on those prayers until you're home again, safe and sound."

With that, she'd turned on her heel, lifted her skirts, and run to catch up to the rest of the wedding party. Who knows how long he might have stood there, watching her link arms with Amos and Janet, if Joe DiMaggio hadn't said, "You're not going with them?"

"No, there's someplace… I need to leave town for a few days."

"Mine business?"

My business, Asa had thought. "Something like that."

Now, his horse snorted, a sure sign that he needed to get his mind back on the road. The reason for the snort, he soon realized, was a rattler up ahead. Tightening his hold on the reins, he unholstered his sidearm and fired a single round, hitting the serpent between the eyes. The shot spooked the horse, and she danced a few steps to the right.

"Easy, girl," he said, gently tugging one rein until she was effectively looking backward. "You're all right," he crooned. "There y'go. Good girl."

She walked right on by the dead snake without so much as a sniff, and Asa decided that she deserved more than a simple pat on the head. He pulled up and dismounted, fished a carrot from the right saddlebag and held it under her nose.

"Doesn't seem right, calling you 'girl,'" he said. "You need a proper name. Any ideas?"

She bobbed her head, inviting a quiet laugh from Asa. "Saw a rodeo in Texas," he said, stroking her forehead, "where a cowboy taught his horse to count. Maybe I can teach you to spell, and you can choose your own name."

Now, she shook her head and nickered.

"Not the schoolgirl type, are you?"

An Overo Paint, the filly had blue eyes and a flaxen mane and tale. "You don't have the best table manners," he said as she gobbled up the last of the carrot, "but you're right pretty."

The horse nuzzled his neck.

"Keep that up, I might just have to call you Miss Flirty."

Mile after mile, he tested names. She didn't react to Princess, Lady, or Blondie, but when he said "Missy," her ears perked, and Asa knew he'd hit pay dirt.

On the fourth night—about three quarters of the way into the two-hundred-mile trip—Asa stopped on the banks of Bijou Creek and set up camp. It was crisp and clear, just the kind of night that stirred the coyotes. If their singing kept him awake, he wouldn't mind. By this time tomorrow, he'd be at Sand Creek.

After tethering Missy to the low-hanging branches of a gnarled cottonwood, he filled a cup with feed, filled another with water, and let her eat and drink at her own pace. Settled beside the campfire, he lay back on his bedroll and stared up at the iridescent sky. Shooting stars flared from left to right, reminding him of stories he'd heard over the years. "Make a wish," said an Irishman who'd shared ranch chores with him in Missouri, "and it's sure to come true." But, according to his own research, the Greeks believed they were bad omens. "Good thing for us," he said to Missy, "we don't believe in fate and signs."

Snorting, she stomped a hoof, as if to say, "You roused me from a nap with foolish talk?"

Yes, Asa decided as he closed his eyes, he'd made a good choice, buying this filly instead of the big black stallion from Sloan Remington's herd.

He didn't know how long he'd lain there, dozing as images of Nell flashed in his mind. But when the eerie sensation of being watched slid over him, Asa opened one eye. He couldn't see much past the arm he'd crooked over his face, but he didn't need his eyes to know that someone was standing to his right, no more than two feet from his holster. He hadn't expected to sleep, and hadn't placed his firearm on his chest, as usual. If he didn't plan his next move carefully, he'd be in trouble.

He rolled left, drew his weapon, and got to his feet in time to see the hem of a long black coat flapping in the breeze as pale boots thudded across the ground. He was quick for a man with a limp, but it didn't take long for Asa catch up. The big man went down with a grunt. He rolled onto his back and held out his hands.

"Don't shoot," he said. "I ain't packin'."

Asa almost didn't recognize the face, thanks to the eye patch. But he would know that voice anywhere.

It took all the strength he could muster to keep his legs from buckling.

"Pa."

Chapter Twenty-five

How long have you been tracking me?" Asa asked as he and his father shared coffee and biscuits.

His father held his gaze for a moment. "How long since Sand Creek?"

While it was a relief to hear that he hadn't imagined the sense that someone was following him, Asa didn't understand.

"What happened to your eye?"

"Lost it in a bar fight," he said, swirling the coffee in his mug.

Asa wasn't surprised; the only question was whether he'd cheated at cards or flirted with the wrong barmaid. "And your leg? Why the limp?"

"Ain't my leg, exactly. Took three shells to my back that night. The doc got two out and sewed me back up. Said the third one was pressed against my spine, and if he went after it, I'd be paralyzed." He patted the leg. "So far, so good." He reached for the last biscuit. "You gonna eat this?"

Asa shook his head.

"Here's the thing," his pa said, taking a bite. "If that shell budges one way or t'other, I could end up a helpless cripple, anyway. Just desserts, I guess you'd say."

It was unnerving, watching as his father gave him the once-over with his good eye.

"You done good, son. I'm proud of you."

Proud. This from the man who'd forced his boys to obey the orders of that cold-blooded maniac Chivington.

"It was good of you to let your brothers off the hook. I heard what they said before you lit out the other day."

So, he knew about the reunion, too? How much else did his father know?

"They were young and scared. Didn't mean what they said that night. Guess you figured that out once that li'l gal of yours brought 'em back to Denver, though, huh?" His pa washed down his final bite of biscuit with a gulp of coffee. "You're more like your maw than me," he said, wiping his mouth on the back of his hand. "She had a forgiving nature, too."

"Nell isn't my gal."

Daniel chuckled. "Even from a distance—and with just one eye—I could see that ain't true." He refilled his mug. "So what's the hold-up?"

Asa raised his eyebrows. "You're joking, right?"

Daniel's brow furrowed. "Joking? About what?"

Asa could only shake his head. "I don't discuss personal business with strangers," he ground out.

"Guess I had that comin'."

"And then some," Asa added.

"Wasn't just you I kept an eye on, you know. I spread it out. Stayed with you for a spell, then moved on to Chester and Edgar before comin' back to you again."

Chester and Edgar had told him that when their pa regained consciousness after the operation, he'd run them off. Asa gave a thought to asking how his pa knew where to find them, but at this point, what difference did it make?

"I done some bad things, and I was a sorry excuse for a pa. Don't think I don't know that."

"You're wrong to say I inherited Ma's forgiving nature."

Daniel nodded. "Reckon I had that comin' too. But you should know, I didn't follow you boys to get forgiven."

"Then why did you?"

"Only way I knew to make up for the mistakes I made was to make sure you stayed safe."

Safe? Asa almost laughed out loud...until the image of the wanted poster bearing his misspelled name flashed in his mind. If his father had truly been on his tail all these years, surely he'd seen it, and knew that outlaw son didn't need his protection.

"Them older two, they had each other. They fell into some good jobs, so I didn't spend as much time lookin' in on them. But you...you were the youngest, out there on your own, carryin' them ugly words in your heart." He nodded. "More than once, I thought sure you'd end up dead."

"Thought the same thing myself a time or two."

Daniel sat quietly for a few minutes before asking, "Mind if I smoke?"

"Suit yourself." Asa remembered smelling smoke, seeing the remnants of paper-wrapped tobacco following each stealthy visit. "You still pounding down pints of Old Crow, too?"

His father looked up from rolling his cigarette. "Ain't swallowed so much as a drop in ten years," he said, glaring with his one good eye. "Believe it, don't believe it, it's the truth."

Asa could hardly believe he was sitting here, having this stilted conversation with the man!

Daniel picked a branch out of the fire and used it to light his cigarette. "I'll tell you who needs to give up the Old Crow," he said, tossing it back into the flames. "That artist who drew up that wanted poster, that's who. Had me a good laugh, first time I got an eyeful of that it." Chuckling, he pointed the lit end of his smoke at Asa. "I know it wasn't you shot those men," he said, "just as I know the good Lord was watchin' out for you. Why, they even spelled your name wrong!"

Asa had never thought of it that way. And if his pa ever shut up and went to sleep, he might just aim a prayer of thanks toward heaven.

The next day, they found the battlefield, despite the thick fog that was reminiscent of that grisly day. But, as his pa pointed out, they wouldn't find Duncan here, because the government had moved the bodies to Fort Leavenworth in '76.

"Didn't know that," Asa admitted. "But I'm not here to visit a grave."

"Then why?"

Two riders, moving fast, kept Asa from answering.

"Chester and Edgar," Daniel said.

"How can you tell in this fog, with just one eye?"

Reminded of his comment at the campfire, his father aimed a half grin at him. "Good to see you have *some* humor left in you," Then he nodded toward the approaching horsemen. "I know 'cause Edgar hunches his shoulders when he rides, same as he did as a boy. Never could break him of that bad habit. It's a wonder he can set a saddle more than five minutes, all tensed up that-a-way."

The brothers slowed their mounts as they approached.

"We figured this was where you were headed," Chester said. "How long has *he* been with you?"

Too long, he wanted to say. "He rode into my camp last night."

"You boys are a sight for sore eyes." Their pa laughed. "For a sore eye, anyway."

Suddenly, a strange feeling rolled over Asa, a sensation like none he'd experienced before. With his pa to his left and two of his three brothers before him, it made no sense to hold on to grudges and past grievances.

"Some ugly things happened to us last time we were here," Daniel continued. "Now, I don't know why the rest of you are here, but I say let's pay our respects to those who died that awful day. And then, after we ride out, we'll never look back or speak of this place again."

His father leaned heavily on the pommel of his saddle as he and Asa's brothers considered his proposition. Then, one by one, the men dismounted, stood shoulder to shoulder, and bowed their heads for several minutes.

No one spoke as they saddled-up again, and they rode until dark, lost in their own thoughts.

It was Daniel who first broke the silence.

"I say we set camp right there." He pointed at a clearing fifteen or so yards from the river.

His sons agreed, and within the hour, they were seated in a circle around the campfire, sipping coffee and poking at the biscuits rising in Asa's skillet.

Daniel held them spellbound with stories of the things he'd seen while following them around. Mesmerizing as his memories were, Asa knew that only one would stick in his mind forever: The conductor whose death had put Asa's face on a wanted poster had not been shot by a member of the James-Younger Gang.

"He had his Schofield pointed at the middle of your back," Daniel said to Asa, "so I got a bead on him with my Henry Repeater and made sure he never had a chance to pull that trigger."

Asa remembered how, when the man hit the floor of the railcar, he'd been looking out the window to his left, not at the outlaws.

Daniel patted the stock. "Never had a gun that shoots straighter."

"A good thing for Asa," Edgar said.

When they'd eaten the last of the jerky and biscuits, Daniel got up and limped around the campfire a time or two. "There's something I need to tell you boys," he said, sitting on a nearby stump. "I'm dying."

Chester shot him a hard glare. "We're all dying," he ground out.

"True enough, but I've got the cancer. Three different sawbones said the same thing, so I reckon it's true. That's why I'm here—to make my peace. Ain't lookin' for forgiveness," he said, "but you boys deserve to hear me say I'm sorry. And that I'm proud, real proud, of the men you've become, no thanks to me."

From the looks on his brothers' faces, Asa realized he wasn't the only one struggling for the right words.

"Y'all need to get married. Livin' alone is fine for grizzlies and cougars, but God didn't make men to prowl around all by themselves." He looked at Asa. "You love that li'l gal, and she loves you. Stop bein' stubborn and make her your wife before that Pinkerton who's been sniffin' around beats you to it."

Asa endured a few minutes of good-natured teasing before his pa turned his attention to Chester and Edgar. A lesson his mother had drummed into his head as a boy came to mind: "Let him who is without sin cast the first stone...." Daniel had admitted that he'd made mistakes—some more grievous than others—but what good would come from holding his feet to the fire now?

"I have a question," Asa said as Daniel rolled another cigarette. "How have you been staying out of sight in Denver?"

"There's an abandoned trapper's cabin near the Cherry River. It ain't the governor's mansion, but it keeps the rain off."

He'd seen the place. That his pa had survived the winter in that falling-down place was nothing short of a miracle. "When we get back, we'll fetch your things, and you'll stay with me."

Daniel shook his head. "You've got only one bed, and I won't put you out of it."

"I'll buy another one. If you're sick enough to hunt us down, you're too sick to be alone. And I won't hear another word on the subject."

Daniel tossed his cigarette into the fire, and as Chester and Edgar nodded their heads, Asa wondered if his brothers had seen what he had: a tear sliding from the corner of their father's good eye.

Several weeks later, Daniel had gone to town for breakfast when Ambrose knocked at Asa's door.

"Had to come tell you what I heard at the Tivoli last night," he whispered.

Asa led him inside, and once he was settled at the table, he asked, "Do you have time for coffee, or are you just here for the gossip?"

"This ain't no joke, Asa," the old man said. "I hate to sound dramatic, but this could be a matter o' life and death."

Asa filled a mug and set it near Ambrose's elbow. "Well," he said, sitting across from him, "don't keep me in suspense. What's got you in a lather?"

"Charlie Hodges and Jack Ford got it in their heads that you boys are about to move a lot of gold, and their plan is to rob you of it between the Holstrom Mine and town. Said somethin' about a big tree with a growth, and how you'll have to take it slow right there where the road bends."

"But there's no way they could know what day we'll come into town."

"That's just what Charlie said when Jack outlined the plot!" Ambrose banged his fist on the table. "But Jack, he just laugh and say, 'What we got to do but set and wait?'"

"Asa gave that some thought. "They're foolish *and* stupid. Everyone in town is wise to them. They can't trade the gold for—"

"They ain't as foolish and stupid as you think. They said they'll take the wagon right straight over to Golden or Leadville, where nobody knows 'em."

"They'd have to kill all of us to make that work."

The minute the words were out, Asa felt the full weight of Ambrose's warning. His heart was beating hard. "You saved our bacon, 'Brose."

"Not yet I ain't. You boys best buy up all the guns and bullets you can get your hands on, so's you won't need to stop and reload on that curve."

"You're sure it's just the two of them?"

"I heard just the two voices." Ambrose got to his feet and shuffled toward the door. "If there was more in on it, they kept mum. I best be gettin' back. And *you* best be makin' a plan."

Asa had no doubt that Ambrose had heard clearly. He knew Charlie and Jack, and the whole thing might be nothing more than a whiskey-inspired daydream. But it couldn't hurt to take Ambrose's advice and make the trip well-prepared.

"When it's over," he said, opening the door, "we're going to pay you enough so you can retire in luxury."

"What?" Ambrose laughed. "Is you crazy? What this ol' man gonna do if he don't play piano down at the Tivoli?"

Asa laughed, too. "All right, then—you'll just have to settle for a fancier suite at the Remington."

Ambrose shook his head. "You really want to thank me, you spend that money on a weddin' ring before Gus Anderson beat you to it."

Asa closed the door behind him and shook his head, wondering how many others agreed with his pa and Ambrose—and if Nell might actually say yes if he took their advice.

When Asa approached his father and brothers with the news Ambrose had shared, they agreed to err on the side of caution. They were well-armed and ready for battle, should they encounter trouble at that bend in the road. It was a simple plan, really: Shaina Remington's brother Earl had volunteered to take the lead, her brother Ben, the rear. Chester would drive the wagon, with Daniel facing rear behind him, his Repeater at the ready. While Edgar watched the right side, Asa would watch the left. Six men—each wearing two fully-loaded pistols—should have no trouble holding off two whiskeyed-up ne'er-do-wells.

Despite careful planning, the tension was high as they hitched up the team and hefted sacks of gold into the back of the wagon, and they eased their fears as best they could with tomfoolery and jokes.

"Just one left," Edgar said, tossing his bag on top of the others.

The men blotted sweat from their brows and gulped water from canteens as Asa said, "I'll get it."

He'd no sooner had he lifted the bag than he heard a shout, and another, followed by a volley of gunshots—so many that he lost count.

The first thing he saw when he ran out of the shaft was his pa, shouldering the Repeater. "It's them or us, boys!" he bellowed.

"Watch it, Charlie!" Jack shouted. "He's got 'im one of them confounded sixteen-shooters!"

But Jack's warning came a tick too late, for the Repeater had already put the robber down for good. Daniel pivoted right and silenced Jack, too, but not before spending every round in the chamber.

When the smoke cleared, Chester said, "What made them show up here instead of jumping us at the bend in the road?"

"Don't know, don't care," Edgar said. "We stopped 'em. That's all that matters."

"Anybody hit?" Asa asked.

The men took stock. Ben had taken a shot to his gun hand, but everyone else appeared to be unharmed.

Daniel slumped to the ground, and Asa collapsed beside him. "They're both hit!" Chester said.

"Pa's gut shot," Edgar said, "and they got you three times, Asa."

Yes, it was registering now…in the shoulder, in the chest, and in the neck.

"Wagon's already hitched up," Ben hollered. "Let's get 'em to town 'fore they bleed out!"

The men eased Daniel into the wagon, right on top of the gold, then put Asa in beside him.

"Well," Daniel slurred, "I'd rather go out this way than inch by inch as the cancer eats at me."

"Don't talk that way," Chester said, signaling Ben to move forward. "You're not dead yet."

"I'm sorry I wasn't a better father, but I'm glad I got the chance to say I love you. And I'm proud of the men you've become."

Asa reached over, grabbed his father's hand, and gave it a hard squeeze. "And we're proud of the man you became, too."

Father and sons enjoyed a moment of familial laughter before Daniel and Asa slipped into unconsciousness.

Chapter Twenty-six

He was gone even before you reached the clinic," Doc Wilson told the brothers. Asa could hear them, but wasn't able to move, not even to open his eyes.

"I'm sorry for your loss," Wilson added.

"We half expected as much," Edgar said. "He didn't budge once the whole way."

"What about Asa?"

The doctor faced Chester. "I patched him up best I could. If he survives the night, our biggest fear will be infection."

Asa couldn't believe he wasn't expected to last till tomorrow. He'd show them!

"If he survives…?"

Wilson only nodded. "Has anyone told Nell?"

"No, not yet."

Elsie removed her bloody apron and, wiping her hands on it said "I remember how awful it was, finding out that Abe was shot during the train robbery. It'll be easier to hear, coming from a woman."

Asa prayed that Nell would receive the news with the same faith she'd shown in the face of every other hardship.

When the doorbell rang at ten o'clock, Nell couldn't imagine who could be calling at this hour.

"Elsie?" she asked when she opened the door. "What on earth are you doing out at this—"

She stepped into the foyer and closed the door behind her. "Come sit with me," Elsie said, grabbing Nell's hand.

"What's wrong? Did something happen to Abe?"

"No, Abe is fine. It's—" She bit her lower lip, then slid an arm across Nell's shoulders. "It's Asa. He's at the clinic. There was a robbery. At the mine. They killed Daniel Stone and shot Shaina's brother Ben in the hand. And Asa...he just got out of surgery."

Elsie had said so much in such a short time that Nell couldn't process it. Heart hammering, she got to her feet and started pacing the floor. "What are you going on about? A robbery? But... but they were bringing...."

She hid behind her hands. Daniel Stone, dead? It couldn't be. A tremor set in, starting at her toes and rolling straight up to her scalp. Nell shivered and sat back down. She grabbed Elsie's shoulders. "Did Amos...was he...did he operate?"

"Yes, Nell, and—"

"Were you there? Did you assist? How bad is it?"

"Why don't you come with me?" Elsie said. "When he comes to, I'm sure there's no one he'd rather see than you." She grabbed a shawl from a hook near the front door and draped it over Nell's shoulders, then led her to the door. "Where's Birdie?" Elsie asked, looking around.

"With the Helds. Their boy has been taking care of him. He's become quite attached, and I didn't have the heart to separate them. But why are you asking? You don't think Birdie was out at the mine, too, do you?"

"No, and it's good that he's with the Held boy. Asa will be very happy to hear that."

"So, he's unconscious?" Nell asked as they walked toward the clinic.

"Yes."

"But he'll be all right...? You were there, so you saw the...the damage. So you know. He'll be all right?"

Elsie patted her hand and quickened her pace. "It's chillier than I thought it would be," she said. "Makes me wish I'd grabbed a heavier shawl."

Nell decided not to ask any more questions. Soon enough, she'd see for herself what shape Asa was in.

She felt weepy and rubber-legged, but she couldn't give in to that now. If he came to—no, *when* he came to—the last thing he needed to see was a whimpering weakling.

Please, Lord, keep me strong, for Asa's sake.

"It's important that he doesn't move around too much," Amos said when she arrived at the clinic. "The bullets did a lot of internal damage, and I'm afraid one of the sutures might come loose."

"I have nothing but time to devote to him," Nell admitted. "Anything he needs...just tell me what to do. I'm not going anywhere. You can give Elsie the night off."

"That's good, very good, because infection is his worst enemy now. It won't be easy, getting water and broth into him, but it's just what he needs. A lot of it, a spoonful at a time." Amos smiled. "Janet has always said you were good for him. If he pulls through this, I'm going to make sure he knows it. No more of this nonsense about men minding their own business."

He turned to leave, but Nell grabbed his arm. "Wait. What do you mean, *if* he pulls through?" Then she looked over at Asa, lying still and pale on the narrow hospital bed. "Of course he'll pull through. He's strong and stubborn. He'll be fine. You'll see."

Amos gave her shoulder a slight squeeze—and an unmistakable look of sympathy for her idealism. Still, she refused to accept that Asa wouldn't get better.

Once Amos was gone, Nell pulled a chair close to Asa's bed and held his hand between hers. "You're going to be fine. I'm going to see to it."

She hugged his arm, and thanked God for every steady beat of his pulse thumping near her ear.

When Nell woke in the same position hours later, the room was dark and the clinic halls were quiet. She worked the stiffness out of her neck and walked to the window.

The full moon glowed bright and white in the inky sky, reminding her that God was powerful enough to keep it up there, yet gentle enough to meet the needs of tiny sparrows in the trees. He knew better than anyone what a good and decent man Asa was, and she'd trust Him to heal Asa completely.

A noise behind her caught her attention, and she returned to his bedside. Beads of perspiration had formed on his forehead, and his hands were hot and clammy. Everyone had gone home, save one tiny nurse who now dozed in a big chair near the clinic's entrance. The wall clock read five in the morning. Amos and Elsie would be back soon, but Nell couldn't wait two or three hours.

She found a big bowl, filled it with water, and carried it into Asa's room. She'd seen stacks of washcloths in the closet outside his door, and grabbed a few. While one was soaking in the cool water, she blotted his forehead with another. And when that one grew warm, she swapped it for another cool one.

She filled a big mug with water, too, then eased Asa's head onto a second pillow. He couldn't open his mouth to swallow a spoonful of water, so she dipped another cloth in the water and gently daubed it to his parched lips.

"As soon as Elsie gets back," she told him, "I'll ask her to bring you some broth." Blinking back the tears that stung her eyes, she finger-combed dark waves of sweat-soaked hair from his brow.

Oh, Lord, she prayed, *how I love this man!* "*Ask, and ye shall receive,*" You said. *Well, I'm asking—no, I'm begging—You to heal the infection that's causing his fever.*

But his fever did not break, and the following afternoon, he remained unconscious.

"He lost a lot of blood," Amos explained, "and he's very weak. But as you pointed out, he's strong and stubborn, so he could rally."

Unlike Amos, Nell believed those words.

Two days passed, and the only marked change was a spike in his fever. She'd recited Scripture to him as she massaged his feet and calves, the way Elsie had shown her, to prevent bedsores and keep his circulation going. She'd prayed silently and out loud and read him the newspaper, hoping some bit of news, or one word or another might rouse him.

It had not.

So she took to pacing, singing the hymns and silly songs she'd taught her students, reciting poems she'd memorized as a girl. Amos caught her at it, and joked that if she kept it up, he'd either have to find her a bed in the clinic, or replace the floorboards when Asa was released.

"Go home, Nell. Have a proper meal and get some rest," he'd said. "You won't be any good to Asa if you collapse from exhaustion. I give you my word, if there's any change, I'll send for you."

She had agreed, but only to get him out of the room. Nell had no intention of leaving this room. It was a five minute walk between the clinic and her house. Even if all she did was eat a piece of cheese and change her clothes, she'd be gone for at least half an hour. A lifetime to someone in Asa's condition!

But Amos had made a good point about resting. She slid the chair right up close to the bed, took Asa's hand in hers, and closed her eyes. It wasn't likely she'd sleep, but if by chance she nodded off, any small movement would wake her.

More than an hour passed as she dozed, head resting beside his arm. Asa stirred, and when Nell opened her eyes, she saw that tears had dampened the pillowslip beneath his head.

"Oh, Asa," she whispered, wiping them away, "are you in pain?" He licked his lips, gave the barest nod of his head.

"I love you," he wheezed. "More than life itself."

"You're delirious," she said, tidying his covers. "And after days without eating or speaking, you sound like a grizzly bear." She dipped a cloth in water, then pressed it to his lips. Dousing it again, she laid it across his forehead.

"You need to know...."

"Hush, Asa. You need every ounce of strength to heal."

"But...you should know...who I am."

Breathing seemed a great effort, and with every word, the struggle increased.

"I know who you are," she assured. "Now please be quiet, all right?"

"Ran with the James-Younger Gang," he rasped. "Never shot anybody. At least, I don't think I did...."

Had he forgotten telling her all of this when they were snowed in at the cabin? But thankfully, he'd stopped talking. *Good*, she thought, *you need your sleep*.

But he was only gathering strength, it turned out, not sleeping. "I don't...deserve...."

Awareness dawned like the brightest of mornings: Asa really *did* love her; but, because of his past, he'd convinced himself she was too good for him. If she'd figured it out sooner, instead of self-centeredly nursing uncertainty and hurt feelings, she could have spared him all that worry. Could have told him that she loved him, too, secret past and all!

"You're wrong, Asa Stone," she interrupted. "You couldn't be more wrong, and when you wake up, I'm going to say it again." She squeezed his hand. "I'm going to say I love *you*, too!"

He inhaled a deep breath, let it out slowly, and his grip on her hand relaxed.

"Sleep, dear Asa," she whispered, replacing the compress. It wasn't hot. Nell pressed her lips to his forehead and realized that *he* wasn't hot, either.

Amos strode into the room just then, wearing his Serious Doctor face...until he looked at Nell.

"His fever broke, didn't it?"

She returned his smile. "Yes, finally. And his breathing seems less labored."

"Good signs. All good signs." He aimed a forefinger in her direction. "But he's not out of the woods just yet."

"Oh, I know what you mean. It won't be easy, keeping him in bed until he's capable of more. If I know him, as soon as he can sit up, he'll want to stand. Then walk. And—"

"Nell!" Elsie rushed into the room. "Have you heard yet? Did they find you?"

"Who?"

"The school board. And the principal. They want you back. It seems Miss Kimball just isn't working out. Isn't that wonderful?"

"Wonderful?" Amos repeated.

"Oh, stop looking like a grumpy old grandfather." Elsie gave him a sisterly shove. "I didn't mean that it's wonderful she isn't working out. Or that the children don't like her. What I mean is, it's wonderful that they want to rehire Nell." She grabbed Nell's hands. "You'll do it, right? Go back to the classroom?"

"Why is it so important to you?" Amos wanted to know. "You don't have any children."

"Yet," she corrected, patting her still-flat belly. "It's important because Nell has gone through so much lately, and she was never happier than when she was teaching." She faced Nell. "Will you do it?"

Nell glanced at Asa and noticed that the color had returned to his cheeks. "If they can wait until he's on his feet again, I might."

"When they approach you, don't let on that I told you. Just act surprised and say yes."

"I have other patients to see," Amos said, taking Elsie's elbow, "and you, sister dear, need to put your feet up, or Abe will never let me hear the end of it."

A nurse delivered some broth, and as Amos left, Nell promised to see that Asa ate it.

"It isn't as tasty as mine," she whispered, touching the spoon to his lower lip, "but it's nourishing, and that's all that matters right now."

"I know," he whispered. "I know."

                                                                     ⌢

Asa's condition improved steadily, and he knew exactly whom to thank. From Elsie and Amos alike, he'd heard daily recitations of everything Nell had done. "If she left your side for more than thirty minutes, it was a long time!" Elsie had told him.

Chester and Edgar promised that when he was well enough, they'd take him to see their father's grave. "I think he'd like what we put on his marker," Edgar said.

"'We're Proud of the Man He Became.'" Chester said with a grin.

It hadn't been so long ago that Asa had wondered if the day would ever come when his life would right itself. Well, it seemed that day had come.

Three weeks into his recovery, Doc Wilson gave him permission to leave the hospital, but only briefly, and only to walk up and down the path out front. "When you build up some strength," Amos said, "you can stay out longer and go farther."

After a few days of walking, Asa ventured to Tryner's Jewelry Store, where the owner showed him a few precious gems. None said *Nell.* Then he noticed a plain band, topped by a daisy-shaped decoration. "I'll take that one," he said, *because daisies are Nell's favorite flower.*

The next day, he paid Cooper Preston a visit and bought a new blue shirt.

And this very morning, he'd stopped at the barbershop for a shave and a haircut.

As he stood at the rear of Nell's classroom, he remembered how flustered they'd both grown when one little girl named Emily asked if he was Nell's beau.

"Look, Miss Holstrom," Emily said now. "He's got a cane." She turned to Asa. "My grandpa has one of those, and he says he needs it because he's old. Are you old, too?"

Laughing, Asa said, "Lately, I've felt that way." He walked to the front of the classroom. "Good afternoon, Miss Holstrom."

She curtseyed. "Mr. Stone."

Facing her students, Asa said, "I'm going to teach your teacher a few things. Is that all right with you?"

"Are you kiddin'?" said a boy up front. "She was about to give us an arithmetic quiz. Go right ahead!"

When the giggling stopped, Asa picked up a piece of chalk. "Do you remember how, when you worked at Stone Hill Inn, you left a note?"

"Yes…," she said tentatively.

Asa faced the chalkboard and wrote, "Will you marry me, and let me be the guardian of your heart?" Then he sketched two squares, adding "Yes" beneath one, and "No" under the other. He fished the ring from his pocket, slipped it onto the piece of chalk, and held it out to her.

She drew a heart in the "Yes" box and handed him the ring.

"How long have you been planning this?" Nell asked, holding out her hand.

He slipped the ring onto her finger. "Since the day you walked into the inn and pulled that ad out of your pocket."

Nell stepped into the circle of his arms. "You did a pretty good job, keeping it a secret."

"Maybe that should be our motto: 'No Secrets.'"

And then he kissed her, the way he'd been wanting to kiss her for months, the way she deserved to be kissed.

Book Group
Discussion Questions

1. Did you like Asa better than Nell, or the other way around? Why?

2. Which secondary characters did you like best? Why?

3. If this novel becomes a movie, who do you see in the roles of Asa Stone and Nell Holstrom?

4. Thinking about Asa's past, do you think he turned over a new leaf before the story ended?

5. What would you say is Asa's strongest character trait?

6. What's his weakest trait?

7. What did you like best about Nell?

8. What was Nell's least attractive character trait? Can you cite an example of it?

9. Consider for a moment the modes of transportation, tools and utensils, forms of entertainment, appliances, and styles that were commonplace during the 1880s. Would you struggle or thrive under those conditions? Which modern convenience would you miss most?

10. Is there a scene or situation in the story that you closely identify with...or one that you'll always remember? Which one, and why?

11. What did you think of the characters' tendencies to turn to God in different situations? Do similar circumstances draw you close to Him, too?

About the Author

With nearly five million 4- and 5-star-rated books in circulation, Loree Lough has been called by reviewers and readers alike a "gifted storyteller whose novels touch hearts and change lives." *Guardians of the Heart* follows *Currency of the Heart* in the historical series Secrets on Sterling Street, published by Whitaker House.

Loree lives near Baltimore and enjoys spending time with her husband, daughters, and "grandorables" at their cabin in the Allegheny Mountains, where she delights in showing off her skill at identifying critter tracks. She loves interacting with readers on Facebook, Twitter, and Pinterest, and via e-mail (she answers every letter, personally!) at loree@loreelough.com.

Welcome to Our House!

We Have a Special Gift for You ...

It is our privilege and pleasure to share in your love of Christian fiction by publishing books that enrich your life and encourage your faith.

To show our appreciation, we invite you to sign up to receive a specially selected **Reader Appreciation Gift**, with our compliments. Just go to the Web address at the bottom of this page.

God bless you as you seek a deeper walk with Him!

WE HAVE A GIFT FOR YOU. VISIT:

whpub.me/fictionthx

WHITAKER
HOUSE